WITHDRAWN

DOWN THE
DARKEST
STREET

A PETE FERNANDEZ MYSTERY

DOWN THE DARKEST STREET

A PETE FERNANDEZ MYSTERY

ALEX SEGURA

POLIS BOOKS

Copyright © 2016 by Alex Segura
Cover and jacket design by 2Faced Design
Interior designed and formatted by E.M. Tippetts Book Designs

ISBN 978-1-940610-75-7
eISBN: 978-1-943818-09-9
Library of Congress Control Number: 2015958673

First hardcover publication April 2016 by Polis Books, LLC
1201 Hudson Street, #211S
Hoboken, NJ 07030
www.PolisBooks.com

POLIS BOOKS

For Guillermo, past and present

"The past was filling the room like a tide of whispers."

—Ross Macdonald, *The Instant Enemy*

PART I:
DIVE FOR YOUR MEMORY

CHAPTER ONE

Pete Fernandez didn't see the kick coming. The boot crashed into his jaw, sending him farther into the dank alley. The two men paused to see if Pete had any plans to fight back. He didn't. He felt blood trickle down his face.

Pete tried to stand up. His feet gave way. He slipped and landed on his ass, slamming into the metal garbage cans that lined the alley. He wasn't sure where the pain was coming from anymore. The Miami air felt thick and heavy around him. His breathing was fast. Short, quick gasps.

Bile rose in Pete's throat. He could taste some of the Jim Beam shots he'd downed over the course of the evening. He tried to wipe some of the sweat—and whatever else—from his face, but stopped when he caught a glimpse of his hand. Shaking and bloody, gravel and dirt embedded in his left palm.

DOWN THE DARKEST STREET

One of the guys laughed as the other walked up and grabbed Pete, lifting him up by his shirt. The guy reeked of cheap beer and cheaper aftershave. He spit a wad of mucus at Pete's face, most of it splattering on his left cheek. The guy let Pete drop and turned toward his friend.

Pete watched the duo lumber away, their curses muffling the sound of their footsteps. He wiped the gunk off his face and let out a jagged breath.

It had been another Miami scorcher. One of those days where you don't want to consider leaving the house, or wearing pants. Where you get sunburned taking out the garbage. Where your shirt sticks to your slick body before you even get to your car. Pete's phone had said ninety degrees that morning but it felt closer to a hundred. The evening had only brought a small respite—dimmed lights in a sauna. The rare, tropical breeze a teasing gift—a sweet whisper in your ear. Miami. Even the brightest sun and neon lights couldn't change it. The place was fucked. Dirty. Corrupt. A nightmare happening in broad daylight.

Pete was on all fours now. His head hung down. A quick cough turned into a dozen and soon he was lying on his side, spittle dripping out of his mouth, his eyes out of focus and his body writhing in the dirt.

He tried to get up, his vision blurring. He got his footing and paused to catch his breath, his body leaning on the grime-covered wall. He tried to concentrate. On his hand, pushing himself off the wall and toward the end of the alley. On each foot—left, right, left— as he started to walk. On what had led him back here, outside the Gables Pub, bloodied, drunk, and alone.

2

The night had started off routine. Standard. Pete needed to get out. Do some reading. His friends weren't around anymore. He didn't care. Fuck 'em. He was fine sitting at his favorite bar, reading his dead father's worn copy of *Night Shift*. Shuffling the pages back every few minutes, having forgotten what he'd read, too proud to give up. The pub was on the fringe of what people considered Coral Gables— meaning it wasn't as nice as the mansions and high-rise buildings that meshed with the tiny city's old Spanish décor. Just a few miles from Miracle Mile, the pedestrian-friendly heart of the Gables, the pub felt like another world: dark, dirty, and out of place. Time passed. He had a few whiskey shots to go with his seven or eight beers and felt rough. Not smooth, like he used to feel after a few rounds, when the buzz glowed around his face and made him smile without thinking about it. No, he felt rough and grimy, like bare feet on a dirty sidewalk.

The two guys were big, but not built. Ex-frat boys with nothing to do but get wasted on a Tuesday night. The television perched over the bar was playing Dolphins football highlights from the night before. Jets 35, Dolphins 7. The two guys and their girlfriends were a few seats away at the other end of the bar, cursing at the screen. Pete found what little concentration he had disrupted. He put his book down and scowled at the double date. They shrugged and kept yapping. Pete groaned and ordered another round. Beer and a shot. The whiskey went down warm. He could feel it coating his throat and stomach.

Next thing he knew, he was sitting next to one of the women, his hand on her leg. Where were the guys? He wasn't sure. Whatever. The other girl—chunkier, louder, obnoxious—was yelling something. She seemed upset. Pete swayed. He tried to play off how drunk he was to the girl, tried to make it seem intentional. His hand went too far. She tossed it off. He tried to stand up, one hand on the bar, his other swinging a bottle of Heineken around. That's when he felt a hand gripping his shoulder. He remembered being pushed out the front door and into the street. It was the two guys. He'd thought they had left. Wrong.

Pete remembered mumbling an apology, but that was lost. Lost in the noise of the two guys yelling and lost as he felt himself being shoved into the alley. It was narrow and wet, dark and empty. That's when he felt the first kick to his midsection. He was splayed on the ground, and trying to get himself back to standing only resulted in a weird push-up. The second kick hit him in the face.

Pete now tried to will the memory away but failed. He wiped his wrist over his mouth and found more blood.

He inched down the alley, away from the pub, toward the backstreets that would allow him some semblance of cover from the shame he knew was starting to kick in. He moved his tongue around his mouth, checking for missing teeth. Relieved to find there were no unwanted gaps.

He reached the end of the alley. Pete had parked his banged up Toyota Celica on the street a few blocks north of the bar, past a small parking lot. It was dark enough outside—a few hours past sunset— that he could limp to his car and not make too much of a scene.

He didn't see any people or cars. Pete let go of the alley wall and began to half walk, half hobble across the street that intersected with the end of the alley. He was out of breath by the time he crossed the street and stopped to lean against the short cement wall surrounding the parking lot.

The sound of an engine cut through the quiet evening.

Pete turned to meet the noise. A van was approaching from his left, the clank-and-growl sound coming from under its hood getting louder as it approached. He stepped back. His first thought was that the two guys were back, this time with wheels. The van was close enough to Pete that he wasn't sure he could risk darting back across the street. He was also unsure he could "dart" anywhere. His head throbbed and the pain in his side had become sharper. He considered the hospital for a second but pushed the thought out of his mind. He just wanted to get home.

The van was now close enough for Pete to see inside. He let his eyes wander over it, his vision hazy and blurry. As the van came up beside him, the driver came into focus—a tall, thin white man with longish brown hair. Pete couldn't tell much else about him in the darkness. The driver didn't notice Pete, watching the road instead. But then the van stopped for a second. Pete and the driver looked at each other. The driver nodded his head. He thought Pete wanted to cross the small street—which he had, but the arrival of the van threw him off. Pete motioned for the van to continue. At first he'd only noticed the driver, but as the vehicle drove on past him, Pete realized there was another passenger—a teenager, curled up in the front seat. The girl was petite—couldn't be over sixteen, Pete figured—and her hair looked rumpled and disheveled.

Pete stepped back. The evening's silence was replaced by the sound of rubber tires on asphalt, as the van accelerated and was gone.

CHAPTER TWO

His hands tightened on the steering wheel. A bead of sweat formed at the edge of his scalp. The drunk man had caught him off guard, stepping into his path like that. The last thing he needed was to hit a pedestrian and make a scene. No matter. They were almost at the spot. The Voice would be appeased and grow quiet again.

The girl was splayed out on the passenger side, her head at a weird angle. He noticed the bloody smear at the base of her skull. He hadn't wanted to do that, but she would have fought. She would have screamed. He thought back to a few hours earlier. Dadeland Mall—a giant eyesore located in suburban Kendall in southwest Miami. A giant block of stores and restaurants that looked more like a prison than anything entertaining. He'd followed the girl and her friends. They were window-shopping. Eating at the food court. The usual. He'd wooed her for days via e-mails, Facebook messages, and the occasional text *message. His method hadn't failed him. He was cautious.*

He turned the van onto the expressway, heading south.

After a while, her friends had left. She needed a ride home. He texted her from the disposable phone he'd purchased that morning. From "my friend's phone." Meet me outside, we can get a soda. *She was hesitant. He watched from the van. The only thing he'd held onto since the darker times. Since New Jersey. Virginia. Georgia. He changed the signage on the side every month or so. Some months he was MONSON ELECTRIC. Other months, it was ANDREA'S BRIDAL.*

He spotted her standing outside of Macy's, near the Lot C parking lot, alone. He got out of the van and approached her from behind. He tapped her on the shoulder. She turned around with a start, a confused look on her face.

"Excuse me, young lady?"

"Yes?"

"I'm Steve's uncle. Have you seen him? He said he was meeting a friend."

She looked concerned.

"Oh, well, he said he was going to meet me here," she said, with no prodding.

"That's not like him not to show up," he said, his hands sliding into his jeans pockets. "Weird. I dropped him off here a little while ago."

She shrugged her shoulders and checked her phone. Nothing from "Steve."

"Have you spoken to him recently?"

"Just a few minutes ago."

"Hmm," he said, rubbing his chin. He'd cleaned up a bit in anticipation of the encounter. His longish hair was tied back, his stubble

trimmed to a reasonable length. He was as clean-cut as he had to be. "I'm going to take a quick swing around the parking lot and then maybe the other side of the mall. Want to come along?"

She hesitated. It sounded safe; he could see her debating it in her head.

"It's up to you," he said, shrugging and beginning to walk away. "I'm just getting a little worried about him. I can tell him you were looking for him, too—when I find him."

"No, no," she said, speeding up her pace to catch up with him. "It's OK. Let's go."

He'd left a piece of pipe by the front passenger side tire. As she opened the van door he swung at her skull with force. She let out a slight yelp and tumbled forward. He pulled her up and pushed her into the van, looking around and confirming no one had seen him. He settled her into the seat, positioning her to look like she'd just dozed off. He allowed himself a moment to caress the hair framing her young face.

He turned off on the exit for Campbell Drive.

The girl whimpered. A slow, low moan of discomfort. He realized she would be awake soon and stepped on the accelerator. A little more speed was OK. They were almost there. And then he and the Voice would be sated for a little while longer. He turned the car radio on. The oldies station. The sound of Harry Nilsson's smooth baritone came through the van's scratchy stereo system.

"Remember . . . life is just a memory, remember . . . close your eyes and you can see . . ."

CHAPTER THREE

"Hi. My name's Pete, and I'm an alcoholic."

The words echoed around the cold room, which was on the basement floor of St. Brendan's, a Catholic church a block away from Pete's house in Westchester, a quiet and small West Miami suburb that looked more like Pleasantville, USA, than an offshoot of a major metropolis. Pete used to hate living here. Now the calm and quiet kept him alive.

The room was used for storage most of the time—a place to house donations and stuff the church was looking to sell at the next, inevitable bazaar. Pete was seated in a small circle of chairs with about a dozen others. He scanned the faces that surrounded him. The variety had surprised Pete the first time he'd come by—teenagers, businessmen, burnouts, stay-at-home moms. The group was like a random sampling of people living within a fifteen-mile radius of the church. They responded with a wave of nods and a unified "Hi, Pete!" He smiled wanly before he spoke.

"Thanks. I'm happy to be here," Pete said. "Really happy. It's . . . uh . . . it's been a rough few weeks. But I'm sober. It's been eighty-six days and I feel better."

He paused for a second and scratched the stubble he'd allowed to form over his face.

"I was not in a good place a few months ago," Pete said. "And I don't think I'm in a good place now. But I can at least see what I've been doing wrong. That's a start. I haven't had a drink, and that's good, too. Thanks."

The group responded with a more scattered, less focused collection of thank-yous and applause. Pete nodded. The meeting was almost over, and as the last few people took their turn and shared about their home life, their days sober, or why they had to pray for serenity on the Don Shula Expressway, Pete let his mind wander. He still had trouble with meetings. Looking for them, going to them, and talking when he did decide to show up at them. But for whatever reason, the collection of people, all struggling with the same affliction that tormented Pete, made him feel better. Better enough to get on with his day.

The circle of people stood in unison. Pete stood up a half second behind the rest of the group. They joined hands and said a prayer. Pete mumbled along, feeling disingenuous for not really believing the words they were saying. The circle broke and splintered off into smaller groups as the attendees began to socialize—shaking hands, giving each other updates. Pete made a beeline for the exit. He felt a wave of relief overtake him as his hand touched the doorknob, which would lead him to the stairwell, which would—in turn—lead him to the outside world and away from here.

Pete felt a tap on his shoulder. He turned around, hoping for a mistake but bracing himself for more AA babble from one of the other members.

It was Jack, an older, slightly chubby man with wispy, thinning hair and a salt-and-pepper beard. Pete had seen him at a few meetings and they'd exchanged pleasantries, but nothing more. The meetings were only a thing Pete did—for now. Maybe later, when he'd gotten under control, he wouldn't even have to come.

"Hey. Pete, right?"

"Yeah, hey, Jack," Pete said, slipping his hands into his pockets.

"Good meeting, huh?"

"Pretty good, yeah. I always feel better after these things, for some reason," Pete said.

"Keep coming back. It gets better," Jack said. "Got a quick question for you."

"All right," Pete said. Having only spoken to Jack once or twice before, he wasn't sure what to expect. Admonishment for his lax attendance? An offer to hang out? Pete could do without both. He already knew he wasn't a star pupil. But he was still vague on the yeas and nays of Alcoholics Anonymous. Was it possible to be kicked out of AA for anything beyond drinking? Pete wasn't sure.

"You wrote that book, right?"

"Book?"

"Yeah, the book about the, uh, the killer, the silent killer."

Pete hesitated for a second.

"Nah, I didn't write it," Pete said. "I'm in it, though—yeah."

Jack's eyes widened, as if he were in the presence of a minor celebrity, as opposed to a washed-up newspaper reporter whose only bit of fame had come over a year ago.

"Was it all true, though? You killed the Silent Death? That's some heavy shit."

Pete sighed. Part of him hated the sliver of fame he'd attained over the last year. The losses were too great. The rest of him got a weird kick out of being recognized for anything other than being a drunk. In a past life, he'd been a sports copy editor for the *Miami Times*. Before that, he'd been a sports reporter in New Jersey. He'd built a rep as a strong enterprise writer with a knack for investigative pieces. He could zoom out and put the pieces together. He had a flair for finding the story others couldn't see. He was on the rise for a while. The drinking—coupled with the sudden death of his father— had derailed that and brought him back home to Miami. It was at the *Times* where he helped a fellow reporter, Kathy Bentley, bring down the mob hitman known as the Silent Death, a masked vigilante who killed for the highest bidder. The adventure had cost Pete the life of his best friend and his job, and had sent him spiraling into a tailspin he'd only started to pull himself out of.

The case created a burst of media attention, and Kathy rode it as far as she could, writing a tell-all book, *The Silent Death: Unmasked*. She'd returned to her old employer, the *Miami Times*, as a local columnist. Pete used the money he got from consulting on the book to get ahead on the mortgage of his dead father's house (now his) and to avoid anything that resembled a job. Unfortunately, that had left a lot of time for drinking. Now, for the past two-plus months, it left a lot of time to think about drinking.

"It's mostly true," Pete said. "But I'd appreciate it if you didn't broadcast who I am to the people in the rooms." Pete had come to learn that "in the rooms" was a nice way of saying "among the drunks at AA meetings."

Jack waved his hands in a dismissive, oh-don't-you-worry way. "No, never," he said. "Just curious, is all. You're probably tired of talking about it."

Pete felt a pang of guilt, but wasn't sure why.

"No, it's fine," he said. "It was just an intense time. A lot of what I'm trying to do is—well—involves trying to get past all that."

"Do you still do that, though?"

"Do what?"

"Like, investigate things. Cop stuff."

Pete coughed, giving himself a few seconds to mull over an answer.

"No. Not really," he said. "I just stay at home. Read. I work at a bookstore on Bird Road a few times a week."

"Well, listen," Jack said. He pulled out a tiny notebook from his back pocket and wrote something on a sheet before tearing it off and handing it to Pete. "Here's my number. Call me anytime. Even if you just want to chat. I know it can get weird out there."

Pete noticed a flicker of sympathy cross the older man's eyes. Jack nodded and smiled kindly before sidestepping Pete and heading out the way Pete had hoped to go earlier. Pete stood in front of the door, as if waiting for someone to sidle up to him and start a conversation.

But that didn't happen, and he turned and left, taking the steps two at a time and almost working up a sweat before reaching the street. He was about a block from his house but he didn't feel like going home. His cell phone rang. It was Emily, his ex-fiancée. She was moving in. Today. It was part of the reason Pete was at the meeting. The idea of Emily living in his house wasn't exactly keeping him stress-free. It was complicated, to say the least. These things always were.

"Hello?"

"I put some boxes in the utility room," she said. "They didn't all fit in the guest room. Just wanted you to know."

Pete frowned and thought before he responded. He had to tread carefully.

"Thanks for checking after the fact," he said. He regretted the petty remark immediately.

"Well . . ." She paused. "OK. You're right. I'm sorry. What are you doing? Are you coming home?"

"I'm going to work," Pete said.

"Fine," she said. "How was your meeting?"

"It was OK. The usual."

The silence on the other end dragged for a few seconds too long. Pete waited. This relationship was emblematic of how his life was right now: uncertain, undefined, and somewhat tedious.

"Thanks for letting me stay at the house," she said.

"You're welcome," Pete said, a bit surprised at her burst of gratitude and feeling a touch of guilt for being so quick on the draw. "What are friends for?"

"I'll see you later," she said and ended the call.

Pete looked at his phone for a second before sliding it back into his pocket.

He wasn't going to work.

It took him a few minutes to reach the St. Brendan's parking lot and find his car. He turned on the engine and AC and let the repackaged air flow through the vehicle, leaving the windows down for a few moments to try and cycle out the humidity that had accumulated while the car sat outside under a blistering sun.

He closed his eyes for a second and let his mind wander back to the meeting. Nothing really stood out to him as memorable, but he felt somehow cleaner, or more focused. He didn't want to overthink it. He opened his eyes and looked over his hands. He still had a few scrapes and bruises from the brawl with the two guys four or five months back. And even that hadn't been enough to make Pete hop on the wagon. He wasn't sure what exactly got him out of bed and to a meeting that day.

The night before he quit had been like many others: a few drinks at lunch, meeting up with some friends amidst the fading glory of Coconut Grove for happy hour. The stretch of land near the ocean full of tourist-trap food and drinking spots had seemed much cooler to Pete when he was younger. Now it made him feel old—the college kids using their fake IDs to score Long Island Iced Teas and the cheesy bars with their faux Irish pub décor and fruity drinks. Every bar was packed and every drink was overpriced and every person seemed like someone's idea of what was cool. Sad people pretending to be happy in the hopes of becoming happy with each other.

This had been followed by a swerving twenty-minute drive to the neon lights and dirty streets of South Beach. Another round or five on the main strip, Lincoln Road—a pedestrian oasis in a town that forced even the blind and dead to drive. Where had they gone? Zeke's, maybe? Or was it the Abbey again? The suggestion of karaoke.

Another ill-advised drive farther down the beach. A few songs he remembered—"Scenes from an Italian Restaurant," "Love Shack," "Old Man."

Strangely enough, the clearest memory Pete had of the evening wasn't the early, sober stages but the very end, when he found himself squirming in a booth packed with people, all of them screaming and singing and gesticulating at each other. They were doing karaoke at the Shelbourne Hotel on Collins Avenue—an off-white building that had seen better days, but was still desperately clinging to the glitz and glory of a time no one remembered. They were in the hotel's tricked-out basement area drinking $15 rum and Cokes with a $10 chaser shot of something fruity, and singing about Brenda and Eddie. In that moment, Pete realized he was totally alone. He didn't know anyone around him. He wasn't sure how he'd gotten to the bar, and he was even less sure about the girl whose hand he was holding. His head was already hurting—a residual hangover now snowballing into the next one, and he hadn't showered since the morning before. *What if I die here?* he thought. He'd gotten up and stumbled to the shadowy men's room—and had rested his hands on the sink. He scooped up a handful of water and splashed it on his face, letting it drip down his cheeks and chin. He didn't care.

When he came to, probably a minute later, he was on the bathroom's muted peach linoleum floor. His neck hurt. His legs were splayed out in front of him. A man wearing a dark striped shirt and a lot of gold jewelry was looking down at him as he washed his hands.

Pete started to look up, but felt his head spinning. He checked his shirt. Reflex. He hadn't thrown up on himself.

"You all right, man?"

Pete tried to respond, but his tongue felt numb—as if he'd just shoved a bag of cotton balls into his mouth. Eventually, he croaked out a response.

"Do I look all right?" he said.

"Hey, just asking," the guy said, raising his arms in mock defense, water splashing on Pete. "You should probably go home. Sleep it off. Press RESTART."

"What?"

"RESTART, bro. You ever play Nintendo?"

"Yeah," Pete said. "When I was a kid."

"Your system ever freeze up on you, man? Like, it won't take any games, won't let you get past the level you want to get past?"

"Sometimes."

"Well, sometimes you got no choice. You can't take the game out, 'cause it's stuck. You can't use the controller because it's jammed. All you can do is push that RESTART button, man. Then you're back at square one. But shit, at least you're moving, you know?"

Pete wasn't sure what to say, if anything.

The man dried his hands and helped Pete to his feet.

"You take care of yourself, man," he said as he tossed his used paper towel into the trash and walked off.

He'd made it home somehow, strangely sobered by the experience—at least, sober enough to sneak past his "friends" and to his car. He didn't remember the drive home, or the moments before he passed out again, this time on his couch. The next day, he'd done a quick Web search and found the nearest AA meeting.

The memory of his "bottom"—or lowest point—was a mixed bag of shame, anxiety, and optimism for Pete. He considered this for a second as he pulled his car out of the parking lot. He turned the radio on loud, trying to drown out his thoughts. The playlist popped on mid-song. Pavement's "We Dance." Pete hummed along as he hopped onto the 836 heading west, toward Coral Gables—about a twenty-minute drive with no traffic. From middle-class bliss to hoity-toity excess. The drive—once Pete hopped off the exhaust-coated wasteland that was the 836 expressway and returned to Coral Way—was scenic and transformative. The office parks and giant grocery stores were slowly replaced by carefully landscaped trees and lawns, which surrounded large mansions and the gigantic landmark that is the Biltmore Hotel. This was old Miami, classic, historic, with a coat of paint over something darker and more dangerous.

The sun was shining and the sky was cloudless. Another perfect Miami afternoon. He squinted as he drove, his sunglasses still in the glove compartment. He wondered how long Emily would be staying with him. If she and her husband, Rick, would be able to work things out. If things *could* be worked out after what had happened between them. He wasn't sure how he felt about seeing her at all. Before Rick, she'd been engaged to Pete, and if not for Pete's drinking and the death of his father, they might still be together. After the events of the last year, they'd managed to revive an uneasy friendship, and Pete had been hopeful they could at least remain polite and work from there. He hadn't expected her marriage to implode. Even less expected was that she'd turn to him for a place to stay while she "sorted things out." He didn't press the question—the best thing he could do was to be there for her, for once.

He didn't allow himself the nostalgic rides through past relationships as often as he had when he was drinking. The whiskey-coated memories of his engagement to Emily were now harder to revisit, and less romantic. But there was no denying he still had a connection with her, and a longing for her. His mind and body—and heart—were not cut out to be dealing with this now.

The playlist wound down—silence replaced the final chords of Sleater-Kinney's "Let's Call It Love." The song—long, loud, emotional, and ragged—fit Pete's mood. He felt raw. He felt alone. But he also felt alive for the first time in years. He turned the car onto Giralda, a small street off Miracle Mile. He was in the heart of Coral Gables, surrounded by townie shops and franchise restaurants. He drove for a few minutes and turned into a cramped parking lot next to an overpriced Thai restaurant. He got out of the car and locked the door. He walked across the street, looking around. He pushed open the main door to the bar—aptly called The Bar—and walked in.

It was dark, in contrast to the bright, sunny, living world outside. The place was empty, too. The bartender, an older woman named Lisa who often worked the day shift, was wiping down the counter. She looked up at him and nodded before she went back to cleaning. Pete slid into a stool at the counter and cleared his throat. Before he could speak, a pint glass of Bass ale was placed in front of him. Lisa lingered for a second before moving across the bar to wipe down the other side.

Pete turned the pint slowly, admiring the amber liquid, watching carefully as it jostled around the glass. He moved his hand back and reached for his wallet. He pulled out the photo with care, unfolding it as if in slow motion. It was about three years old.

"You gonna drink it?" Lisa yelled from the kitchen, out of sight. "Or just stare at it, like usual?"

Pete didn't respond. He placed the photo flat on the bar next to the glass, careful not to get it wet or dirty. The photo was dark and out of focus, taken in a watering hole like a million others—possibly the one Pete was sitting in. It was Pete and his friend Mike. Happier times. Their eyes were both at half-mast, always a sign of a good night. Pete's arm wrapped around Mike. He didn't remember many of the details of that specific evening. The picture was one of the few he had of his friend.

His memories were invaded by the vision of a car enflamed. A funeral. His best friend caught up in a mess of Pete's creation. A mess that cost others their lives, too. He let out a long sigh as his fingers wrapped around the glass of beer. It would be so easy, he thought. Just pull it closer and take a sip. It wouldn't have to be like the last time. Or the time before that.

He let go of the pint glass and pushed the thought out of his head. He set the photo on the bar. The creaking gears inside the jukebox began to grind together.

CHAPTER FOUR

The Book Bin was a small used bookstore on Bird Road, caught between a Checkers cheeseburger joint and Antonia Nunez's real estate office. It was cold, cramped, overstocked, and smelled of paper, wood, and age. Pete liked being there. In a town where everything seemed to be a long drive away, the fact that the Bin was near his house also helped.

He pulled his car into the parking lot and grabbed his tattered copy of *The Shining* from the passenger seat as he got out. Pete felt like his entire life these days fell under "spare time." He got a lot of reading done. A couple of books a week. Working at the store involved plenty of sitting around and reading. Every few hours someone would wander in—some looking for a specific book, others asking if they had a greeting card section or sold coffee. The job was relaxing but left a lot of time for thinking. Pete didn't like thinking too much.

The sound of chimes greeted him as he entered. The place was empty, which was pretty standard for early in the afternoon. Pete took his seat behind the register and opened his book. A few minutes later he heard whistling.

Pete raised his head from the book as Dave Mendoza stepped into the main foyer/cash register area, his burly body passing with minimal grace through the narrow aisles which were bloated with paperbacks and dusty hardcovers—the bookshelves looking like they'd cave into each other with but a tap. Pete couldn't help but smile as his friend came into view: Thin Lizzy T-shirt, large round sunglasses worn indoors, and beard more out of control than usual.

Dave ran the Book Bin. It was a little pet project his parents had left him when they realized that, despite their best efforts, the Bin would never be a huge earner on par with some of their more lucrative investments—like fusion restaurants on Lincoln Road or twenty-four-hour laundromats. For Dave's parents, a nonstarter was not an option. But the chance to give their burnout son something to do? An acceptable loss.

They left him alone and he didn't sink the store. The agreement had held firm for a few years. Barely.

Dave was carrying a stack of romance paperbacks a few books too high when he turned to Pete as if he'd just realized his friend was there. He stopped whistling and dropped the stack on the floor. He walked toward Pete, his left hand raised for a high-five.

Pete responded in kind, and smiled.

"Sup, brofus?" Dave said, scratching at his puffy beard. "Didn't think you were in today."

"I'm not," Pete said, leaning back in his seat. "But I figured you could use some time off. Y'know, give you a break."

Dave shrugged. "Man, I haven't had anyone walk in once today. But, hey, whatever, dude," he said, turning and picking up some of the paperbacks splayed on the floor. "*Mi casa, tu casa.* Just don't bill me for too many hours. You know how weird my dad gets."

Pete nodded. He sometimes forgot Dave was at least five years younger than him, despite the beard, cloud of weed smoke, and slight potbelly.

Dave was one of those guys Pete had known of for years—they ran in the same circles and seemed to know a lot of the same people. But it wasn't until about six months ago that they became what Pete would consider friends. Pete had popped into the Book Bin to kill time—during one of his attempts at staying sober that didn't stick— and Dave recognized him. They got to talking and Pete left with a part-time job offer and a new friend—the latter being in short supply.

"I'll do the usual," Pete said. "I just needed to get out of the house."

Dave turned, eyebrows slightly raised.

"Emily moving in making you feel strange?"

"Nah, it's fine."

"Dude, dude—seriously. It's OK," Dave said. "I mean, I get the appeal—Emily's great. Smart, funny, pretty. Total package. But there's history there, bro. You guys have baggage. And she's a mess right now. Just sayin' you can talk to me whenever."

"I know. It's all good."

"Don't know how you do it, man."

"Do what?"

"Letting a woman that did you so wrong move in with you," Dave said, looking over each paperback as he picked them up, re-forming the stack from earlier. "Can't be good for your *cabeza*."

Pete shrugged and let his attention return to the book. He longed for some music. The stereo at the Bin had blown out a few days before, the victim of one final, epic Rush marathon, courtesy of Mr. Dave Mendoza. A meticulously curated playlist explored at full volume. Pete was thankful when the speakers drowned out Geddy Lee with their own shrieking death wail before conking out for good.

"You read the paper this morning?"

"You know I don't read the newspaper," Pete said, not looking up from the book.

"Yeah, I know," Dave said. "But did you check it on the Internet or some shit? Do you try to keep up with the wild world around us?"

"What're you getting at?"

"Some girl's been missing for a few weeks—maybe more," he said, flipping through the pages of another used paperback. It featured a long-haired, bare-chested man pulling a woman to him. She seemed OK with that. "Went to Dadeland to shop with her friends, never came home. Weird, huh?"

"Stop."

"Stop what?"

"This," Pete said, putting his book down, open-faced, on the counter. "Giving me a headline or news bit and trying to get me to involve myself. I don't do that."

"You do, though," Dave said, wiping his index finger on a shelf and checking the dust. He didn't seem pleased at what he found. "You used to investigate stuff for work, right? Hell, even after all this psycho killer stuff, you took some random cases."

"Every blue moon, when I need cash. Never anything serious. Cheating husband, stuff like that. It wasn't for me. The only one that was close to being a 'case' was a complete disaster," Pete said. The case—which involved a lawyer friend enlisting Pete to help find a missing child—had ended in tragedy, and cemented Pete's belief that dabbling as a detective might not be the best idea, even if the work gave him an unexpected rush and meshed with skills he'd honed before. Even worse, it all went down when Pete found himself spiraling further into his own private, alcohol-fueled hell. It was a few weeks after the case ended that Pete found himself on the floor of the Shelbourne Hotel bathroom after a bad round of karaoke. "I don't even have a license for that kind of shit."

Dave didn't respond. *He's annoyed,* Pete thought.

"Look, I'm not a detective. I don't want to be one. We've been over this. Can we just let it drop?"

"Whatever, dude. I was just making conversation. Thought you like to know about stuff like that. Crime. Whatever. Missing girls seem to be your thing."

Pete winced.

An awkward silence followed. Pete went back to his book, Dave returned to collecting the paperbacks and restacking them somewhere near the back of the store. The door chime sounded. Pete took a second to finish the sentence he was reading before looking up. He dreaded actual customers—their questions, quirks, and weird attempts to befriend him. Manning the Book Bin register was generally easy and the store had a regular, if sometimes erratic, clientele, but every once in a while you'd get someone asking for an obscure fantasy novel series or inquiring where they could sell their used DVDs.

It took a second for Pete to recognize Emily's husband, Rick Blanco. His eyes were wide and his shirt was soaked with sweat. He looked thinner, and the stubble surrounding his face was new. He seemed worn-out and unhealthy. Pete set his book down and stood up. Rick was standing in front of the counter.

"Rick," Pete said. "Hey. What's up?"

"I need to talk to Emily. I know she's staying with you."

Pete's eyebrows popped up.

"You have her number."

"I've been calling her. She doesn't answer."

"Well . . ." Pete tried to slow things down. He didn't hate Rick. He'd always struck Pete as a nice, if somewhat boring, guy. Still, he had a sinking suspicion—based on the bits and pieces Emily had shared with him—that the root of her sudden departure from her home and husband had to do with Rick's own straying. Pete wasn't going to bend over backwards to make Rick's life any easier. "I think that's pretty telling in its own way, don't you?"

"You're loving this shit."

"What?"

"This," he said, waving his arm in Pete's direction. "You won. Or you think you did. She's with you now and your sad sack act worked. Well, good for you, man."

Pete stepped back and raised a hand in defense. "Look, I don't want to get in the middle of this."

"That's a new tactic for you. I guess you don't have to meddle once the damage is done."

"What are you talking about?"

"Don't fucking play with me," Rick said, leaning over the counter now. Pete saw Dave in the background, concern in his eyes. "This is what you wanted. And fine, I fucked up and made it easier for you. But she's my wife."

"If she wants to talk to you, she will."

Rick grabbed Pete's shirt and tugged him forward, his breath hot on Pete's face. He smelled of cheap wine and dirt.

"You think I want to go through you first? I've tried to find her—at work, at your house," Rick said. "I need to talk to her now."

Pete pushed him away and tried to regain his composure. He took a soft fighting stance, ready for Rick—who, despite his disheveled appearance, was a good three inches taller and better built than the scrawny Pete—and hoped this wouldn't turn into an actual, honest-to-God fight. Rick pulled him in close again, their faces almost touching. Pete could see the vein jutting from Rick's forehead. *Was he on something?* Then Rick's anger turned to surprise.

Dave.

"Who the fuck do you think you are, bro?"

Rick let Pete go, allowing him to back up a few paces and notice that Dave was holding a gun—a Sig Sauer P220, no less—to Rick's head, his arm stretched up and his wrist tilted down, the casual stance of someone who's held—and fired—guns before. Pete remembered why he liked Dave so much. Behind the hippie, who-gives-a-shit-let's-just-smoke-a-bowl veneer was one mean dude. One who had seen his share of scraps and had been down some dangerous parts of Miami. Dave considered himself semiretired, in the sense that he no longer trafficked in the areas that used to be his livelihood—dealing heroin, crack, and lots of weed—and stuck to running the used bookstore his rich parents gave him. But the criminal was there. Always would be.

"That's right, bitch," Dave said, his hippie drawl coating the profanities in a way that made Pete almost crack a smile. "Step back like the stank pussy you are. I can smell it from here."

Pete fought back a laugh and averted Rick's frightened, wide eyes. He waved a hand at Dave. Dave nodded and slid his gun behind his back, holstered on his waistband. He gave Rick a slight shove and walked casually back toward the stack of paperbacks, his eyes still on Rick.

"You need to calm down," Pete said. "I can let her know you came by. Maybe she'll want to talk."

"Are you guys fucking nuts? Pointing a gun in broad daylight?"

"Shut your mouth," Dave yelled from across the store.

Pete shrugged in a what-can-I-do? way.

"Tell her it's about Alice," Rick said, dusting himself off, shaken. "Tell her Alice is missing. Maybe dead."

"What?" *Who the fuck was Alice?*

"She'll know who I'm talking about," Rick said.

Pete tried to form a response, but his thoughts were drowned out by the sound of the Book Bin's door slamming shut.

"The hell was that about?" Dave asked as he walked toward the counter.

"Fuck if I know. You always carry a piece in the store?"

"Yeah, why not?"

"I dunno," Pete said. "Seems a little extreme, don't you think? We're in the suburbs."

"You never know what's gonna pop out at you," Dave said, sliding his fingers through his beard. "Seemed like that dude was pretty pissed at you. Who was that?"

"Emily's husband."

Dave shook his head. He did not approve.

"What?" Pete said, sitting back down.

"That's what you get for messing with someone's lady, man," Dave said. "Don't dance with an MW."

"MW?"

"Married woman. *Muy malo.*"

Pete laughed. "Get a grip, man."

"I'm serious, dude," Dave said, exasperated. "She's living in your house. Can you blame him for being pissed?"

"I guess not," Pete said. "But we're not together, and she was with me before she was ever with him."

"Ah, so that's it."

"What?"

"You feel like you had dibs."

"Grow up."

"'S cool, man," Dave said, scratching his stomach. "You gotta do something with your time, now that you're not drinking yourself stupid every night."

Pete leaned back and opened up his book, but couldn't bring himself to read. Why had Rick come to see him? Who was Alice? He slid his hand into his front pants pocket and pulled out a business card. It was worn and bent from being carried in whatever pair of jeans he was wearing on a given day. It was the only one he carried. His name was on it, with the words PRIVATE INVESTIGATOR in bold under it, a phone number—his cell—on the left side of the eggshell-white piece of paper. Emily had ordered a box over a year ago, after the Silent Death. He sighed and flicked the card toward the garbage can near the entrance. The card missed, bouncing off the edge and landing face down near a day-old edition of the *Miami Times*.

CHAPTER FIVE

Julian let a soft yawn escape his mouth as he parked his van a few blocks from his place. He'd lived in the dingy Overtown apartment for close to a month; it was all he could find for the money he had and the privacy he needed. Overtown, in the northwest part of Miami, was a poor area. Despite repeated efforts over the years, it remained plagued by crime and struck him as the perfect spot to hide.

He proceeded to his first-floor one-bedroom apartment. Julian never spoke to the Voice directly—that was not possible. But his Messenger reached out to him when the Voice needed him, wanted him to act. Erica Morales had been good. A slight smile formed on his face as he turned on the living room light.

He sat down at the edge of his small used couch. A few minutes before he arrived at the site, she had awoken confused and mumbling, slipping in and out of consciousness. She was talking about her Spanish test. She wasn't supposed to wake up yet. He slammed her face forward on the dashboard and heard a soft thud. She slid to the right, moving with the car as it turned into the site, and that was it for Erica.

The phone rang.

Julian got up with a start. He picked up the landline receiver. He waited.

"Hello?" It was the Messenger.

"You're not supposed to call me here," Julian said.

"I know, but—"

"Hang up. I will call you."

"Wait, I have—"

Julian slammed the receiver down, the force of the motion shaking the small, flimsy table the phone rested on. He made a mental note to cancel the phone line and to begin preliminary searches for a new place to live. A connection now existed.

He walked over to his tiny computer desk and grabbed a small plastic bag from under it. He pulled out a disposable cell phone—one of about twenty that were in the bag—and began to dial a number he knew from memory. He'd just finished the latest quick-drop on his way back—leaving a series of phone numbers for the Messenger so he'd know where to call. Yet he calls his home line? Foolish.

"Hello?"

"Speak."

"Oh, OK," the Messenger said. It was awkward-sounding and hesitant. "Um, I spoke to, uh, to our friend. He's happy with, uh, um . . . with your work. He likes what you did. He hopes you're staying careful and busy."

"I am. I am very careful. He should know that."

"He sees all and knows you're serving him well. He is happy."

Julian cleared his throat. "Good. I'm waiting for word from him. About what to do next."

"No need to wait," the Messenger muttered. "You must refine the method. Channel your focus back to where you started and move on that quickly. Think of the Voice. Let him fuel your behavior. Spread his message with whatever you do."

Julian closed the cheap disposable cell and let it fall to the floor. He dropped his heavy boot on the phone and watched as it splintered and chipped.

Julian felt content. Not only had Erica accepted him inside her, and become another piece of his tapestry, but the Voice had reached out. It had been months. It was a time for good news and celebration.

He let his shirt and pants drop to the floor and sat down in front of his computer, a cheap, rudimentary mini-laptop that he replaced often. A shiver trickled down his spine as he began his search. He hunted. He would find the next one and continue the mission he had been tasked with. And with each step—with each check marked in blood on the wall—he would build a chorus of voices so loud that the future would be as clear as the present, open for him to see and feel.

CHAPTER SIX

Who *the hell is Alice?* The words screamed in Pete's head as he walked through the door. It still felt like his father's house, Pete thought as he slid his keys into his front pocket. He heard a rustling sound. His cat, Costello—named for Elvis, not Lou— appeared from under the large dining table in the middle of the main room. The table stood next to an old couch, a dark red recliner, and a beat-up coffee table. The cat started rubbing his face against Pete's leg. He put his bag down on one of the dining chairs and picked up the cat, rubbing the cat's chin as he walked toward the kitchen.

"Hello?"

Where was she? he wondered. The house looked the same—she hadn't left many signs that she'd just moved in, Pete thought.

He let Costello drop to the floor and walked to the kitchen

counter. That's when he heard a drawer closing in her room. She was getting dressed.

He picked up the stack of envelopes on the counter and scanned them. Two pieces of junk mail. A telephone bill that was already a week overdue and a letter addressed to him. He looked at the return address: The Carver Family. Pete felt a tightening in his chest. He looked across the kitchen to the opposite wall. Near the landline phone—which existed for no other reason than Pete's desire to keep the house as close to what it looked like when his father lived there— was a calendar for the month of October. Circled was the twelfth, a week from tomorrow. A year since his best friend Mike Carver had died, overcome by flame and metal as his car exploded around him. An explosion Pete should have seen coming. An explosion that was Pete's fault. He knew what the card was: a memorial of some kind. He let it drop back on the counter as he turned to the hallway.

Emily stood in the doorway to the kitchen, her head turned to Pete, having just noticed him on her way out. She was wearing a black skirt, black heels, and a short-sleeved white blouse. He could smell her perfume. He hated himself for still being able to name it. He hated her for not changing it. She was going out.

"Oh, hey."

"Hey," Pete said.

"I didn't hear you come in."

"Heading out?"

"Yeah, actually," she said. "I'm going to meet Susan for a drink. She got off work early."

Pete tried to smile, but produced an awkward half-smirk instead.

"Rick came by the store today."

"What? Really?"

"Yup. He wants to talk to you."

"Well, no. That's not going to happen," she said, her arms crossing. "I have nothing to say to him."

"He seemed pretty desperate to talk to you."

"Was Dave there?"

"Yeah, why?"

"Did he stay calm?" Emily asked. She'd known Dave as long as Pete had, which was to say, not very long, but long enough to know he had a short fuse and wasn't afraid to let people know about it.

"Who's Alice?" Pete asked.

Pete noticed Emily's face flush at the mention. He didn't need her to answer to know who Alice was.

"He mentioned *her*?" She stretched out the last word a split second too long.

"Briefly," Pete said. "He didn't look good. Seemed shaken up. We didn't talk long."

"What did he say?"

"What I said," Pete said. "He wants to talk to you—about Alice."

Emily stood in the doorway, her stare blank, brow furrowed. She wasn't going to respond.

"So Alice is the girl he fucked around with? That's why you needed to stay here?"

Emily's distant gaze found focus on Pete's face. Her eyes narrowed and he noticed her fists clench. He'd seen her dance close to this line before, but that was in another life. He didn't have to take it in this one. He raised his hand.

"Don't go postal on me," Pete said. "I'm just telling you what happened and making a reasonable assumption."

"Why do you have to be so fucking logical about everything?"

"Would you be getting like this if Alice was his cousin from West Palm, Em?"

She let out a sigh and entered the kitchen, grabbing a glass from the cabinet and sidestepping Pete to get to the fridge. As she poured herself some water, she spoke.

"Yes, Alice was the girl he 'fucked around' with. Jesus. You're so crude."

"OK," Pete said. "So, why would he mention her? Why would he want me to ask you about her? He seems worried about this person."

He thought about mentioning that Alice was missing, but hesitated.

"I don't know what's going on in his head. I've hardly responded to any of his e-mails or texts or calls," Emily said. "I just moved out of our home. So he's trying to get to me through you. He must have found out I'm staying with you."

For some reason, the words stung Pete. *Staying with you.*

"It just seemed weird," Pete said. "What do you know about this Alice?"

Emily drained her glass and put it in the sink. She turned to Pete.

"What does it matter?"

"Humor me."

"She worked with Rick. She was young. Right out of college. She was basically the new girl in the office. He said they 'connected,' and things evolved from there."

She stormed past him, grabbing her purse from off the dining room table. She opened the door in one swift move and gave him a quick look.

"It's not your fault," she said. "It's his. But it still hurts and I still feel like a chump."

She didn't give Pete time to answer. The door slammed shut. Costello leapt onto the dining room table and ran off. Pete looked around the empty, quiet house. He didn't have anything to do for the rest of the day.

He checked the time on the gaudy gold-colored clock hanging on the wall across from the front door. Almost six. If he hurried, he might catch her.

CHAPTER SEVEN

"I need a favor."

Kathy Bentley took a big bite out of her bacon cheeseburger and looked at Pete from across the grimy booth at Kleinman's, a dive sports bar a block away from the *Miami Times* offices, Pete's former and Kathy's current workplace. Pete wouldn't stand a chance at getting hired there again. Kathy was already back. The bar was tucked into a half-abandoned condo building near the Venetian Causeway, a stretch of highway that connected Miami's downtown to the beaches. Pete remembered many a night—and morning—spent here. The place smelled of fried fish and cheap beer.

Kathy chewed her food and wiped her mouth with a napkin before responding. "I hope it's something exciting."

"Don't think so."

Kathy shrugged and took a long sip of her gin and tonic. Pete looked at the glass. He shouldn't be here, he thought. Hanging around in bars. Watching her drink. It triggered things that he needed to leave alone.

"Should I not be drinking in front of you?"

"What do you mean?"

"You're not drinking."

"So?"

"So, I've never seen you not drink in a bar before."

"I'm just taking it easy. I'm not drinking today."

"Yeah? What about tomorrow?"

"I don't know."

She reached out and patted Pete's arm with her hand. She gave him a half smile.

"I think it's a great idea."

Pete didn't respond.

"If anyone knows the symptoms of someone trying to quit drinking, it's me. My dad drank nonstop until he died. But it's not like he didn't try to stop, once or twice."

Kathy's dad, Chaz, had been a newspaper columnist for the *Miami Times*. About a year ago, he'd asked Pete to find Kathy, who had gone missing. What Pete didn't know at the time was that Kathy had been kidnapped and that Chaz was just a small part of a bigger puzzle, one that had links to the Miami underworld and eventually led to the deaths of Chaz and Pete's best friend. Still, he had found Kathy alive. Kathy wrote a best-selling book with Pete's help. Because of that, he could afford to live off Kathy's overly generous consulting fee and his pittance of a salary at the Book Bin while he figured out what to do next, if anything.

Pete nodded, waiting for the moment to pass. He'd told no one, aside from Emily, that he was going to meetings for his drinking. He liked Kathy. Even considered her a friend. But they weren't there yet. He gave her a dry smile in response.

Kathy looked up at one of the many TVs set up above the bar at Kleinman's, checking the time on the all-day CNN newscast. She turned to Pete.

"So, what's the big favor you couldn't ask me over the phone? I have to head back to the newsroom in a little bit. I owe them a column."

"I need to find out some stuff about a person that works with Rick Blanco."

"Emily's Rick?"

"Yeah."

Kathy finished the rest of her gin and tonic and slid the glass toward the opposite end of the table.

"Why, pray tell, do you want to investigate Emily's husband? Is this some weird guy thing?"

"Guy thing?"

"Yeah, guy thing. Where you somehow delude yourself that you, through whatever weirdness you've concocted, can win Emily back."

Pete took a deep breath. "It has nothing to do with that," he said, sipping his Diet Coke. "I just had a weird run-in with him today, and he said something that I can't get out of my head."

"Did he say this while threatening to kick your ass for sleeping with his wife?"

"We're not sleeping together."

"Oh, I know."

"Then why . . . Wait, what's that supposed to mean?"

Kathy let out a chuckle. "Just because you're not sleeping with her doesn't mean you don't want to be, or that her husband—who, from what little I can tell, is a jealous dude—doesn't think you are. But yeah, I know very well you're not."

"How do you know that?" Pete said.

"That's not the point," she said, playing with her fries. "So, OK. Rick shows up. Then what?"

Pete looked at his hands. What was he doing? He should be at a meeting. Or at work. Or trying to find better work. His savings were running out, and even though his father's house was paid for, there were other bills to pay. Still, something gnawed at him about the encounter with Rick, so he did what he'd always done: he dug around until he found something. It was an instinct he'd honed as a reporter, before alcohol and the death of his father had sent him spiraling to what he now referred to as "the bottom." It was the instinct that had helped him find Kathy the year before.

"Then what?" Kathy said, pulling Pete back to reality. "I have to get back to work."

"Right," Pete said. "Then he started asking about Emily."

"OK, so far this sounds amazingly predictable, dear. What a shocker that Emily's husband, with whom she is no longer sleeping or living with, came to you, her ex-fiancé, with whom she is now apparently living, to find out about his wife. When does your story— which, mind you, is far from worth this watered-down drink you bought me—get interesting?"

Kathy always got to the point, in every aspect of her life. Her father may have been a deadbeat dad and an alcoholic, but he was a hell of a reporter once, and it had stuck with his daughter. She knew how to sniff out a story, and when to realize there wasn't one.

"Well, he just looked off," Pete said. "I've known Rick for a bit, and he's always been very, well, I dunno—clean-cut? Never a hair out of place. Always dressed to impress. This time he looked like he'd just come out of a bar. And he smelled like liquor."

"That's just your AA mind projecting."

"I don't think so," Pete said, no longer trying to keep up the appearance that he wasn't in recovery. "Trust me, he looked off. Dave had to pull a gun on him."

"Ah. Dave. The paunchy weirdo," Kathy said. "Anyway—you were saying? Rick was looking rough and asking about Emily? Like I said, not a shocker so far."

"Then, after Dave forced him to back off hurting me, he told me to mention someone named Alice to Emily," Pete said. "That she would know what he meant."

"Did you?"

"Did I what?"

"Mention this Alice person to Emily."

"Yeah," Pete said. "Alice was the woman Rick cheated on her with. Rick said she was missing and might be dead."

"Well, that last part is weird," Kathy said. She checked the time on the CNN screen again. "Fuck. I'm late. What else can you tell me about Alice?"

"She worked with Rick; he does construction in Homestead. Blanco Properties—I think that was the name of his company. That's a start."

"Got it," she said, making a mental note. "Why do you need me to do this?"

"You've got access to the *Times*. I don't."

"Right. You're stuck with Google like everyone else these days."

"I wouldn't go back there if they paid me," Pete said, nodding in the general direction of his former workplace.

"That's the thing," Kathy said. "They wouldn't."

She got up, but not before sliding the check over to Pete's side of the booth.

"Thanks for dinner, darling," she said, kissing him on the cheek before walking to the exit.

Pete watched her go. She was an attractive woman. Smart. In good shape. She kept Pete on his toes when they sparred. He replayed their conversation in his mind. His eyes wandered toward the bar. He reasoned with himself. He was only checking to see the bottles Kleinman's had stocked. For old times' sake.

He dropped two tens on the table and drained his Diet Coke. He nodded to the bartender as he walked out into the hot Miami evening.

The call came a few hours later. Pete was home, trying to read his book. He picked up his phone and checked the display. Kathy.

"Hey."

"Hola," she said. "So, it turns out your story is more interesting than you made it out to be."

"How so?"

"Lady's name is Alice Cline," Kathy said. "Ring a bell?"

It did. Alice Cline had been one of Pete's earliest clients in the aftermath of the last year's chaos. Although not licensed or very experienced, Pete had muddled his way through a few small-stakes cases, even before he had decided to quit drinking. The cases consisted of Pete sitting in cars and following spouses around to see if they were being unfaithful.

Alice Cline's case was a little different. Back then, she'd been engaged to Jose Martinez, the youngest son of a prominent Miami politician. When they'd broken things off, the younger Martinez couldn't handle it. He showed up at Alice's apartment, called her constantly, and started harassing her friends. It was a relatively easy case, as far as these things went. Pete met Martinez's father—City Councilman Miguel Martinez—in the parking lot of Casa Pepe restaurant on Bird Road and handed him a manila envelope that included a mini-drive loaded with his son's voice mails, a printout that included a list of local reporters Pete had in his Rolodex, and a few black-and-white photos of his son acting the fool. Jose didn't bother Alice again. Last Pete heard, he'd moved to New York to join a prestigious law firm.

That Alice ended up being Rick Blanco's mistress was a strange coincidence. He felt the pieces start to click into place—forming something that Pete could almost see. But was Pete starting to look into this—and enlisting Kathy's help—because he was just that good a guy? Because he needed something meaningful to do? Or did the idea that maybe Emily's picture-perfect husband was a bit tarnished hold some appeal? Pete tried to prevent his mind from wandering down that path.

"Yeah, actually," Pete said. "I worked on something for her almost a year ago."

"Yeah, according to what I could dig up, she was tight with Jose

Martinez," Kathy said. "And then, suddenly, she wasn't. You have anything to do with that?"

"You could say that."

"Well, looks like after all that went down, she needed some cash," Kathy said. "So she took a secretarial—excuse me, executive assistant—job in Homestead, working for Rick."

"Any idea how long she's been missing?"

"Not sure. I made a few calls," Kathy said. "She lives near Sunset Place, with a roommate. No family in Miami. They're all in Philadelphia. No siblings, parents divorced. A few traffic infractions, but beyond that, her record's squeaky clean."

"That's all you got?"

"You realize the Internet is not a magic genie bottle, right? There are limits to what I can dig up, even misusing my work database."

"Fair enough," he said. "You got a home address?"

"I do," Kathy said. "But before I pass that along, can I ask what it is you're doing here, Mr. I-don't-do-PI-work?"

"I'm curious."

"Is that a synonym for *stupid* these days?"

"Are you going to give me the address or not?"

"On one condition."

Pete sighed. "What?"

"Let me help," she said. "And if we find anything worthy of press, I call dibs."

Pete thought about it for a second. "Sure, that's fair. I don't imagine we'll stumble across Atlantis or anything remarkable by just talking to a missing girl's roommate."

"You never know," Kathy said. "The cops have probably talked to her, though."

"The cops are clueless," Pete said. His track record with the police was spotty at best, despite his pedigree as the son of a lauded homicide detective. "And I have a condition of my own, if we're going to do this."

"Oh? What?"

"You don't hold out on me," Pete said.

"Excuse me?"

"Keep me in the loop," Pete said. "You have sources. You know things. And I can tell you're only giving me part of the story. What else did your calls dig up?"

Kathy was silent on the other end.

"Rick's been asking around for her," Kathy said. "Her roommate, her old job, her family."

"Doesn't sound like something a murderer would do," Pete said.

"Right, which makes it the perfect thing for a murderer to do," Kathy said.

"Are you free now?" Pete said.

"I have to file my column, but that's close to final," Kathy said. "I hate writing these feel-good pieces. This one's about a kid who discovered his grandmother's stamp collection, which apparently helped his family keep their house. Nice, but a dime a dozen."

After the death of her father and her eventual reinstatement at the *Miami Times* following the Silent Death case, Kathy now held her father's old job: local Miami-Dade columnist. The hours were flexible, the work was easy, and the pay was good, so Kathy tolerated it. But the parallels to Chaz's life did not escape Pete. He could tell she was bored.

She rattled off the address to Pete.

"Meet me at her apartment in an hour?" he said.

"Make it forty-five."

CHAPTER EIGHT

Sunset Place, a once-proud mall and haven for hoity-toity shops that had faded into a series of empty storefronts and chain restaurants, was about a half-hour drive from Pete's house in Westchester. Shoehorned between South Miami and Coral Gables, Sunset Place—and the surrounding bars and restaurants—was cluttered with University of Miami students looking for fun and South Miami residents looking for the perfect crib for the baby's room.

Pete turned the volume up on his car's shitty stereo. Mick Jones sang about being lost in the supermarket. Pete nodded to the beat for a few seconds. It was happening again, he thought. That weird instinct that told him he had to be involved in something. Except it was electric, not like before, clouded and muffled by alcohol. No, this reminded Pete of his days covering sports teams and investigating the next big enterprise piece. The coach who lied on his résumé. The player who had somehow hidden his DUI arrest. He could sense there was a question that needed to be answered. He just wasn't sure what it was yet, or if he'd like the answer once he figured it out.

Alice Cline's apartment was a few blocks north of the central Sunset Place stores, off US1 and across the street from Fox's Lounge, a dive bar that served a great French onion soup but had seen better days. Pete pulled into a guest parking space adjacent to the small four-story apartment building and noticed Kathy's silver Jetta a few spaces over. She was in the car, earbuds in and oblivious to the world outside. Pete got out and walked over, rapping his knuckles on her driver's-side window. She reacted with a start. She yanked the buds out of her ears.

"You're here early," Pete said, as Kathy's window slid down.

"Does it surprise you that I didn't want to stay a second longer at that place?"

"Can't blame you."

"What took you so long?"

Pete checked his phone.

"Impatient much?"

"Not at all," Kathy said. "Just bored. All I had in the car to listen to was Amy's Pixies playlist, which—apologies to Kim Deal—gets boring on the hundredth listen."

Pete didn't comment. Amy, like Mike, had been murdered by the Silent Death—a final casualty before Pete confronted the killer and uncovered his true identity: Pete's high school friend, Javier Reyes. Amy had been Kathy's best friend, and they'd all worked together at the *Miami Times*—Amy as the Books editor. She was tough, smart, and her help had been integral to finding Kathy. It had been over a year since her death. Kathy rarely mentioned her.

Kathy got out of the car, slid her bag over her shoulder, and closed the door before turning to Pete.

"The roommate's name is Janet Fornell. Her parents are Cuban, like you and everyone else in this godforsaken town," she said. "She works down the street at Fox's Lounge, a bar—"

"I'm familiar with it."

"Oh, right. Of course you are."

"I'll take that as a compliment."

"You should," Kathy said. "You seem different. It's nice."

They started to walk toward the elevator, located in the middle of the first-floor lobby, which was empty and dilapidated. Pete didn't notice much activity, either. There were a few cars in the lot, but he'd yet to see an actual person.

"It's amazing what not drinking a bottle of vodka a day will do for your disposition," Pete said. He pushed the UP button on the elevator.

"How long has it been?"

"A while. A few months."

"That's something."

They stepped inside the elevator and Pete pushed the button for the third floor, exchanging a concerned look as the old elevator creaked to life. He let out a breath as the doors opened on Alice's floor. They made a left toward the building's west side, where the apartment was located—3H. Kathy knocked a few times and backed up, waiting for what was inside.

"Who is it?" a soft voice on the other side of the door said.

"Ms. Fornell?"

"Yes?"

"My name's Pete Fernandez. I was wondering if you'd have a few minutes to talk about your roommate."

They hadn't discussed strategy beforehand. Pete hoped Kathy would follow his lead.

The door didn't open. Kathy crossed her arms.

"Are you with the police?"

"Not exactly," Pete said. "I'm a . . . I'm a private investigator."

Pete didn't have to look at Kathy to see she had a smirk on her face.

They heard the latch and another lock turn, and watched as the door opened. Janet Fornell smiled as she backed into her tiny apartment, a signal for Pete and Kathy to come in. She was wearing sweat pants and a Voltron T-shirt, but they couldn't hide her fit body and simple but strong facial features. Pete reminded himself to focus. Being smitten this early in the game wasn't healthy.

"This is my colleague, Kathy Bentley," Pete said.

"You write for the newspaper, no?"

Kathy nodded. "Yes, but that's not why I'm here."

Pete noticed that Janet's expression had gone from somewhat welcoming to concerned.

"She's a friend," Pete said. "This isn't for a story. She helps me on cases when she's not working on the paper."

"Sounds like bullshit, but OK," Janet said. "Everything here is off the record. So, don't go quoting me anywhere. I'm not some *balsero* that just came ashore."

She walked them over to the apartment's tiny living room. Pete and Kathy took a seat on the IKEA loveseat and Janet pulled up a chair from the dining room set that filled out the rest of the space. The kitchen, also connected to the living room, was off the main hallway. Pete didn't notice many pictures, but one caught his eye: on a small table to his right and next to the couch was a framed photo—taken at a bar, Pete guessed, based on the giant mugs of beer Janet and Alice were hoisting up. They seemed happy. Alice's dark brown hair flailed around wildly, and both of them wore a variety of beads. He pointed at it.

"Mardi Gras?"

"Right, but not in New Orleans," Janet said, rubbing her palms on her sweatpants. "We just went down to Titanic, that UM bar a few miles from here."

"I know it," Pete said. "They do craft beers and burgers?"

"I think so, yeah. So, we were there," Janet said. She looked at Kathy, then at Pete. "Tell me, what can I do? Are you trying to find Alice?"

Kathy turned to look at Pete.

"Not exactly," he said. "I know Rick, Rick Blanco."

Janet's expression darkened.

"I don't think I want to talk to you, then."

Pete raised his hand.

"Hear me out first," he said. "I know Alice. Do you remember when she was being stalked by her ex? And she hired a PI? That was me. I was the guy that helped her."

Janet seemed appeased, but not fully convinced. Pete looked over at Kathy, as if to say, "Help me out here, will you?" but only got a slight shrug in response. He was on his own.

"OK," Janet said. "But that doesn't explain why you're working for Rick. That guy's a big-time asshole. For all I know, he hurt Alice."

"That's the thing," Pete said. "I'm not working for Rick."

"Then why are you here?"

"I'm worried about Alice, and I want to make sure she's OK."

"Just like that?" Janet said, her shoulders rising and dropping, her body talking along with her mouth. "I'm supposed to just tell some random dude everything I said to the cops?"

"So you *did* go to the police?" Kathy said.

Janet hesitated.

"Yeah, I mean, of course I did," she said. "I had to file a missing person's report. She hasn't been home in over a month. The last time I saw her, she was going to have dinner with Rick. His wife was out of town or something, so they could actually spend time together. He'd gotten a nice room at a hotel on the beach—the Eden Roc. She was really excited."

"How often would they see each other?" Pete asked, trying not to lose the momentum of the conversation, to keep Janet talking.

"Depends," Janet said. "Sometimes a few nights a week, if his wife was busy, sometimes once a month. He was really cagey about it. He definitely didn't want to end his marriage. But he seemed to like Alice. He told her that maybe, down the line, they could figure something out. But he couldn't leave his wife just yet."

"They always say that," Kathy said. "But it's never true."

"Yeah, tell me about it," Janet said, her eyes distant, reliving a painful memory. "But you can only tell your friend so much before they have to learn this shit for themselves, you know? She was in denial. Thought Rick was some kind of shining knight when he was really just a dude who'd gotten bored of fucking the same blonde *americana*, so he wanted another, different one."

53

Pete bristled at her description of Emily, but let it go.

"Did Alice have problems with Rick?"

"Yeah," Janet said, almost laughing. "What do you think? Everything was a problem. You've met Alice. She's a pretty girl. Smart, too. She didn't want to share her man. But she fell hard for this dickhead and he knew it, so he played her. She'd go to him every time he could spare a minute. And wow, try to take that girl's iPhone away. She'd be texting him all day, all night."

"Do you think Rick would hurt her, though?" Kathy said.

"I don't know," Janet said, her voice lowering. "I met the guy a few times, when he'd come over really late at night. Seemed OK. I could tell he liked her. But like I said, anyone can want you. It's the guys that actually do shit for you, beyond opening doors and their wallets, that count. This guy was just a player."

"Is there any chance Alice went to stay with relatives?" Pete said, racking his brain, looking for any logical explanation for her disappearance. "Friends? Has she ever just up and left like this?"

"Nah, never. She's the kind of girl that would always tell me where she was going and when she was coming back, even if it was clear I didn't give a shit," Janet said, her eyes watering. She clasped her hands together.

Pete flashed back to something in his blurry memory. Alice had heard of him through Kathy's book and the related news coverage. Pete had been struck by her beauty when he first met her at his house, to talk over the case. He'd been drinking heavily then—waking up with a vodka on ice to get through the morning, and doing his best not to leave the house. She seemed scared and surprised when she saw his living room: bottles collecting around the garbage can, newspapers stacked near the door. Someone lived here, he wanted to say. Someone else had made this mess. He'd been struck by her intelligence; she got to the point and spoke with conviction. Soon, they'd agreed to terms and Pete was ready to start. "Ready" being relative.

"You sure you're up to this?" she'd asked.

"Yeah, of course."

"All right, man. Just don't fuck up and make me regret this."

They'd laughed. But now, thinking back on the exchange, Pete felt empty; sitting on the tiny couch in Alice's apartment, a space she might never fill again, he felt like a complete waste.

"She's dead, isn't she?"

Janet's question shook Pete out of his reverie and he noticed Kathy's concerned look—one that was mostly sadness but also said, "What are we getting into?"

He had no answer. For either of them. He looked at Janet, his eyes locked in on her, trying to provide whatever comfort he could muster and send it to her.

"I don't know."

"What can I do?" Janet said.

"Can you tell us anything else about Alice, about what she was doing before she disappeared?" Kathy said.

Janet thought for a moment, her hands rubbing together as if that would help jog her memory.

"Not really," she said. "We were going to split soon."

"What do you mean?" Pete said.

"Like, we had to find our own places," Janet said.

"How come?" Kathy asked.

"I'm moving to New York, got a job doing social work," Janet said. "I graduated last semester and tried to find something here, but *nada*. Our lease is up in a month."

"So she was looking for a new apartment?" Pete said.

"Yeah, she had a few leads. I'm not sure. Nothing was definite."

"Is her computer here?" Pete said.

"Yeah, why?"

"Can we take a look at it?"

Kathy plopped herself in front of Alice's iBook and opened it. A light cloud of dust appeared as Kathy jostled the computer. Alice's room had just enough space for a double bed, a dresser, a small desk, and a tiny TV on a stand. Still, it was neat and no-frills. A few framed photos rested on the nightstand next to Alice's bed, one of Rick alone and another of Alice and what Pete presumed was her family at the beach, all smiles and looking up at the camera. He pulled up a chair next to Kathy, and he and Janet looked over her shoulder as she typed. She clicked through the keys and Pete had to focus to keep up.

"I doubt we'll be able to find anything of note," Kathy said, her eyes on the screen. "But at the very least, we can check her history and see what sites she's been on."

"Do you think that will help you find her?" Janet said.

"Unclear," Kathy said, her hands no longer typing as she scanned a dropdown menu of Alice's browsing history. "But it can't hurt. It looks like she's been spending a lot of time on Craigslist."

"So, she was on there looking for an apartment?" Janet said.

"Or a roommate, or sex—you can get anything on here," Kathy

said, beginning to type again. "I'm hoping she's lazy like I am and has her password saved on her e-mail . . . yup, we're in."

Pete patted Kathy on the shoulder. "Nice work."

"It was pure luck," she said, shrugging away from Pete's touch and continuing to type. "So, OK. It looks like she was e-mailing with someone: MIAapt4rentSOON@hotmail.com. Not the most unique name, and the fact that the person uses Hotmail indicates they're slightly behind the times, or just using this account for the purpose of finding a roommate. Not a warning sign, just yet."

"I use Hotmail," Janet said.

Kathy's eyebrows popped up in judgment, but returned to normal after a second, her eyes focused on the screen.

Pete and Janet read the e-mails between Alice and the Hotmail account. They seemed harmless. No meetings were set up, no conversation deviated from the professional. If anything, the exchange was dry and without emotion.

"The last e-mail was from two months ago," Kathy said. "And this person asked Alice for her phone number to set up a time so she could come see the apartment, which is supposed to be downtown, near the Performing Arts Center."

The new PAC was also adjacent to the *Miami Times* building.

"What's the address?"

"That's the weird thing," Kathy said, looking frustrated, her typing growing more fevered. "They never give Alice the address, just cross streets. But that could be anything. Saying you live on Biscayne and Twenty-first Street means very little."

"Do you think this person did something to Alice?" Janet said.

"Too early to tell," Pete said, his eyes still on the laptop monitor.

"She could have just stopped responding, or gone to see the apartment and not been interested. We don't have much to go on."

Kathy pushed her rolling chair away from the desk and got up.

"It's a start. I'm not sure we're going to get much else on her computer, though."

"More than the cops did," Janet said as they exited Alice's room.

"Color me surprised," Pete said.

Janet followed Kathy and Pete toward the door. They'd been at her apartment for a little over an hour, but it felt like much longer to Pete.

"Thanks for taking the time," Pete said. He stuck out his hand and Janet shook it.

"I just want my friend back," Janet said.

Pete wasn't sure how to respond.

Kathy shook Janet's hand and slipped her a business card. A few moments later, she and Pete were in the parking lot, heading to their cars. They reached Kathy's first, and Pete lingered as she got in. She lowered her window. "What?"

"I don't have a good feeling about this," Pete said, looking toward the busy thruway that was US1, a block or so away from the apartment complex.

"Neither do I," Kathy said. "But I also don't know anything concrete. She's definitely missing, though."

"She may be dead."

"Yes, Mr. Private Investigator, that's very astute of you," Kathy said. "She may be dead. But all we know at this point is she was looking for a new apartment before she went missing, which I'm sure isn't all that uncommon."

"What the hell is your problem?"

She sighed and began to rummage through her purse.

"This is . . . this is just really weird," Kathy said, motioning at the building with her left hand. "It's like I'm at the other end of what happened to me, and I'm not sure how I feel about that."

She pulled out a pack of cigarettes and lit one, puffing on it before turning to look at Pete.

"Can you understand that? I was missing once, too. And this girl might be where I was. Alone. Tied up to a bed and blindfolded, with no idea as to whether she's going to live to see anyone she knows, much less her family or friends. It's terrible. I wouldn't wish that on anyone."

Pete felt like an idiot. He'd let her come along, was excited for the company, but hadn't considered the implications. Just a year ago, it was Pete who was looking for Kathy, though *looking* was a generous word for it.

"It's OK for you to feel strongly about this," Pete said, trying to be helpful.

Kathy shot him a look. She wasn't the type for lovey-dovey new age advice. She was biting her tongue, though. She took another drag, then pulled the cigarette from her mouth and looked at it. She tossed it out the driver's side window without comment.

"I just need to go home and relax for a bit," she said. She looked up at Pete. "I'll call you tomorrow and we can pick up on this. OK?"

"Sure, sounds fine."

Before he could finish, she was backing her car out of the parking lot and speeding off toward the expressway. Pete walked over to his car and sat in the driver's seat. He didn't start the engine. He let his head fall back on the headrest. He felt strange. A combination of déjà vu and something different. Something bad. It took him a second or two to realize he'd closed his eyes. When he opened them, a slight rain was falling, the drops of water the only noise Pete could hear.

CHAPTER NINE

He knew someone was in the house as he started to get out of his car. The rain hadn't stopped. Pete never carried an umbrella. Storms usually didn't last this long in Miami. The days were hot and the nights only less so.

For some reason, the porch light was off. Pete popped open his glove compartment and took out the gun—his father's Glock, from his days as a homicide detective for the Miami-Dade Police Department. He got out of the car and held the gun low as he crouched toward his front steps. For a moment, Pete felt foolish, creeping up on his own house, holding a loaded gun, but then he reminded himself that he seemed to attract the kind of company that would require this kind of entrance.

His paranoia was confirmed when he got to the front door. It was ajar. He leaned his back on the wall next to it, trying to peer in but seeing only darkness. *Where was Emily?* Still out with friends, he hoped, as he pushed the door open with his foot, careful not to make any sudden moves. No sounds came from inside.

Pete let his head pop in the crack of the door. He saw a figure in the living room, sitting in his father's favorite recliner, which faced away from the front of the house and toward the television set hanging on the opposite wall. It wasn't moving.

"You can put the gun down," the figure said, the voice low and male.

Pete straightened up and stepped into his house. He flicked on the gun's safety and slid it behind his back. He turned on the light switch near the front door and squinted as the living room and dining area were illuminated. Rick stood up from the recliner and faced Pete. He didn't look any better than the last time.

"You do this often?"

"What?"

"Break into people's houses? New thing for you, huh?"

"Your door was open."

"Bullshit."

"OK," Rick said. "Maybe not. I didn't break anything to get in."

"Parse away," Pete said, closing the front door. "But I think this still falls under breaking and entering."

"Are you going to let me explain?"

"I was hoping we'd reach that point, yes."

Rick walked toward the smallish dining room table. They both took seats and faced each other.

Pete pulled his gun out and laid it on the table.

"Is that necessary?"

"I'll be the judge of what's necessary," Pete said. "This being my house and all, and you being uninvited but still, you know, here."

"Fine."

"Plus, it hurts my back when I have it there and sit down."

Rick ignored the joke and scratched his chin, sizing Pete and the situation up.

"I haven't done anything to Alice."

"Well, that's good," Pete said. "Never said you did."

"The cops think I did," Rick said, cracking his knuckles. "They're asking me for alibis and shit like that."

"That's what cops do, man."

"I didn't do anything wrong."

Pete sighed.

"I'm running out of patience here," Pete said. "I'm tired. I've had a long day. I'm getting tangled in some bullshit I don't want to be tangled in, and I just discovered my ex's husband has broken into my house. And he may be wanted for questioning by the police. This complicates my life. And it bothers me. So let's get to the point before I ask you to leave and wash my hands of the whole fucking thing."

"You wouldn't do that."

"Want to risk it?"

"I know you," Rick said. "That's not how you operate. You're like a dog with a bone—you don't let these kinds of things go."

"How did you figure this out about me?" Pete said. "Considering we've spent, what, maybe five hours together in total?"

"Just because you're not with Emily doesn't mean she never talks about you."

Rick let that hang and Pete let it jab at him. The idea of Emily talking about him, referencing what they once had, comparing that to whatever she had with Rick, made his head pound.

"Get to the point," Pete said. "Where were you the night Alice disappeared?"

Rick's story meandered, but seemed true, at least to Pete. He was up front about the affair with Alice; it had been going on for a few months. She had joined his company as an executive assistant. His assistant, to be exact. So he became the cliché boss that fell for his hot, twenty-something secretary. She "understood" him, got his jokes, enjoyed the music playlists he made her, was supportive of him writing that last great American novel or finally learning to play the guitar. All the shit that Emily, over time, had started shrugging off.

The night in question, Rick had rented a room at the Eden Roc, a fancy luxury hotel on Collins Avenue in South Beach. The kind of place everyone knew, but few stayed at. It was expensive, and about an hour away from his office. It was a last hurrah of sorts. Emily was catching on, and he had decided that he wanted to work things out with his wife as opposed to taking a leap into a relationship with a coworker who got his dick hard. Pete found himself nodding as Rick told the story.

A year ago, if someone had asked Pete what he wanted most of all, it would have been easy—Emily. To be with her again. To make her laugh, to sit around and spend time together doing nothing. Now, he wasn't so sure. The memories—of her stepping into that cab a few days after his father's funeral, of the terse exchanges and distant stares that followed—still stung, but seemed a lifetime ago. He felt both grateful and sad about that.

Rick's plan was to have one last romantic romp with Alice, break the news to her, then propose they have a friends-with-benefits scenario, where neither of them would shoot for a relationship in the long term, but they'd still fuck from time to time.

"Did you really think she'd go for that?"

"Yeah, why not?" Rick said, straight-faced. "She got all the goods and none of the drama."

"You don't think dating a married man involves drama?"

"Well, I'm not sure. It sounded good at the time."

"What happened that night?"

"She came to the hotel, around nine. Emily thought I was working late. I slept at the office every now and then. After Alice came to the hotel, we went to that shithole club, Purdy Lounge. You know, the one by Gibb Memorial? That park?"

"You're kidding me."

"No, no. She liked that scene. Drinking and dancing. We used to go all the time."

Pete looked up at the clock. It was half past midnight. The "case," or whatever he was doing, had taken up most of the day.

"So, we're pretty lit up," Rick continued. "Alice loved those kamikaze shots, so we did a few of those, couple rounds of beers. You know, the usual let-me-get-my-date-ready scenario. We head back to the hotel, do some lines, and I think things are going to go well from there, so we start—"

"Spare me the details, please," Pete said. "Did she leave? Did she spend the night? What happened?"

"We argued," Rick said. "We didn't even get to anything physical. She asked where 'this' was going and I sprung it on her. She flipped;

started throwing shit, yelling. Threatened to call Emily and tell her everything. It was nuts. She went fucking crazy. Finally, she wore herself out and bolted."

"Did you try calling her?"

"No, I just tried to fix the room up and get out of there. I was worried she was going to call Emily, but when I got home and realized she hadn't, I just figured she needed time to cool off."

"You didn't try to reach out to her, then?"

"No, man," Rick said, confusion in his voice. "Why would I? Bullet dodged, you know?"

"You're an asshole," Pete said, standing up. "You can leave."

Rick got up and followed Pete toward the door.

"But why? What am I supposed to tell the cops?"

"Exactly what you told me."

"But that sounds terrible."

"That is accurate," Pete said.

"I need your help," Rick said, his voice pleading. "I could be seriously up shit creek for this."

Pete opened the door.

"I don't care," Pete said. "I used to think you were a good guy. After all the shit I'd put Emily through, I thought, hey, OK, at least she's with a stand-up dude and they're going to have a decent life together. But you're not. You're a piece of shit and you've come to me to get you out of a bind of your own making. You know what? Fuck you. You're not my concern."

Rick seemed taken aback and let out a quick, dismissive sound.

"Suddenly you're this high and mighty force of good? I remember when you'd spend hours on the phone, crying and begging for Emily to take you back. I'm not the sad piece of shit, man, you are."

"Get the fuck out of my house."

"That's it, then?" Rick said, venom in his voice. "You're going to let me dangle because I fucked around on your ex? You know what she's like as well as I do, and after a while, the joke gets old. It doesn't change the fact that Alice is missing, and I could be getting the blame for it. You're going to let her disappear because of some petty vengeance against me?"

Pete locked his eyes on Rick's.

"I'm not going to help you," Pete said. "Your story—true or not—sounds terrible, even if you've done nothing wrong. As for Alice, well, that's different—but none of your business. That goes for Emily, too. Leave us alone."

"She's never going to take you back," Rick said as he turned toward the open door.

It was only then that they noticed Emily standing in the doorway, her arms looped through a half-dozen grocery bags. Her eyes were red. The rain had stopped.

CHAPTER TEN

"Leave us alone?" Emily said.

"Let me explain."

Rick didn't stick around to see the fireworks. Upon realizing Emily had heard most, if not all of their heated exchange, he sidestepped his estranged wife and darted off. *Stand-up guy*, Pete thought.

"There's nothing to explain," Emily said, walking into the house and plopping her groceries on the dining room table. She gave Pete's gun a quizzical look. "Why is that out in the house?"

Her tone gave Pete pause. "The house?"

"Yes, this house," Emily said, her volume rising. "Why is there a gun on the dining room table of this house?"

"Because this is my fucking house," Pete said. "How many times am I going to have to remind people of that today?"

"What are you talking about?"

"Never mind," Pete said. "I thought someone had broken in. I pulled out the gun and found Rick in here."

Emily began shuttling grocery bags to the kitchen and putting the items away. Pete followed her.

"Thanks for the groceries," he said.

"You're welcome," she said. "I got a few things before I met Susan."

"You're pissed."

"Yes, Peter. I am pissed."

She never called him Peter, he thought, unless she was reaching a level of angry no one really wanted to experience.

"What was I supposed to do, kick him out?"

She looked up from the fridge, her eyes dull and red.

"I don't want to have this discussion," she said.

"So, we just forget this happened and avoid each other for a little bit, hoping that things go back to normal?" Pete said. "Just like old times?"

Emily closed the fridge door with a little too much force.

"This is not 'just like old times,'" she said. "You know that. It can never be that way again. You're letting me stay here for a bit, and I appreciate that. I just need some time to think about what to do next, and it doesn't help to come home to find your two most recent exes having a confab about you, one of their mistresses, and who's more deserving of your affection. Such macho, stupid bullshit."

"He's being questioned about this girl's disappearance."

"Alice? You can say her name. I won't go into convulsions."

"Yes, Alice," Pete said.

"So, they think he did it?"

"They're questioning him, at the very least," Pete said. "And I doubt his visit to me is going to earn him any points with them."

"Wonderful," she said. "Fucking wonderful."

She sped past Pete and headed toward the guest room, which was across the hall from the kitchen. She closed the door with a slam.

He decided against prolonging the discussion. He walked back to the kitchen and slowly put away the rest of the groceries. After a few minutes he was done, and exhaustion overtook him. He walked back into the living room, picked his gun off the table, and made sure the safety was on. He stood by the dining room table and scanned the house. The liquor cabinets were empty. That's where his mind went now, he thought. Always to what was missing. What he couldn't have anymore. He pushed the thought away and put the gun on the small table by the front door. He walked down the main hall toward his bedroom, pulling his T-shirt off as he closed the door behind him. He threw his jeans into a corner. He didn't bother to turn on the light. He knew where every book was, where every piece of furniture jutted out. Costello mewed in frustration as Pete fell onto the bed.

His life had become a collection of ghosts from his past mingling with the detritus of his present with a dash of nostalgia and regret. He slid under the covers and fell asleep.

He didn't hear her come into the room at first, but the light from the hallway woke him up. He wasn't sure how much time had passed. The cat was gone, probably distracted by a bird or sound. She slid in bed next to him, sniffling to herself, trying to keep it down. Pete was on his back. He felt her leg loop over him and she was on top, her breath hot on his face as she leaned in to him, grinding her body onto his. He reacted. He remembered her. Them. His hand reached for her sides as his mouth found hers and for a split second they were back—back to a time when this was normal and what they both wanted. Pete pulled away from the kiss and tried to look at Emily's face in the darkness.

"What are you doing?"

"Don't talk," she said, almost pleading. "I just need to feel something, OK?"

Pete didn't respond. She slid her nightgown off and tossed it near his dresser, and any chance of this stopping went away. She leaned back in to Pete, her body warm on his as he guided his hands up her back, cautiously at first, as if it could stop at any moment—then with more abandon.

Responding to his hungry hands, she reached for him, pulling his boxers down and off the bed. They kissed—bumping into each other, getting reacquainted with their movements, texture, bruises, and tics. Soon, like muscle memory, their bodies moved in a rhythm that neither had found since Emily got into that cab, years before. It was in this moment that Pete allowed himself to push past the nervous energy, the rush of paranoid thoughts, and the constant overthink that had invaded his brain since he'd stopped dulling it with alcohol. She was quiet, letting out soft, slight moans in response to Pete from time to time. Both of them focused on what they were doing to each other—and for each other. A momentary respite from the dirge-like existence surrounding them: the darkness, the rejection, the failure, and the sadness that Pete had seen in himself and in her was carefully placed on the shelf for a minute while they dealt with other feelings that had collected a coat of dust: pleasure, affection, comfort, love.

Pete didn't believe his phone was actually ringing until the third chime, and with that, he let out a loud groan. Emily, still on top of him, grabbed both his hands and pinned them down on the bed, willing their bodies to continue.

"Do not answer that," she said, her voice almost hoarse. "I will kill you if you answer that."

Pete pulled her close and kissed her. She smelled the same. She moved the same. He took comfort in the familiarity. Everything was clearer. The phone continued to ring.

"Let it go to voice mail," he said with a smile, as he picked her up and flipped her over, kissing her neck, finally appreciating the moment. It rang twice more.

"Good boy," she half whispered. His fingers, sliding over her face, felt the smile on her lips.

The phone started to ring again. Pete let his eyes glance at the display—it was Kathy. She wasn't a phone person—the fact that she was calling him twice back-to-back meant it was important.

Pete untangled himself from Emily and grabbed the cell phone on his nightstand.

"Hey," he said, out of breath. "You OK?"

"Um, I'm fine," Kathy said. "I guess. You sound like you're not, though. Are you OK?"

"Yeah, I'm fine."

"OK, well, you may want to get down here," she said.

"Where? The *Times*?"

"Yes, the *Times*," Kathy said. "I've been stuck here all night. Have you not watched the news at all? I figured you'd be the one calling me."

Emily stirred. "What's going on?"

"I don't know," Pete whispered to her, then returned his attention to Kathy. "What happened?"

"Is someone there with you?" Kathy said. "Jesus. OK, whatever. It's Alice."

Pete's heart sank.

"They found her? Is she dead?"

"Yeah . . . Yes," Kathy said. Pete could hear her voice crack. "It's just . . . It's terrible. Terrible."

"What happened?"

"She's dead," Kathy said. "Stabbed all over. I've never seen anything like it. They found her—most of her—in a lake. Whoever did this . . . I can't even describe it. She's dead. Alice is dead."

Pete dropped the phone and let his eyes drift up to the ceiling as Emily pulled him closer. He couldn't hear her, but he knew what she was asking him. As he closed his eyes for a moment, the sliver of moonlight creeping into the room went dark.

They didn't talk during the half hour drive from the house to the downtown offices of the *Miami Times*. They'd gotten dressed, throwing on whatever was around. Pete in a T-shirt and hoodie sweater with blue jeans and sneakers, Emily in Pete's Pixies reunion shirt, jeans, and sandals. They looked just like they felt—a couple interrupted. Pete had a playlist he'd put together months ago playing off his iPhone. The third track kicked in, Neko Case. She sang about wanting to die at the drive-in. Emily flicked off the stereo. He looked over at her. She was staring out the window.

"You OK?"

"Yeah," she said.

He thought about reaching out a hand, but he wasn't sure what to make of her. Had their connection been just a thing that happens when you mix toxic emotions with old flames? He wasn't sure. Now wasn't the time to define anything.

"You're thinking about us," she said, still looking out the window as Pete turned onto the 836, taking them east toward downtown.

"Is that surprising?"

"No, that's what you do," Emily said. "You do something, then you think about it forever, then you do something else and think about that for a while."

"You're describing pretty standard human behavior," Pete said.

She turned to him. Even this early in the morning, it was humid and sweaty outside—like walking through an endless wall of lukewarm fog. The night sky had a misty, almost smokelike quality that reminded Pete of mornings spent watching his dad put on his uniform and head out on patrol. When sleep glazed over everything and it all seemed a little fuzzy.

"You're more like yourself now," she said. "It's like you woke up from a bad dream, but you're still in bed wondering if it was a dream or not."

"I guess," Pete said. "I don't know. What are you getting at?"

"Nothing," she said. "I'm just saying it's nice. I wish it had happened sooner."

Pete didn't respond. He pulled the car up by the main *Miami Times* entrance, which was near the expressway and close to the Venetian Causeway, the small bridge that led to the neon glow of Miami Beach. Prime real estate. He wondered when the *Times* would call it a day and finally sell the land. Then he realized he didn't care. Pete had put in a few years as a copy editor for the *Miami Times*' sports desk, after years as an award-winning sports reporter in New Jersey. His tenure at the *Times* could be described as unspectacular to subpar. Had it not been for Kathy's disappearance, he would have probably lasted a few more months, as opposed to getting fired for basically shirking his responsibilities while he went off searching for a woman he barely knew and continuing to drink himself to oblivion.

He parked the car and they got out. Kathy was outside, close to the entrance, huddled, her two-sizes-too-big sweater enveloping her as she took a drag from her cigarette. The *Miami Times* building was a symbol from a bygone era when newspapers mattered, surrounded by half-empty, giant downtown high-rises, luxury condos being rented instead of sold, and a looming performing arts center—a faded icon that would soon flicker out completely. Pete thought he could smell a tinge of salt water mixed in with the dust and dirt from the myriad construction sites slowly dragging the city into the present, but he was probably just deluding himself. Despite the sweltering Miami weather, Kathy looked like she was freezing. Kathy scanned them carefully as they approached, a knowing look in her eye.

"Glad you could make it," she said, exhaling a small cloud of smoke. "Emily was up at this hour, too?"

Pete didn't take the bait.

"Is there anything I can do?"

"No; she's dead," Kathy said, whatever anxiety she had been feeling over the phone now gone. "Her body washed up in a lake over in Kendall. Someone had taken a raft out sometime late at night and dumped her there. The bag was sealed airtight, so it floated to shore. Maybe the killer was a moron—but that strikes me as odd, considering all the terrible things he did to this girl. I can't even repeat it. It's the worst I've ever seen. No note, no prints, obviously. No word on DNA. The cops are in a tizzy. And, in case you were wondering, Rick isn't much of a suspect anymore. This was a little too—um—stylish for him."

"Tell me about the scene," Pete said.

"He tied her up, wrists to ankles," Kathy said. Pete could tell she was uncomfortable, choosing her words with care. "I can't. I can't deal with this."

"Where in Kendall?" Emily asked.

"Off 137th," Kathy said. "Townhouse complex—Bent Tree. Kind of nondescript. Kind of old pseudo-condos painted in earth tones to look thematic. Pretty random place to dump a body."

"Unless that's what you want," Pete said.

"Excellent point, Mr. Detective," Kathy said. "But doesn't this strike you as odd? It just seems really random."

"It does strike me, but *odd*'s not the word," Pete said.

"What do you mean?" Emily said.

"It's like a weird déjà vu feeling," Pete said.

"That's not surprising," Kathy said, rummaging through her purse and pulling out a stack of printouts. She handed half to Pete and the other half to Emily. "Look at these. I found them in the news archive earlier tonight while doing some research. Something I never do, so I'm sure red flags galore went up. So, suffice to say, these were not easy to acquire and you're not supposed to be seeing them. Hence our covert rendezvous. So, yeah. No live-tweeting your reading."

Pete tried to stifle a yawn. It was close to dawn. He was surprised by the number of cars in the parking lot, but big news in Miami meant the *Times* had to call in what little staff was left. And the grisly murder of a young, recent college grad fell under big news, even in a seedy place like his hometown.

He flipped through the stack of *Times* clippings. Most were dated from the mid-eighties, and a handful were written by Kathy's father, Chaz, who, before moving up to be the local columnist du jour, had toiled away as a crime reporter, much as his daughter would twenty years later. Pete skimmed the headlines: "Teen girl found mutilated at Crandon Park"; "Tamarac teen feared missing, last seen with mystery man"; "FIU grad dead, stabbed 24 times: police fear serial murderer." For a second, he appreciated the terse, staccato writing of the journalists of the era—trying to inform as much as possible, before the Internet, Twitter, and Facebook were options, when your daily paper was your one main dose of information before the nightly news.

"These sound similar," Pete said, still rifling through the clippings, each one clocking in at about four printed pages—a front section story and a lengthy jump, unheard of now. "But they're from twenty years ago."

"Except this one," Emily said, pulling a page out of her smaller stack. She handed it to Pete.

Pete scanned the single sheet. The byline was a name he didn't recognize: Alexia Sanchez. The turnover at the *Times* was frequent and usually involved interns and temps taking on full-time jobs for less money. The story, unlike the pages from the 1980s, was brief and limited to the front page of the local section. The headline was short, befitting a story buried on the lower right of the page. With only a small mug shot for art, the story was lucky it made the front at all. "Miami High student missing after shopping trip." It was light on details, but did include a call out to the *Miami Times* website "for more information, as it happens." Pete let out a sigh.

"This one's from a few days ago," Pete said. "But kids go missing all the time. It doesn't automatically mean they're connected."

"Fair enough," Kathy said. "But did you read the story?"

He hadn't. The piece was poorly edited. Pete fought the urge to pull out a pen, as he had so many times during his stint at the *Times*, and make corrections.

"The best details are lost in the story," Pete said, more to himself than to Kathy or Emily. "'Morales, seventeen, a senior at Miami Senior High School, was last seen talking to a white male in his thirties in the Dadeland parking lot, adjacent to Macy's off N. Kendall Drive. The man was driving a white van of unspecified make and model.' Why is that in the last paragraph?"

"That's not the point," Emily said. She'd been looking over Pete's stack of clippings while he read the story. "The kids and women in these stories were also last seen talking to a dude driving a van."

"Right, but that was twenty years ago," Pete said. He was confused. He looked at Kathy. She didn't seem confused at all. "What's the deal?"

"You're a bad Miamian," Kathy said. "You're really still drawing a blank?"

Pete hated guessing games. Especially when they involved people's lives.

"Just spit it out," Pete said.

Kathy collected her printouts and shoved them back into her purse before taking out a black folder. She opened it and pulled out a sheet of paper and handed it to Pete.

"Rex Whitehurst," Kathy said. "Does the name ring a bell?"

"Not really," Emily said.

"Pete?"

He looked over the printout, a quick bio of Whitehurst. It was incomplete, as if someone had been in a hurry and had only printed a few pages. But the basic information was there. Whitehurst had killed a dozen women—ranging in age from fourteen to twenty-seven—in the early 1980s, ending his string of murders in Miami, where he ruthlessly killed three girls in a manic spree that led to his capture. Whitehurst was a stabber—and known for leaving his victims in elaborate, sexualized poses.

"So, this is our dude, then?" Pete said, regretting it after the words left his lips.

Kathy snatched the paper back and slipped it into the black folder.

"That's the problem," she said.

"I'm confused," Emily said. "How is this possible? Did this guy somehow escape?"

"No, dear," Kathy said. "This is a much bigger problem."

"Why?" Pete said.

"Rex Whitehurst has been dead for over two decades," Kathy said, her voice emphasizing the last few words. "He was put down via Old Sparky in 1994. Rex is dead and someone is killing women in a sick, twisted homage to him."

PART II:
VENGEANCE IS SLEEPING

CHAPTER ELEVEN

The bitter coffee burned Pete's tongue as he sipped it. He hated this part of AA. The socializing. The exchanging of numbers. The questions, like "How's your day been?" or "How are you holding up?" It drove Pete up the wall. He didn't know how he was holding up. He wanted a drink most of the time.

He'd slid over by the coffeepot, where he figured he could finish his cup of tar, do his time, and sneak out with little fanfare. That was the plan, at least.

"Hey, Pete, how goes it?" It was Jack. Again.

"Not bad," Pete said, sipping the still-hot and still-nasty coffee faster. Plan foiled.

"Meant to tell you this last week," Jack said. "But you seemed a little ruffled when I mentioned the book. Hope I didn't offend you."

Pete stiffened for an awkward exchange.

Jack cleared his throat. "I knew your dad," Jack said. "I was a beat cop—Miami Dade PD. Your dad . . . He was one of the good ones. Great detective. Smart man. Just an all around good guy. I think he'd be proud of you, seeing you right yourself like you're doing."

Pete was caught off guard. He'd been expecting some new age AA babble, or a passive-aggressive guilt trip about how Jack "hadn't seen him around." Not the memory of his father. It felt weird—like his dad was in the room with him, noticing him for what he was. He stammered a bit before responding.

"Well, uh, thanks. Thank you, Jack," Pete said. "Not sure if you're on the money there, but I appreciate it. My dad was a good man."

Jack poured himself a cup of coffee.

"You been keeping up with the news?"

Pete tossed his cup into the nearby trash bin.

"Sure."

"People are talking about that dead girl," Jack said, sipping his coffee with none of Pete's hesitation. "Some of my old buddies on the force say the brass is freaking out."

"Yeah? Why's that?"

"Lots of reasons," Jack said. "Smells of a serial, first of all. Especially with that other girl missing."

"What other girl?"

Jack seemed surprised.

"Morales," Jack said.

Pete nodded and grabbed another empty cup. The church basement had cleared out by now, with the exception of a few stragglers helping put stuff away.

"Yeah, I read the story," Pete said, pouring himself another half cup for lack of anything else to do. "But what's that got to do with a serial killer?"

"You're cagey," Jack said, laughing. "I'm not trying to grill you, man. I'm trying to talk shop a bit. You're the closest thing to a cop in this room, and I get nostalgic for the water cooler talk in my old age. Beats going down to John Martin's and knocking back a dozen Guinness."

"That's fair, sorry," Pete said. "I'm just paranoid by nature. Been a nutty year or so."

He was wary of Jack. Of all the people he'd met in the rooms Jack was the most persistent. And now he kept bringing things back to the murders. Was he looking to talk shop, or was there more to it? Was Pete just being paranoid? He wasn't sure yet.

Jack gave Pete an apologetic smile.

"The name Rex Whitehurst mean anything to you?" Jack said.

"A bit," Pete said. "Been reading up on him lately, actually."

"What they did to that Cline girl," Jack said, pausing for a beat. "That's Whitehurst. 'Cept it can't be. He's been dead for about a decade."

"Yeah," Pete said. "But he's not the only person to ever slice people up."

"Fair enough," Jack said. "But I was there when Rex came to town. I remember what he did to those girls, and what he was like. It wasn't just about posing a girl in a sexy way, like a porno. He posed them in a way that said 'I did this. I won.' When we brought him in, he was talking nonsense—about a dark age that would last thousands of years, and how he needed to stop it. Crazy shit. But this is a mirror image of his work. If I hadn't known people who saw him get fried, I'd think he was back at it somehow."

"I was young," Pete said. "But I remember bits and pieces. The press was all over it. It wasn't 'Summer of Sam' crazy, but everyone in the city was looking for that guy. Surprised he was on the run as long as he was."

The room was empty now, and Pete wondered how much time they had to shoot the shit before someone semiofficial came to usher them out.

"He was smart," Jack said. "But he was crazy. In custody he kept going on about the collapse of society. He'd rationalized it to himself in his mind. He'd started off molesting kids at the school he worked at, up in New York. Then he went too far and killed one, went on the run. Think he had over a dozen or so bodies under his belt by the time we got him."

"You think we have a copycat?" Pete asked.

"I dunno," Jack said. "Could be a one-off, could be more than that. Sure seems like an homage, at the very least. What'd that girl ever do to anyone except break a few hearts?"

"What do you mean? I'm not following you."

"She's pretty, is all," Jack said, giving Pete a confused look. "Or was."

"Yeah," Pete said. The comment struck him as odd but he let it go. "It's a tragedy."

Jack nodded and started to head for the door. "Well, I gotta get home," Jack said. "Mona's gonna cook up her usual and I have to sit down and pretend to love it. Marriage, huh?"

Pete waved as Jack walked out. He felt on edge. He needed to do something. But what was he already doing? He was researching Rex Whitehurst, talking to the people around Alice, and trying to figure out who was behind her death. He knew this feeling. It had paid off when he found Kathy, he thought, but it'd also cost him the life of a close friend and two others. He didn't want to put anyone at risk again. But did he have faith in the Miami police to do anything?

He made it to his car and grabbed his worn-out leather carrying case. Inside it, Pete had been collecting documents for his ad hoc research. Copies of the clippings Kathy had found, a few other printouts Pete had made the night before, and a legal pad with some scribbled notes. He sat in the driver's seat and tried to focus. He'd settled back into the routine of a reporter with little rust or hesitation—research and all. He still found the library visits tedious, but even that was almost bearable.

Still, there was something about the information that wasn't gelling, and something that Kathy had said that was buzzing around his brain—ever-present, but impossible to pin down. Why was she surprised about Pete not recognizing Rex's MO? He pulled out one of the newspaper clippings, this one from 1984. The headline read "Boca girl, 13, still missing." The subhead gave a bit more information above the Chaz Bentley byline: "Approached by white male driving nondescript van." A van. Surely that wasn't unique amongst killers, or anywhere, Pete thought. But the information stuck with him.

He felt the pieces begin to click into place in his brain. But instead of relief, his body was shrouded by a deep, creeping fear.

CHAPTER TWELVE

He bit into the small red apple. He chewed and watched as Fernandez pulled his car out of the St. Brendan's church parking lot. Fernandez wasn't a fool, Julian thought. He'd notice if he was being followed. He let it drop.

He hadn't expected the remains of the first girl to wash up so soon. Bagging her like that had been a mistake. A subconscious ploy to get attention. He should have just buried her with the rest of them. But the only way to build toward the powerful moment he needed was with more. The clarity he gained through these ceremonies let him see what was next.

He waited a few more minutes and pulled his tiny Dodge Neon out of the parking lot and headed toward the expressway. This was his second vehicle. The "day-to-day" car. It stuck out less than the van. His hands itched under the leather gloves he was wearing. His eyes on the road, he slid his right hand into the grocery bag on the passenger side. He pulled out a cell phone.

"Hello?" the Messenger said. He sounded tired.

"I have a problem," he said.

"What happened?"

"The detective's son. He's bothering me," he said, both hands on the wheel, the flimsy temporary cell phone cradled on his shoulder.

"You have bigger things to worry about," the Messenger said. "You were sloppy. You should have stuck to the plan."

"There is no plan," Julian said. "I honor the Voice, I don't copy it. Now, tell me you'll handle this new annoyance."

"I'll handle him," the Messenger said after a few seconds. "Just lay low for a bit. We need more time."

"Time is relative," he said. "It's only through actions like this that I can open my eyes and see what's coming."

"You need to slow down."

"It is not an option. Fix the problem or I will," he said, his terse, whispery tone the only signal that he was upset.

"Wait—"

Julian lowered the driver's side window and tossed the phone out. He saw it rattle down the street and disappear under a car in the carpool lane. He looked up at the rearview mirror and smiled. The girl was still squirming, her body laid flat on the backseat, her eyes blindfolded and her hands and feet bound by twine. She whimpered. He held his breath. She'd pissed herself. He could hear her sobbing, unable to lift her face up.

"What a mess you've made."

He lowered the window, letting the Miami breeze hit his face as he pulled onto the expressway.

CHAPTER THIRTEEN

L ight flooded The Bar as Pete shoved the door open. He walked up to the counter. The bar was dark and humid. The jukebox was playing Mission of Burma—the cascading guitar held down by the trainlike drums. The music was turned low, probably under the control of the staff and a brief respite from the pop and dance music most late-night patrons were fond of. Pete fought the urge to scan the liquor bottles lining the area behind and above the bar register. The Bar was empty aside from Lisa. Her eyes met his and she nodded. She didn't seem happy.

He sat down at the bar and pulled out the picture of Mike. The quick jolt of pain hit him. It happened each time he did this. It was becoming a weekly ritual. The jolt came first, then spread until it formed a general ache that he felt he'd never be rid of.

Lisa set the pint of amber beer in front of Pete, not bothering to stop for small talk as she sometimes did. Pete was OK with that. The noise from the local news—it was close to six in the evening—filled the empty bar. It'd probably start to get crowded around seven, when the two-for-one happy hour made it worth anyone's time. Otherwise, it was just another expensive, faux-authentic bar in the Gables, except without waitresses or live music. A few notches above the pub, but still a dive and seeming more out of place amongst the gourmet restaurants, wine bars, and cocktail lounges that were taking up more and more space.

Pete thought back to almost a year ago. The day the bomb went off and killed his best friend. He had just found Kathy, tied up and trapped by a madman in the Keys. They'd come to Fort Lauderdale to hole up at Mike's apartment until they could figure out what to do next. Pete hadn't even stopped to consider that by coming to Mike, he'd brought the danger along with him and put his best friend at risk. The bomb, which had been meant for Pete, destroyed Mike, his car, and any chance Pete had of returning to a normal life.

Pete stopped himself from reaching out to the glass and taking a sip; his instinct was still strong, but he had to resist. Old habits die hard, and coming here—tempting himself—didn't help. But the torture of the act was a small fee, he thought, for the guilt he felt. He noticed Lisa watching him. She looked away, embarrassed.

"I knew you weren't a cheerful guy, but this is straight up torture, dude."

Pete turned around. Dave took the stool to Pete's left, skipping pleasantries. He waved Lisa over and waited for her to come up to the bar.

Pete took a second to compose himself.

"Hey," Pete said. "Sorry, this isn't, it's—"

"You haven't touched that beer," Dave said, "so I'm guessing you're not going to. Am I supposed to think this is admirable somehow? This weird self-torture?"

"What do you mean?"

Dave motioned to the unsipped Bass ale.

"This," Dave said. "This weird ritual. That's your friend, right? Mike? The dead one?"

Pete grabbed Mike's photo and slid it into his pocket.

"Yeah," Pete said. "I was . . . I just took it out for second."

Lisa approached the bar and leaned over to Dave.

"He does this every week," she said, both annoyance and sympathy in her voice. "It's weird. What are you having?"

"It is weird," Dave said. "I'll take a Boddingtons." He turned to Pete. "So, seriously—this is what you do when you're not at work or at home? You sit in a bar and feel bad for yourself?"

"I'm not feeling sorry for myself," Pete said.

"Dude, I've worked with you for a few months now," Dave said, grabbing the beer as Lisa placed it in front of him and taking a long pull. "You're either at the store, reading for hours and not really doing the job I'm sort of paying you for, or you're at home, living with your smoking hot ex, and not making a move on her. Then I find you here—a guy who doesn't drink—sitting in a bar, looking at a photo of your dead friend with a fucking full pint in front of you. If you're not feeling sorry for yourself, what are you doing? Because you definitely aren't having fun. Look at you."

Pete let out a quick laugh.

"You're not responding because you're either going to punch me, which I don't suggest if you still want to hold on to your job, or because I'm right," Dave said. "And I know I'm fucking right." He downed his heavy British ale in a few large gulps. Still swallowing, he motioned for Pete to pass his own untouched beer over. Pete complied.

"Yeah," Pete said. "You may be right."

"Billy Joel," Dave said, "is always the answer."

Pete laughed.

"Why are you here? Did you follow me?"

Dave smirked. "Another one of your lesser, more unappealing traits is your belief that everything that happens around you happens because of you. No, I didn't follow you here. Why would I follow you? I had to swing by my dad's office and pick up some papers. It just so happens that this here bar, better known as *The* Bar, is one of my favorite shitholes. And one of the few I'll humor with my presence in the Gables." Dave shot a toothy smile to Lisa, who rolled her eyes and went back to counting the bills in the cash register.

"Say no more," Pete said.

Dave wasn't paying attention. Instead, his eyes were looking upward at the television screen mounted above the bar, still playing the early evening news. It was an NBC station, and a forty-something Cuban woman Pete recognized but couldn't name was giving the top news item.

"Another few weeks and another dead girl has been found," the newscaster, Sara Guzman, said as her name popped on the screen. "The body of seventeen-year-old Erica Morales was found by authorities mere hours ago in an abandoned field in rural Homestead. WTVJ reporter Hansel Vela has the latest. Hansel?"

The screen cut to grainy footage of the scene. Vela, a fit and gruff-looking man in his late thirties, was off to the right. In the background, Pete could see officers roaming around the desolate field, overgrown with weeds and littered with junk.

"Sara, it's a sad day for the Morales family, as their daughter, Erica, who had been reported missing weeks ago, was found," Vela began. "After days of frantic searching and an unprecedented outpouring of support from the community, it was off-duty police officer Christian Orr who found her when he decided to cut through this vacant Homestead lot, discovering Erica brutally stabbed to death, her body tied to the front of an abandoned car. Police declined comment when asked about the state of Morales's body and have yet to confirm any link between the death of Morales and the earlier murder of Alice Cline, but we will keep you posted. Back to you, Sara."

Morales's photo was on the screen for a few moments before the TV flickered off. Pete looked down and saw Lisa, the remote in her hand. Pete saw something in the photo. He'd seen Erica before, he thought. Once. He wasn't sure where.

Lisa let out a loud hissing sound. "Disgusting," she said. "There's a sicko out there and all people can do is sit back and watch."

She tossed the remote on the bar and went back to the register. Pete kept his eyes on her, unable to process. She caught him staring.

"What?"

He snapped out of his trance and shook his head. "No, nothing."

"What do you think?" It was Dave, sipping his new beer, not as quickly as the last, a pensive look on his face.

"I don't know enough to have an opinion," Pete said. "The murders could be related."

"If they're related, we have a problem," Dave said.

"We?"

"Well, Miami. The world. Society." He shrugged.

"I think we'd have that problem anyway," Pete said. "But if the murders are connected—and my gut tells me they are—then it means a few things. One: Rick didn't kill Alice Cline, which I suspected, no thanks to his attitude and being an ass. Two," Pete continued, counting the points off on his right hand as he spoke, "we may have a serial murderer on our hands, or at the very least a spree killer of some kind. Three, someone should have seen this coming a while ago."

"Pretty insightful for someone who doesn't do PI work."

Pete ignored the comment and continued. "There's a pattern," Pete said. "Girl goes missing, time passes, girl turns up dead and posed in an obscene way. It's almost ritualistic. It's only two bodies, sure, but that just means two have been found."

"OK, cool," Dave said, no sense of urgency in his voice. "Then what?"

"Then nothing," Pete said, forcing himself to fight the temptation to signal Lisa for a beer. "We have a psycho on the loose and who knows how many bodies are out there, or how many he'll take before he's caught."

CHAPTER FOURTEEN

Pete left Dave after a few more minutes. He walked the few doors down to Randazzo's, a decent Italian restaurant in a town that didn't have much good Italian food. The early evening provided a break from the weather, adding a cooling wind to the sludgelike heat of earlier. He tugged at his shirt, which was sticking to his body, hoping the fabricated breeze would cool him off a bit. The streets were empty and quiet, aside from the sounds of passing traffic and piano music coming from the restaurant. It was still on the early side—before the Gables nightlife kicked into high gear. A lull between the happy hour brigade and the late dinner crowd.

Pete stood outside and checked his phone. He was a little early. He slid his phone into his front pocket and peeked into the restaurant's main window. It was empty aside from the waitstaff and a few tables. For years, the place had been in the regular rotation for him. He'd had a birthday party here, about four years back. He and Emily had been in town, visiting from New Jersey. They'd just gotten engaged. His father was alive. They'd toasted to the future. It seemed so long ago. Pete could almost taste the bottle of pinot noir they'd split and smell the garlic bread on the table.

He watched as a couple—neither over thirty—sauntered past him. Designer dress, nice suit. They were drunk. The man opened the door for his date, his feet slipping a bit as he leaned in to get the door.

He saw Emily across the street, walking over from the parking lot in a blue dress. He'd never seen the dress before, which at first struck him as odd, until he reminded himself that there was a gap of time where she'd been—and, well, still was—married to someone else. She reached Pete and smiled.

"Hey," she said.

"Hello," Pete said. He felt underdressed. He hadn't been sure what Emily had in mind when she'd suggested dinner. After their night together, they'd reverted to their platonic roommate-esque behaviors—sleeping in their respective rooms, not spending much time together. Pete was OK with it being what it was, he supposed, but he couldn't say he didn't think about it often. When she'd texted him, asking if he had dinner plans, he took it to mean they'd order a pizza or grab some Cuban sandwiches from La Carretta by the house—something easy and platonic. When she suggested one of the restaurants they'd frequented as a couple, he wasn't sure what to make of it.

"Am I overdressed?" she said, her eyes widening a bit. She was nervous.

"Oh, no," Pete said. "The ball is about to start."

She punched him on the shoulder as he opened the door and they walked in.

I guess it was kind of random."

"I'm not complaining," Pete said.

Their conversation was interrupted by the stocky waiter. He handed each of them a dessert menu before shuffling back to the kitchen.

"You didn't seem very upset, no," she said, her eyes scanning the menu, looking up after a moment, a slight smile on her face. "Unless I misread you."

Pete took a sip of his ice water.

"You didn't misread me," Pete said. "But . . . "

"But what?"

"Well, what does it mean?" Pete said.

"Doesn't me being here, in this restaurant, with you," Emily said, "show you what it means?"

"I'm not sure," he said.

She put the menu down and folded her hands in front of her. "You seem different," she said. "More like you were when we first got together."

Pete nodded.

"I forgot how much I missed you," she continued. "And seeing you and Rick in the same room, it just, I don't know, clarified it for me."

"That you want to be together?"

She moved her hand across the table and on his waiting palm.

"Let's just take it easy," she said. "I just wanted to sit with you here—in this restaurant we both like—and let you know that's what I was thinking. Does that make sense?"

"Yeah, on some level," Pete said, wrapping his hand around hers. Did it, though? A few days ago they were at each other's throats. He did miss her, that he was sure of—the good and the bad. The moodiness and cutting remarks were washed away by her good heart and crackling brain. But this was moving fast; he needed to hold onto something.

He moved his hand back to his side of the table.

"Do you want dessert?" he said.

"Not here."

Costello jumped on Pete's side of the bed, rubbing his face on Pete's arm, purring. He scratched the cat's chin in the darkness. Costello was receptive until he decided there was more to do around the house. He hopped off the bed and scurried away, his tiny paws thumping on the hardwood floor. Pete turned to his right, where Emily was curled up next to him, her head resting on his arm. She felt him move and positioned her body closer to his. He pulled the bedsheet up over her shoulder. Pete let his head drop back onto the pillow. He looked up at the ceiling, hard to make out in the dimness. The evening had been wonderful. Pete wasn't sure he remembered what "wonderful" was like. Dinner was good. Conversation was lively and familiar. Everything he'd wanted—or remembered wanting—had been laid out on the table for him to take. The only woman he'd ever thought to marry was sleeping in his bed. He had enough money to get by for the time being and he felt like, for the first time in years, his life had momentum. He felt recharged. He pulled Emily closer and kissed her on the forehead, smelling the remnants of her perfume and feeling her warm skin touch his.

But if everything was where it was supposed to be, why did he feel so uneasy?

His phone, resting on the nightstand next to the bed, vibrated. A text message. He grabbed it and turned on the display. Kathy.

KATHY: You awake?

Pete typed a response with his one free hand: **Yeah. What's up?**

KATHY: I'm talking to Erica Morales' family tomorrow. Wanna come with?

Pete paused. What was he agreeing to do? **What for?**

KATHY: What do you think? To help me figure out who's killing these girls.

Pete moved out from under Emily and sat up. She grumbled to herself, half asleep. He responded to Kathy, typing with more speed: **You don't need my help. You're smart.**

KATHY: Cut the bullshit. Do you want to help me or not?

OK. When/where?

KATHY: I'll pick you up in the morning. Be ready by 7:30. That means stop fucking your roommate and go to sleep.

Pete laughed and set the phone back down. He slid back into bed and turned to face Emily. Her face was focused and serious when she slept. He remembered the first time he'd told her that, how she'd laughed and called him a creep. Years later, she admitted that had been the moment she knew he was a keeper, knew that he cared.

He felt a pang of guilt as he pushed a strand of her blond hair away from her face.

CHAPTER FIFTEEN

Erica Morales grew up in a tiny but well-kept three-bedroom house in Little Havana, a few blocks from 8th Street—or Calle Ocho. That's where they were heading. Calle Ocho was the heart of the Cuban exile community of Miami—a stretch where English was a second language and people were more interested in the politics happening ninety miles from U.S. soil than what was going on in Washington. Where a comment that even remotely made it sound like you agreed with a certain bearded dictator could get you pummeled. West of downtown, Little Havana was an extension of a Cuba that no longer existed—an idealized version of a country many had left behind in haste and fear. The pace was slow, the salsa music was loud, and the *cafecito* was strong.

The bright morning sun beat down on the silver Jetta as it darted through weekend traffic—a cacophony of honking horns, changed lanes, and slow-moving Cadillacs and Buicks manned by grumpy senior citizens. Kathy drove while Pete fiddled with the satellite radio. It was a little past eight in the morning. In his right hand, Pete clutched an extra-large coffee, which he'd purchased after a quick *cortadito* made at home. He'd left Emily sleeping, telling her he'd be back later. She seemed to understand, in her hazy, half-asleep state, but he expected a questioning text or call in a few hours. Her freelance design work gave her a fairly flexible schedule that made room for sleeping in when needed. He was happy Emily was back in his life and that he was better equipped to handle it. It reminded him of the early days of their relationship, without the arguing and histrionics that would become all too common toward the end. Though she was the one who packed her bags and left, Pete was as much to blame— drinking at all hours, working late, and distant when he was around. He'd never expected a second chance. He took a long sip from his lukewarm coffee.

"Are we there yet?" he said.

"Shush, you," Kathy said, her eyes on the road. "My GPS is busted and you know I don't come down to Cubatown all that often."

"Aren't you a reporter?"

"I was, my dear," she said. "But now I'm an all-important 'local columnist,' so I needn't worry about remembering where things are. It's about *how* things are. *Comprende*, my little *café con leche*?"

Pete laughed and pushed a button on the satellite radio. The Decemberists came on. It was a relatively obscure track—the band's lead singer, Colin Meloy, doing a Morrissey song. It took Pete a second to remember it.

"'Jack the Ripper,'" Pete said.

"Pardon?"

"That's the song."

"The Morrissey song?"

"Yup."

"This is a shitty cover," she said.

"I like it more than the original," Pete said.

"You would," Kathy said. "It's more emo than the original."

Kathy pulled the car into a parallel parking space on a residential street. After turning off the engine, she leaned back in the driver's seat, as if to announce, "Yeah, I did that."

"Do you want a prize?" Pete said, sliding his half-empty coffee into the car's cup holder.

"You wish you could park like me," Kathy said, smiling. She opened the door and stepped out of the car. "OK, so what's the plan, mister?"

Pete got out and looked at Kathy from across the car.

"I follow your lead," he said. "I'm just a special guest star."

She let out an exasperated sigh.

"Fine, whatever," she said. "But turn your brain on. I brought you here for help, not comic relief."

Pete waited for Kathy to come around the car before walking to the house.

"My story is slated to run tonight, and I want it to be more than a 'wah-wah look at the dead girl's family' piece," she said, opening the front gate to the quaint Morales house, not noticing the older woman standing in the front yard. Her face showed that she'd heard Kathy's flip remarks. "Oh, shit. I'm sorry."

Pete looked at the lady and waited for a heated, angry response, but saw only confusion. He looked at Kathy for a second before opening his mouth.

"*Hablas inglés, señora?*"

The lady's look changed from confusion to relief. "*No, ni un poco. Pero mi hermana, sí. Con que te puedo ayudar?*"

Kathy looked at Pete, uncertainty in her eyes. "She doesn't speak English," Pete said, looking at the lady and smiling politely before looking back at Kathy. "Her sister does, however. Thankfully, she wasn't here to hear what you said."

"Rub it in while you can, little man," Kathy said, smiling at the older woman. "Ask her if she has a few minutes to talk."

"*Señora, somos reporteros del periódico Miami Times,*" Pete said, his Spanish rusty and not coming to him with much ease. "*Tienes un momento para hablar?*"

The woman didn't respond. She knew why they were at her house.

Before the old lady could respond, another woman, younger and smartly dressed, appeared next to her.

"Can I help you?"

"Yes, I'm Kathy Bentley," Kathy said, sticking out her hand to the new arrival. "I'm a writer for the *Miami Times*. I'm working on a story about Erica Morales, your niece. We wanted to know if you and your sister had time to talk about her for the newspaper. We're very sorry for your loss, but if you have a moment to spare, we feel it'd be an important story to share with our readership."

The younger woman scrunched up her nose and looked at Pete, as if to say, "Who is this?" She wrapped her arm around her sister. "Erica wasn't my niece," the woman said, her voice lowering. "She was my daughter. I'm Odalys Morales. Her mother. This is my older sister, Olga. She just arrived from Cuba, so you'll have to forgive her lack of English skills."

Pete felt foolish and figured Kathy did, too.

"And who are you?" Odalys asked, her eyes on Pete.

"I'm Pete Fernandez." He stuck out his hand, which Odalys glanced at before ignoring. "I'm a colleague of Kathy's."

Odalys let out a long sigh and whispered something to her sister. She motioned her head to the house. Olga nodded and walked into the house, not bothering to say goodbye. Odalys rubbed her temples and closed her eyes before looking at Kathy and Pete.

"What can I do? I've already talked to the police," she said. "My little girl is dead. I really just want to be left alone."

"I apologize for intruding, ma'am," Kathy said. "I'd only need a few minutes of your time."

"For what, lady?" Odalys said. "You and this guy show up like nothing? To chat with me about my dead daughter like it's no big deal?"

"We didn't mean any offense—" Kathy started.

"You didn't mean any, but it happened anyway," Odalys continued.

"We think we can help you," Pete said. "If we write this story, draw some more attention to your daughter, maybe someone will come forward with information. It's the best thing we can offer you now, which isn't a lot, I know. But information is key. If we get anything that could help the police or get someone to come forward, it'd be worth your time. We don't want this to fall through the cracks."

Odalys's shoulders slumped in resignation.

"All right," she said, turning around and heading toward her house. "Let me make some *café* and we'll talk."

The Morales home was small but welcoming; the furniture and decor reminded Pete of his own grandmother's house. The lighting was low, to conserve whatever cool air the ancient air conditioner was still able to spit out, and the shelves were stacked with books two-deep. A quick scan showed various volumes focused on the plight of the exile community and many histories of Cuba—essential reading for any educated household this close to the epicenter. They sat in the cozy living room, Kathy and Pete on chairs brought over from the dining room, Odalys sitting across from them on a colorful couch that didn't look very comfortable. She rubbed her palms on her black pants and nodded to Kathy, as if to say, "Let's go."

Kathy took the cue and pulled out a notepad and tape recorder. "Do you mind if I record this?"

"Not if it means you won't misquote me," Odalys said, no sign of humor in her voice.

Kathy clicked the record button on the tiny device and slid it toward Odalys, resting it on the long coffee table between them.

"Odalys, can you tell us a little about what Erica was like?"

Odalys cleared her throat and waited a few seconds before speaking.

"Erica was a good girl," Odalys said. "She did well in school, she had good friends from around the neighborhood. She was well behaved, never talked back, never drank, didn't do drugs . . . " She trailed off.

"Did she have a boyfriend?" Pete asked.

"No, not that I knew of," Odalys said, hesitating. "But I wouldn't know. She was always on her phone, texting, tweeting, e-mailing. You know. Every kind of distraction. But she still managed to get her homework done and do her chores. She wasn't away enough to have a boyfriend, I don't think."

"Did they recover her cell phone?" Pete asked.

Odalys's face jerked at the word "recover." It was a reminder that her daughter wasn't just on a school trip—she was gone. She closed her eyes. A tear started to slide down her face before she wiped it away.

"No, they didn't," she said, her voice hoarse. "They didn't find it."

"I realize a lot of this you've already discussed with the police," Pete said, choosing each word with care. "But it's very helpful to us. Do you remember the last time you saw your daughter?"

Odalys covered her face with her hands and began sobbing. Quietly at first, but soon she was shaking. She pulled her hands away and Pete could see her face, splotched with tears and red. She wiped her eyes with her arm and spoke, her voice shaking.

"She wanted to go to the mall," she said, gasping after every third word. "I thought she needed to do some stuff around the house—clean her room, help me in the yard. But she insisted. She wanted to see a movie, she wanted to meet her friends there. So I let her go. She's such a good girl. She never asks for anything."

Pete didn't correct her tense when discussing her daughter. He motioned for her to continue.

"I forgot to ask her who she was meeting," Odalys said. "She said she was going to take the bus and one of her friends was going to bring her back. I didn't think anything of it. The one time I didn't press her to tell me everything, and this happens." She nearly yelled the last two words.

Pete looked down at his feet. He hated this.

"Did you talk to any of her friends?" Kathy said. "Did any of them know who she was meeting?"

"None of them were there, except this one girl, Silvia Colmas, *Silvita*," Odalys said, spitting out the last word like it was sour.

"You don't seem very fond of her," Pete said.

"She's not a good girl," Odalys said. "She was a troublemaker. I didn't like for Erica to hang out with her. But she did what she wanted when it came to Silvita."

"So, she was with Erica at the mall when she went missing?" Kathy asked.

"Yes. Yes, I think so," Odalys said. "The police have already questioned her. She didn't know who Erica left with. She didn't see her leave with anyone. She just 'lost track of her.' *Maldita*."

Pete didn't need to translate the word for Kathy to know what it implied.

"Did Silvita go to school with Erica?" Pete asked.

"Yes, they both went to Miami High," Odalys said.

Pete looked at Kathy. "Do you have anything else to ask?"

Kathy seemed confused by Pete's question. "Um, yes, actually, I do," she said. "Did you have to be somewhere?"

Pete stood up and looked at Odalys. "Ms. Morales, did Erica have her own computer?"

Odalys seemed confused, but tried to focus. "No, no," she said. "She used the computer in our office, next to her bedroom."

"Do you mind if I give it a look?"

"Well, no," Odalys said. "The police already looked it over. They thought Erica had run away until . . . until they found her."

"You guys continue," Pete said. "I'll go to the other room and check the computer."

"This is standard newspaper procedure?" Odalys asked.

Kathy frowned. "Not really," she said. "Pete is a colleague, we used to work together. He's also a private detective."

Pete didn't try to correct her.

Odalys wrung her hands together and looked at Pete, who was still standing in front of her. "Do whatever you need to do," she said, looking down at her lap.

Pete nodded and headed to the office, which was off to the right from the small dining room. The room was a converted bedroom, and appeared to be where Odalys's sister stayed. She'd escaped to the kitchen after meeting Kathy and Pete. Pete sat down in front of an outdated PC. He tapped the space bar and waited for the computer to wake up.

Pete moved the mouse and started the computer's Web browser— Internet Explorer. He checked the program's history and found what he would expect to find on a computer used mainly by a teenager: Facebook, Twitter, Instagram, celebrity gossip sites, Gmail. Nothing out of the ordinary. He expanded the search to go back a week and discovered a few Craigslist hits. It looked like Erica was also scanning the Miami apartment listings. But for what? Pete thought. The ads Erica had looked at were innocent—young girls looking for roommates.

Pete switched back to Erica's Gmail account. Erica had been smart enough not to save her password on the computer, but it didn't take Pete very long to find the light blue Post-it note in the desk drawer on the right with "GM PW" scrawled on it. He typed in the combination of letters and punctuation and logged in as Erica. He typed "craigslist" into the search field at the top of the page and waited.

After a few seconds, the screen loaded up about a dozen e-mails, each with the same subject line, referencing low-rent housing for students. Pete read through the e-mail conversation. Erica had e-mailed one of the posters from Craigslist in reference to one of the ads and in the hopes that the poster would have more listings. But why did she want to move out?

Pete continued to read. The poster, "Steve," seemed to be Erica's age, but something struck Pete as odd. The notes were being hit too perfectly, he thought. The pop culture references came across as more forced than real. This "Steve" person seemed a half-step behind. Pete sent the e-mails to print from Odalys's creaking LaserJet. As the pages cranked out of the old machine, Pete continued to read. "Steve" insisted he had a "great deal" for Erica. But they needed to talk in person, since he would have to have his "uncle" sign for her.

Erica's reasons for wanting to move were vague, but it was clear she didn't get along with her mother, feeling stifled by her conservative upbringing. Her plan, or at least what she relayed to "Steve," was that she and her friend—Silvita, Pete assumed—were going to quit school, get easy jobs, and save money to move to LA and "start a new life."

Pete frowned. Erica didn't strike him as the flighty type. He grabbed the pages from the printer and folded them so they fit in his back pocket. Who was "Steve"? The e-mail address he used, CheepApts4Students@yahoo.com, didn't match the MIAapt4rentSOON@hotmail.com e-mail of Alice Cline's pen pal, but both were from e-mail services that required minimal identification to start an account. He shut down the computer and double-checked to make sure he had the pages in his pocket. When he returned to the living room, Kathy was hugging Odalys near the front door.

"I was just about to go get you," Kathy said. "I'm done."

"How'd it go?"

"Good, I hope," Odalys said, looking more at peace than when Pete left the two of them. "I hope talking about my Erica will help find the monster that did this, wherever he is. Did you find anything useful on the computer?"

"A few things," Pete said. He'd found it much harder to lie since he'd stopped drinking. It made moments like these a bit more difficult. "But I doubt it was anything the police didn't find."

Odalys nodded.

Pete stuck out his hand and was surprised when Odalys drew him in for a hug. She held onto him for a second or two longer than he'd expected.

"If you or *la gringa* need anything," Odalys said, "please call me."

"You got it," Pete said, walking outside of the house with Kathy.

As they stepped down the porch and toward Kathy's car, Pete looked back to make sure Odalys was out of earshot before speaking. "Well, she seemed to be in a much better mood."

"We connected," Kathy said, no sign of sarcasm in her voice.

"You what?" Pete asked, opening the car door and getting into the passenger side. "Connected?"

"Yes," Kathy said, starting the car. "It turns out Erica wasn't as good a girl as Odalys wanted us to initially believe. They were constantly at odds. Erica threatened to move out a number of times. She'd run away before, too, which is why the cops weren't very responsive when Odalys reported her missing. I talked to her about my drama with my mom—and how, after a time, we started to get along again. I told her that it would have happened with them. That her death wasn't her fault."

Pete couldn't think of anything to say. He waited for the car to start moving.

"Did you find anything?"

"Huh?"

"On the computer," Kathy said. "Anything useful?"

"Yeah, actually," Pete said. "But nothing you could really run in the paper."

"I'll be the judge of that, thank you very much," Kathy said.

"Well, she was e-mailing with someone via Craigslist," Pete said. "The exchange was similar to Alice Cline's, but whoever she was e-mailing with seemed . . . off. I don't know."

"What do you mean?"

"Well, with Alice's e-mails, it seemed more formal, like two adults conducting a business transaction," Pete said. "Here, it read to me like two teens, except one of them learned how to be a teenager by watching *Saved by the Bell* reruns."

"Someone impersonating a teenager?"

"Just a feeling I got. The way he talked was . . . I dunno. Off," Pete said.

Kathy hesitated before turning onto the street. "You think it's the same guy, then?"

"Yeah, I don't see any other explanation."

"Well, people look for apartments via the Internet all the time," Kathy said. "Let's not get ahead of ourselves. This could be a really weird coincidence."

"True, but do two of the people looking up apartments end up dead?" Pete said.

"You're probably right," Kathy said, accelerating down the street. "And if you are, then this could get very bad."

CHAPTER SIXTEEN

Pete stepped up to the podium and felt a hundred degrees warmer. His black blazer wasn't helping. He pulled out a few crumpled note cards from his jacket pocket. He scanned the small crowd that had gathered in the ballroom. Mike's parents had planned the memorial, and they'd asked Pete to take point on reaching out to Mike's friends and colleagues—people Mike's parents were not very familiar with—to make sure the people Mike had cared about were present. They'd also asked Pete to speak, something he'd managed to avoid a year earlier at the funeral. Pete spotted Emily standing off to his right, near the front. She looked more curious than sad, her eyes on Pete. He met them and she smiled. His eyes drifted and landed on the glasses people were holding. Wine. Beer. Liquor. He tried not to think about it. He hadn't been to a meeting in a few days and he was feeling on edge.

He noticed Kathy slipping into the ballroom and standing at the rear of the small crowd. She'd barely known Mike, Pete thought, but Pete had invited her anyway. Their fates had been intertwined.

"First off, I'd like to take a moment to thank Reed and Kelly for putting this together," Pete said, his voice shaky. He hated public speaking. "Mike was important to all of us, and it's a wonderful thing to take a moment to recognize, once again, what a great friend, brother, and person he was. I hope we can do it again as the years go by."

Pete swallowed. He waited a second before continuing. He looked to Emily and saw her taking a deep breath.

"Mike was the best person I've ever known," Pete said. "And I didn't deserve a friend like him. That kind of sums up how I feel about this." He paused and looked around the room. "He was there whenever I needed him. He was the rock that I never expected but always relied on. In a time where everyone is soaked with cynicism and sarcasm, where you have to think twice whenever anyone does something nice for you, Mike was a beacon of genuine good. He was a kind person. I regret every day that he can't see me trying to be. Not just for him, but because of him."

Pete felt his throat tighten. His eyes began to well up. He pushed the note cards farther away on the podium and held onto each side, trying to steady himself. He was almost done, he told himself. Almost there.

"I wake up most mornings and feel an aching emptiness," Pete said. "And it's because so many people that meant so much to me and defined what I am are gone. It's easy to make this about me, but it isn't. We're here for Mike. Because of Mike. I miss him all the time.

Losing my best friend was like losing a part of me that I used every waking moment, and now, moving forward, it's like learning to walk and live all over again. I miss you, man."

Pete saw his hands shaking as he collected the cards from the podium. It took him a moment to notice the applause, soft at first, then more pronounced as he reached the ballroom floor. Emily met him and took him by the elbow to a nearby corner. He felt her hand rubbing his back and her warm breath on his neck.

"That was good," she said. "He would have been happy."

"Thanks," he said, his face turning to see hers close to his. They turned their attention to the next speaker. Her hand slid into his, gripping it.

He felt a poke at his shoulder. He and Emily both turned to find Kathy behind them.

"Sorry to interrupt the latest edition of Puppy Love Revisited," Kathy said, her voice low, trying not to interrupt the proceedings. "It's a pleasure to see you both again, really, especially in full Hallmark mode. But I need to talk to Pete here for a second about our . . . case— for lack of a better, more realistic term."

"Case? What?" Emily said.

"The murders," Pete whispered to Emily, hoping that would pacify her.

"You're working on them? Like, officially?" Emily was not pacified.

"No, not really, I was just helping Kathy," Pete said. He didn't sound very convincing, he thought. "I can explain it all later."

"Yeah, let's try that," Emily said, pulling her hand away from Pete and folding her arms. She turned to face the stage, signaling for Pete to handle whatever he needed to handle.

He followed Kathy outside. The ballroom was a reception area at the Rivero Funeral Home, where Mike's funeral had been held. The parking lot was mostly full and, even this late in the evening, not much cooler than the packed ballroom.

"What's up?" Pete said.

"Did I get you in trouble or something?"

"I'm not sure," Pete said, annoyed. "I don't know. Don't worry about it."

"Done and done," Kathy said. "I figured you'd want to hear this."

"What's going on?"

"Well, my sources in the police department tell me that they're freaking the fuck out over the Morales case," Kathy said, pulling out a pack of cigarettes from her purse and lighting one up. "They're worried this isn't just two linked murders but two in a series—like, serial killer time. There are things that they're holding back from the press that are proving they're connected—things that only the killer would know, that are repeated. Not just the posing."

"What else?" Pete asked.

"The girls were posed sexually, that we know and the press knows," Kathy said, looking around as if she were about to share a deep secret. "But both scenes featured mirrors. Lots of them. Some in the bag underwater with Alice Cline—some placed around Erica Morales's body in the lot, facing each other. That was also a trick Whitehurst used toward the end. When he was still in some control."

"What do the police think all this means?"

"Well, it means that the killer is definitely the same guy," Kathy said.

"That's kind of what we were thinking, too."

"Kind of, but hoping for the opposite," Kathy said. "The fact that the murders resemble one of the last serial killers brought down in Miami isn't helping matters."

"So, what does that mean for us?"

"Nothing, really," Kathy said, taking a long drag. "My story about Erica Morales ran today and I got a few calls, but nothing substantial, just your usual ranters and concerned geezers complaining."

"But why would this dude be copying Rex Whitehurst?" Pete said.

"Not fully sure he is copying him," Kathy said. "Whitehurst was skewing much younger by the time his mystery machine rolled into Miami. This guy's only taking things he seems to like from the Whitehurst playbook."

"True," Pete said. "But Whitehurst mostly preyed on college and high school girls, right? Even Bundy went extra nutso toward the end of his spree, grabbing a younger girl for his last kill."

"Hmm, I'm impressed," Kathy said. "Seems you've been doing some extra-credit reading. Did you reach the Ann Rule section yet?"

"I've done some research," Pete said, more annoyed than amused by Kathy tonight. "So, what do we do next?"

"I don't know," Kathy said. "It just means that these murders are on the police radar. Which means they'll probably be on the FBI radar, which means our snooping around will end up on someone's radar before too long, which is not good."

"Why's that?"

"Well, you're not exactly on the Miami PD's Christmas card list."

She was right. Part of the fallout from Pete and Kathy's adventures the year before, and the book that was published a few months later,

116

was the revelation of deep-seated corruption and unethical activity among Miami-Dade's finest.

"We'll figure it out," Pete said.

"Will we? Sounds like your old-slash-new girlfriend is taking issue with you dipping your toe in this," Kathy said. "You backing out?"

"Backing out of what?" Pete said. "I'm just trying to help you. I'm not investigating anything. I'm just trying to help."

"You said that, darling. And, sure, however you want to explain what you're doing, that's fine," Kathy said, dropping her cigarette and rubbing it out on the pavement with her heel. "I'll call you tomorrow and see whether you can 'help' me or not."

"Okay," Pete said. She didn't respond. She was already halfway to her car.

Pete hesitated before turning to walk back to the funeral home. He needed to clear his head. He walked toward the far end of the parking lot. There were fewer cars around there. A slight breeze. He kicked a small rock and watched it hop a few feet away; his shadow loomed large thanks to the fluorescent light of a nearby streetlamp. He looked at his shadow again. It was too big, he thought. There was something else there.

The fist hit his face as he turned around, and the punch floored him. His head smacked the parking lot pavement hard, snapping forward and slamming into the ground again. He was flat on his back. He could smell blood in his nose and saw a dark figure hover over him. The man had a black ski mask on and everything else he was wearing was dark and muted. Leather jacket. Black jeans. Black gloves. He was of medium build, about Pete's height. Pete's vision was blurry; the bump on the asphalt had shaken him up. A cold knife was at his throat, near his chin. He tried to speak, but the man in black held up a finger with his free hand.

"I talk, you don't," the man said. "Just listen, you deluded fuck."

Pete tried to move. The man pulled the knife back, returning with his fist—two swift punches to Pete's face. He felt something loosen in his mouth. He let out a soft groan, and the knife returned, preventing him from curling up into a fetal position.

"You're in way over your head," the man said. "What you think you know—that's not even the half of it. If I killed people for fun—just because they bothered me—you'd be dead. Problem solved. But I don't. What I do is more important than that. It's pure. These people need to die. I need them to build a harmony together. The closer they get in death, the closer I get to him, and to seeing what I need to see. I can't expect you or your stupid friend to understand that. But I will not let you make it any harder for me."

The blade dug into Pete's skin. He felt the sting of it. Felt his blood trickling out. His eyes darted around, looking for anything—a tool, a rock—to help him.

The man grabbed Pete by his hair and slammed his head on the pavement again. Harder this time. Pete felt his vision fade in and out.

"No one can hear you," the man said. "They're all in there celebrating your dead buddy. Now, I need you to listen very closely. I will not repeat myself. Leave me alone. Step away from me and I won't hurt you. Because I can. I can hurt you. I can destroy the people around you and build a beautiful chorus of pain that you will never recover from."

He grabbed Pete's left hand by the wrist and brought the knife to his palm. The man slashed into it, his eyes widening under his ski mask, Pete's hand gushing blood. The cut was deep—Pete could feel the blade on both sides, cutting into him. Pete couldn't move, he was pinned down and he was having trouble staying conscious. He let out a pained scream. The man got up, sending a swift kick to Pete's midsection before turning and walking toward the street. Pete brought his hand closer and saw his own blood flowing. He reached for his neck and felt a smaller trickle coming from the cut under his chin. His face felt sore. His good hand reached back and felt his head: more blood. He tried to sit up, but a wave of dizziness hit him, forcing him to roll over, his cheek scraping against the dirty parking lot. That's when he saw Emily—his view capturing her from a sideways angle. She had walked out, probably looking for him. She was running to him. He was on the ground, no longer able to even hold himself up. She was closer to him now. He could hear her.

"Oh Jesus, Pete," Emily said, sliding down next to him. "What the hell? What happened?"

"Some guy," Pete said, having trouble forming words. "Out of nowhere."

"Did they rob you? Are you shot?"

The edges of his vision got darker and spread inward until everything was black and quiet.

Pete's eyes fluttered open. He felt a dull pain in his side. It was dark. He looked down at himself. He was in a hospital bed. His head hurt and his tongue felt thick and heavy. The only light was from the TV set propped up on the wall, playing the evening news on mute.

Next to him, in a chair that looked very uncomfortable, was Emily—
her sleeping body leaning on the chair in an awkward position. A
beeping sound chimed every few seconds. Pete reached out his hand
and took hers before closing his eyes and falling asleep.

"**Y**ou look like shit, dude."

"Thanks," Pete said, dropping his bag behind the counter at
the Book Bin. Pete wondered how Dave could have even concluded
that Pete looked like shit, so intently was he organizing books on the
far side of the small store. Still, he did notice. Pete looked better than
he felt, which meant he felt like a lot of shit. It'd been a week since he'd
been attacked, and he was stepping out into the real world for the first
time. He wasn't sure how he liked it. He winced as the strap on his
messenger bag yanked at the bandage wrapped around his left hand.
He caught a glimpse of his reflection in the storefront window as he
sat down behind the counter. A pretty spectacular black eye, a busted
lip, and a painful-looking scratch/cut near his chin. Not to mention
the giant slice down his left palm. That wound was thankfully out of
sight under the white gauze. Pete closed his eyes.

"Could be worse," Dave said, the noise of books dropping on the
counter echoing through the empty store.

"How's that?"

"Well, you're alive," Dave said, picking up another, smaller stack
of books farther down the counter and walking toward one of the
aisles.

"I appreciate your optimism," Pete said, his voice louder to make
up the space between. "I needed to get out of the house. Sorry for
missing a few shifts."

Dave walked over and placed his free palm on the counter, facing Pete.

"Please don't give me the martyr bullshit," Dave said. "No one in their right mind would come to work after what happened to you. I'm glad you're OK. Next time, wander the Miami streets with a buddy."

"Duly noted, boss," Pete said. "What's on tap today?"

Dave ignored his question.

"How's Emily?" Dave asked.

"Why do you ask?"

"She seemed pretty shaken up when she called to say you were in the hospital," Dave said. "So I wanted to see if you'd screwed anything else up in the last week or so."

They smiled at each other.

"She's OK," Pete said, humor turning into frankness. "She's really pissed about me sniffing around these dead girls."

"That sounds disgusting."

Pete laughed. "Yeah, so, she's pissed."

"Are you gonna stop . . . whatever you were doing?"

Pete didn't respond.

"You kidding me?" Dave said.

"I have to talk to Kathy," Pete said. "She asked me to help her. I think it might have been the killer who attacked me."

Pete let the words hang in the air, like a puff of smoke.

Dave looked at Pete.

"What?"

"Whoever attacked me wants me to think it was the killer," Pete said. "But the whole thing rubs me wrong. I dunno. Maybe it was the killer, changing his MO to throw me off."

"How would you even know it was the killer?"

"He basically said so," Pete said. "He told me he would have killed me if he could murder for fun. But what he does is 'pure.' "

Dave shook his head as he grabbed a copy of the latest Chabon book and walked over to the front window display of the store.

"I'm guessing you told the cops this, right?" Dave said, his back to Pete. "Please tell me you told the cops." Before Pete could respond, Dave spoke again. "You expecting anyone?"

"Huh?"

The door chime sounded as two men stepped into the store. Both were tall and fit; one was older, past fifty, with salt-and-pepper hair. The other one looked Hispanic and was probably younger than Pete. They looked like cops.

The older one walked up to the counter and gave Pete a knowing half-smile.

"You Pete Fernandez?"

"Who're you?" Pete responded, not standing up from his seat.

The younger one stood behind his older partner and scowled. The older man pulled out a badge.

"Robert Harras, FBI," the man said, folding his badge and sliding it into his back pocket. "This man here is my partner, Raul Aguilera. Also FBI. Now, will you answer my question?"

Pete stood up and extended his good hand.

"Pete Fernandez," he said. "Not FBI."

"Could have fooled me," Aguilera said, a sneer on his face. "The way you've been acting."

"I didn't realize it was junior varsity week at the FBI," Pete said.

Harras raised a hand as if to quiet Aguilera. He gave Pete an apologetic look.

"Listen, we'd like to chat with you for a minute if you have time," Harras said. "It's related to the deaths of Alice Cline and Erica Morales."

"Sure," Pete said. "What about them?"

"I need to know what info you've collected during your little vigilante escapades with Kathy Bentley," Harras said, his eyes cold. "I know you've been dancing around the PD's case—talking to the family, et cetera. I also know you were the victim of a fairly severe beating a few nights ago."

"I got mugged."

"Yet you didn't report anything stolen," Harras said. "See where I'm going here? You're interfering with a police investigation."

"Not the first time," Aguilera said, standing behind Harras with his arms folded.

"You've got the menacing thug thing down pat," Pete said.

"You think you're hot shit because of all that went down last year," Aguilera said, this time ignoring Harras's subtle pleas for silence. "But you're not. You're not a cop. You're just a hotshot, like your father."

Pete was more confused than insulted by the agent's remark.

"You didn't even know my father," Pete said. "And you haven't given me a single good reason why I should talk to you. All I know is you're being an asshole—which, news flash, isn't good."

"Stop right there," Harras said. "Raul Aguilera Senior knew your dad—he was on the force with him and Carlos Broche, your father's partner. You remember him, right?"

Pete nodded. Broche had been like an uncle to him, until he was revealed to be as corrupt and traitorous as the rest of his department.

The memory of the old man collapsing from a gunshot wound to the head, courtesy of the Silent Death—and of the others lost during the whole affair—hit him. Mike. Amy. Broche. Chaz. The list of people lost in those few days was long.

"Yes," Pete said. "And while I'm always up for doing some past-life regressions, can we get to the point here? I'm at work."

Harras gave the store a cursory look, nodding at Dave, who was still stocking books near the front window display—and probably doing it just to listen in on as much as he could.

"Ah, right," Harras said. "Your job. My deepest apologies for interrupting your important work."

"You guys really know how to butter someone up," Pete said, sitting down again. "But I have to ask, what brings the FBI into this? I mean, I'm just some dumb hotshot, right? I may be nuts, so stop me if you've heard this one before, but if the FBI is involved, that means whatever the Miami PD is investigating crosses state lines— or might. Which means our potential serial killer situation might have just gotten confirmed, and also might involve something much bigger than two dead girls in South Florida. Am I getting warmer?"

Harras grimaced. Pete had hit a nerve. He wasn't sure if that was a good thing.

"You're lucky we don't haul you in right now, you smug son of a bitch," Harras said. "Just take this as a first and final warning: This is not your case. You're not a private investigator and you don't have any clients. If you know anything that you think may be of value to us, you'd better spill it in the next twenty-four hours or so help me, you'll be spending some serious time in jail. You're fucking with the wrong people, and you don't have a flimsy newspaper press badge to protect you anymore."

With that, Harras turned around, swung the store's door open, and walked through, Aguilera right behind.

"Later, asshole," Aguilera said.

"Nice to meet you guys," Pete said, waving. His stomach was turning.

"Are you fucking crazy?" It was Dave. He'd reappeared, having heard everything. "Why didn't you tell them what you just told me? Or are you just in the mood to be difficult?"

"I don't know those guys from Adam," Pete said, reorganizing some of the flyers on the counter to keep his hands busy. "And I don't have a great rapport with cops, FBI or not."

"That's for sure."

"They weren't exactly being welcoming," Pete said.

"You weren't either," Dave said, shrugging. "But whatever, that's kind of your thing, isn't it?"

"What do you mean?"

"Being a difficult asshole? That's your thing. It's how people know you now. Like your signature move, or whatever. I'm amazed you have any friends."

Pete didn't know whether to laugh or be upset, so he shrugged and went back to organizing the flyers.

"I'm not trying to rip on you, dude," Dave said. "I'm just being honest. You stick your finger in shit and make a mess, but don't commit. Then you wonder why people get mad at you. It's selfish. You're doing it with this case, you're doing it with your ex/now-not-ex maybe/maybe-not girlfriend and you do it with this job."

Dave began to walk toward the back of the store, not waiting for Pete to respond.

Pete dropped the stack of flyers on the counter and let them slide onto the floor. He picked up his messenger bag with a swoop of his good arm and slung it over his shoulder. He didn't look at Dave as he walked out, the door slamming behind him.

CHAPTER SEVENTEEN

Pete felt out of sorts as he pushed open the main entrance doors at Miami Senior High School. It was early in the afternoon and most of the students were in their last class. Miami High was a school that prided itself on its athletics—basketball, baseball, football—and boasted one of the prettiest high school campuses Pete had ever seen. It also necessitated another visit to Little Havana, albeit the westernmost part of the neighborhood. The school was a landmark, thanks to its refurbished architecture—the high ceilings, terracotta tiles, and cast-stone vent screens made it feel more like a museum than a public school. Though Pete had attended Southwest High, he'd taken his SATs in the beautiful Miami High auditorium his junior year. He had carried a beeper and never left the school grounds to get lunch. Kids today were e-mailing, Instagramming, Facebooking, and Twittering their way through classes. Just walking into the school made him feel like he was closer to sixty, not a few years past thirty.

He walked into the main office. Pete hadn't been much of a student early on, and it was only when he had an unpleasant brush with the law that his father had clamped down and watched Pete's every move. It was then that Pete discovered that school wasn't all bad, and a lifelong love of books, writing, and reading was awakened. Now he envied the students for the time that they had left in school.

He walked up to the long front desk of the main office and waited. Soon, a young girl, her hair in a ponytail and her eyes dazed, walked up on the opposite side. Her eyes widened as she caught a look at Pete in all his post-beating glory.

"I feel worse than I look," Pete said.

"Can I help you?"

"I'm here to see the school counselor."

"Which one?" she responded, her tone flat.

"Melinda Farkas," Pete said. "I spoke to her earlier today."

"All right," the girl said. She turned toward a series of offices on the far end of the large room and yelled, "Yo, Miss Farkas? Some guy here to talk to you."

The girl walked away from the front desk without a word, leaving Pete waiting. He drummed his fingers on the counter and looked around. The interior of the school had seen better days; underneath the fresh coat of paint and polished awards was the wear and tear that came with budget cuts and increased enrollment.

A moment later, a woman appeared behind the front desk. Melinda Farkas was about Pete's age, if not a bit older. Fit and tan, she wore her business suit a size too big; she was probably more used to gym clothes, or T-shirts and jeans, Pete imagined.

"You're Pete?" she said. She gave him a more polished once-over than the student had. "You look terrible."

"Yeah, it's been a rough few weeks," Pete said.

She nodded and motioned for him to come around and follow her into her office.

She sat behind her desk in the cramped space and motioned for Pete to take the tiny chair across from her. She got up and closed the door and sat down again, grabbing a file folder at the top of a stack of what looked like class schedule printouts.

"So, you called about Silvia Colmas," she said, looking over what Pete assumed was the girl's transcript.

"Yeah," Pete said. "I'm working with a reporter at the *Miami Times* on a story about the death of Erica Morales, and our interviews have led us to believe that Silvia was one of the last people to see Erica alive."

Farkas didn't respond, her eyes on Pete.

"Well, let me not waste your time," Farkas said. "I can't let you interview Silvia. It's not our call, it's up to her parents. From what little I do know, she's already spoken to the police, and we don't just let newspaper reporters—even sort of famous ex-journalists like you—swing by and chat up minors. It's just not how we operate."

Pete was frozen. Farkas had done her research. She knew his *Times* story was a weak cover at best.

"Did you really expect to walk in here and talk to a young girl without a problem?" Farkas asked, no malice in her voice. "I mean, I have to ask, because I found it kind of baffling when you called. Also, you don't work for the *Miami Times* anymore."

"I'm actually investigating Erica's murder," Pete said. He figured he'd go with all he had left: some form of the truth. "It's not an official thing; my friend Kathy is a writer for the *Times* and I've been helping her gather information. I spoke to Erica's mother and she said Silvia was the last friend Erica saw before she was taken. I was just hoping to ask her a few questions about that day, see if there was anything the cops had missed. I realize this is a weird request, and a bit of a long shot, but I don't really have much to work with here."

Farkas took off her glasses and rubbed the bridge of her nose.

"At least now—finally—you're being up-front," she said, no sign of anger or emotion in her voice. "Hell, you're probably doing a better job at investigating what happened to Erica than the cops, who've done nothing of note beyond interviewing a few people here and there. Erica was a special girl. Smart. Worked hard. She was one of my favorite students here. She had a real future. She was going to go to a good school, up in the northeast, where she'd have her first kiss, make lifelong friends, and figure out what to do with the rest of her life. All that's gone now, because of some sicko. All that time she had waiting for her? It's gone. And everyone else is left standing around wondering what happened. The people who have to figure it out could care less. They're more freaked about the bad publicity all this serial killer talk is giving the police department. A department, mind you, that you had a big hand in dragging through the mud. So, yeah, you hit a nerve. Lucky for you, I guess. I'm going to talk to Silvia myself. If she tells me anything I think you should know about, I'll pass it along. But only if I think it'll help. If anyone asks me if I talked to you outside of this office, and outside of me saying, 'No, Mr. Fernandez, you cannot talk to one of our students, please leave the premises,' then I'm going to deny it until I'm blue in the face, and it'll be your word against mine. You feel me?"

Pete nodded.

"All right, so there we are." She stood up and stuck her hand out, a slight smile on her face. "Now, Mr. Fernandez, please leave the premises."

CHAPTER EIGHTEEN

Julian checked the clock on his work computer. Ten minutes after five. He could leave. Only the secretary—Myrna, a slovenly bison of a woman—remained, staring blankly at her terminal.

Fernandez seemed to have quieted down. But he couldn't know for sure. It seemed like Kathy Bentley was the only one Fernandez confided in. Perhaps Julian would visit her. He pulled out a piece of spearmint gum and popped it into his mouth.

His job had its benefits. The sheer access it gave him—to people, rental spaces, and a sense of who was looking for a new place to live—was useful. These were the people he needed for his own, higher purpose. A simpleton could execute his tasks as a Realtor.

The Morales girl had been rushed. Too soon after Cline. But it had to be that way. The Messenger was being cautious and skittish. He was weak. But he was Julian's only direct link to the Voice.

He felt his phone vibrate in his pocket. He flipped the cheap disposable open and checked the display. A text message. Nina.

Do you have time to meet to discuss the apartment tonight?

Julian smiled. He took a mental inventory of the situation—he walked through every step of his plan, looking for holes, problem areas. Each part had to be thought out and organized.

He responded, his fingers used to texting on the crappy flip phones by now.

Can we meet later tonight? Sorry, just swamped at work.

Looking forward to getting you a great deal, Nina!

Nina Henriquez checked her iPhone. No new messages. She sighed. It was past ten o'clock, and she was pushing her curfew, again. She'd already had to avoid two FIU campus police officers as they made their rounds. For some reason, this real estate dude, Steve, had asked to meet on the university's Modesto A. Maidique campus—named after the school's Cuban-born ex-president. The campus was huge—about ten blocks long and wide, nestled next to the equally massive Tamiami Park in southwest Miami—a cobbled-together collection of buildings tacked onto the land as the university gained approval to build them, decorated with a sprinkling of standing art pieces, wide swaths of greenery, man-made lakes, and plenty of students. Except now. The area was desolate; the only sound Nina could hear was a distant stereo playing reggaeton. Nina wasn't super-comfortable with the situation, but thought, whatever. She needed to move, and she didn't have time to wait to graduate and get into a good school. She'd had it with her dad, her stupid little brother and his demands, and her bitch of a mother. Wherever she was.

Nina looked older than her sixteen years. She usually wore her long brown hair down and she was fit—as much of a gym rat as you could be at her age. She could pass for a college student, she thought. Most definitely an FIU student. Shit, FIU was like high school continued anyway. But she couldn't live in that house with her father any longer.

She'd signed onto the Craigslist apartment listings one day while in the school computer labs, bored out of her mind. She'd had it out with her dad that morning for the millionth time. He'd come home at two a.m., reeking of cheap wine and even cheaper perfume. He wanted something to eat, but lo and behold, the fridge was empty. Nothing Nina could do about it, no sir. He was having none of that, though, and took it out on her. What had started with a surprise slap and a wave of apologies going on for days and almost weeks was now the occasional full-on beating. Black eyes, broken nose. Nina had gotten good at dodging the swings aimed at her face and running out of the house. But he got her good last time. Rough. Slammed her against the wall, held her there, slapped her face. Called her every name he could think up in his muddled, alcohol-brined brain. *Slut. Whore. Just like your mother.*

Thinking about it now, Nina fumbled around in her purse for a cigarette, but then remembered he'd taken those, too. Part of keeping tabs on her, he'd said. New curfew. No smoking. No drinking. No hanging out after class. *Fuck that guy,* she thought. *He'll feel like shit when I'm gone,* she thought, *living it up in my own place, doing whatever the fuck I please.* She was staying with her aunt—her brother had come along, too. It was a temporary arrangement, at best. She still had a curfew. The rules weren't gone. Her aunt had been clear enough about that when Nina and her brother, Robert, showed up. She didn't have the energy or the space for them beyond a night or two. It was only a matter of time before her father woke up from his stupor and realized he didn't have his butler and maid around to fetch him a beer or grab dinner and keep the change. He'd be hunting them down soon. Maybe tonight.

Her younger brother had even less say in what was going on in their lives than Nina did. She'd had it. With her dad, her brother, everything. It was time to go. Nina would make it work, at least long enough for Nina to come of age and become his legal guardian. In the short-term game, though, she had to get out of there. She needed to survive. For herself and for Robert. If she had anything in common with her mom, a woman she remembered less each day, it was that. She was a survivor. She checked her phone again. Nothing.

She walked over to a small bench area. She felt a chill, even though the weather report predicted another typically warm Miami evening. That's when she saw the headlights from the parking lot directly across from her. They shut off, and she saw it was a white van. Was that him? She wasn't sure. She'd never met Steve in person.

She saw someone approaching the bench. It was a man, normal build. He was waving. She waved back. *Why did I do that?* she thought. She considered leaving. Going to her aunt's and sleeping on the floor. Bracing for the next, inevitable beating or verbal lashing from her father once he found them. Anything normal and comfortable, as fucked up as that was. But she didn't. The man stepped into the dim street light and nodded. He seemed clean-cut. Not fat or skinny.

His hair was parted in a weird, sitcom-dad way. He was older, but everyone seemed older to Nina. He didn't look like a freak at least. He seemed harmless.

"Nina?" he said, his eyes wide, not blinking.

"Hi, yeah," she said. "You Steve?"

He stuck out his hand. She shook it.

"Hi, yes, I'm Steve," he said. Smiling. His teeth were very white. His eyes were still wide. "Glad you could meet me here. Sorry for the late time, just been crazy at the office, as you can imagine."

He sat down on the bench opposite Nina. They were just a few feet apart. She didn't have any idea what questions she should ask of a real estate agent, especially one working basically pro bono, from what he'd told her. Did that even exist? He seemed a little nervous— no, not nervous really, she thought. More excited than nervous. She ignored that.

"So, what now? Do you have, like, an apartment for me? Is that how this works?" she asked.

He smiled. "Well, I do have a few," he said. "It's going to be tricky, especially since you don't have a roommate or the money for a deposit. I figured, if you don't mind, we would drive to a few places and check them out."

"Now? Isn't it too late to be going into apartments?"

"I called in advance," he said, his tone clearer now. "They're expecting us."

"Why don't we go another time?" she said. "I mean, do I just pick a place and you make it happen? Why would you do that for me? I barely have a job."

Steve cleared his throat and folded his hands together. Was he getting annoyed? Nina wondered.

"Well, I'm doing this off the books, you see," he said. "I know you're in a tough spot, so I'm not making any money. I'm just trying to help you. So, I can't really do it during regular work hours."

Nina nodded. "OK, that makes sense," she said. "I guess I just thought it'd be weird for people to be waiting around in the apartments they wanna rent for some dude and a girl to show up to check it out, you know? But I don't get this apartment hunt shit." She let out a dry laugh.

"Please don't curse."

"What?"

"Your language," he said, a forced smile spreading across his face. "Please don't curse. It doesn't become you."

"The fuck you talking about, man?" Nina said. She stood up. "You know what? Fuck this. You're weirding me out. What kind of a creeper meets a teenager this late and then wants to go on a tour of Miami?"

Steve stood up and took a step toward Nina. She backed up.

"I'm sorry," he said. "I didn't mean to weird you out; I'm just really old-fashioned when it comes to some things. I apologize. Let's just see a few places; maybe you'll really like the first one. I just want to help you out."

Nina felt a bit calmer. But she couldn't shake the uneasiness. Why had she come here?

"I don't think I can," she said. "I gotta get back home. My dad's waiting for me."

Steve shrugged. He seemed disappointed, but understanding. "No problem," he said. "At least let me drive you home, or to your bus stop. It's the least I can do, for making you come out here."

"I don't think so," Nina said. "I'll call a friend to give me a lift."

"It's up to you," Steve said, motioning to his van.

He was about to say more when he stopped and reached into his pocket. He raised his other hand in Nina's direction—telling her to wait a moment—while he walked a few steps away, talking softly into his phone. A few moments passed. He ended the call and returned to where he'd been standing.

"Sorry, that was my girlfriend," Steve said. "She needs me to come home. She's not as cool with me working twenty-four/seven as I am. I have to go home and fix things."

He let out a self-deprecating laugh. In that moment, he seemed so normal—so mundane and boring. Nina almost felt bad for this nerdy guy. He shrugged and started to head for his car before turning back.

"Sure I can't give you a lift? We can drive by a few places I wanted to show you on the way—depending on where you live," Steve said, his tone flat. He didn't care one way or the other it seemed. "We won't have time to go inside since my girlfriend needs me, but you can get an idea of what I had in mind. Your call, though."

Nina paused for a second before responding. "Sure, OK, let's go," she said. "I live near the water treatment plant, on Sixty-third Street. Is that too far?"

"Oh, not at all," Steve said, starting to walk toward the parking lot. "It's right on my way home."

Julian tightened the black cords wrapped around Nina Henriquez's wrists. He was humming to himself. She'd been out for the better part

138

of an hour. He dragged her farther into the storage area and toward a small set of stairs that led below.

The space wasn't much, he realized, but it met his requirements. Quiet. Inexpensive. Out of the way. In addition to its unique two-floor setup and a fairly accessible main storage area there was also—via a small set of stairs—a basement.

He yanked Nina up and carried her down the small staircase. The room was the size of a large closet. He set her against the far wall onto a dirty, uncovered twin mattress and untied her arms. She let out a confusing series of sounds as he bound her wrists to her ankles with Velcro rope. She was tied up, but could move somewhat. Within her reach were a few boxes of cereal, some bottled water and a bucket.

He stood up and looked over the cramped, dark space. He walked up the rickety stairs and closed the hatchlike door above the tiny room, enveloping the small space in darkness.

CHAPTER NINETEEN

Pete stifled a yawn as he unlocked the Book Bin's front door. It was just past six in the morning and he had the unenviable task of opening the store. He hadn't spoken to Dave since their argument a few days before. It was fine. Dave was a friend. Friends argued. He put his coffee cup on the ground and crouched down to gather the bundle of *Miami Times* that waited near the door. That's when he saw the headline: "Miami PD search for girls' killer still drawing blanks."

He let the door swing open while he pried a single copy loose from the pile. It was a column by Kathy, no less. He skimmed the story at first, then began to read more closely. It was almost a blow-by-blow account of their investigation so far. Kathy didn't quote him. Still, she was laying out the bits of information they'd collected via their interviews with Alice Cline's roommate and Erica Morales's mother, including the detail about the killer using mirrors around the two bodies—something that Kathy had gleaned from a confidential source—one that probably wouldn't be as willing to feed her inside dirt next time. The bits from the interviews included information that Pete had no idea was on the record, and stuff the police might not even have—or want out there for the public or killer to recognize. Kathy was intimating that he, Pete Fernandez, "the amateur who brought down one of Miami's deadliest mob enforcers," thought the Miami-Dade police were inept: look at all the info he found while working with his sometime partner Kathy.

What was she trying to do? What little advantage they had was now in black-and-white newsprint, plastered all over town and on the Internet. They'd blown their sources, their trust—for what? For a headline that would disappear in a few hours from the *Miami Times'* rinky-dink website, or be lining a birdcage in a week or two. He threw the paper down on the floor and kicked his coffee cup down the sidewalk, spilling the brownish liquid in front of the store entrance.

Pete dug his hand into his front pocket and pulled out his cell phone. He tapped Kathy's name in his contacts. She picked up on the second ring.

"*Miami Times*, Kathy Bentley speaking."

"What the fuck did you just do?"

"Pete, let me explain."

"How could you do this? You blew any cover we had. All our info is out there. Now the cops know everything we know. He knows everything we know now. This is seriously fucked up. What were you thinking?"

"Are you going to let me talk, or just get all your pent-up, repressed alpha male anger out?" she said. "Let me explain before I just hang up on you."

Pete didn't respond. He watched as the coffee he spilled spread around in front of the store, soaking the stack of newspapers. He'd have to pay for those, he thought. He didn't care.

"Are you there?"

"Yes," Pete said.

"Oh, I see," Kathy said. "I guess this is 'Pete mad' mode. Well, look, I had no choice. My editors needed a story on these murders. They knew where I'd been and who I'd spoken to. So it was either write the best column I could, and hope it prods the damn police to do some actual, oh, I dunno, fucking police work, or face the wrath of my editors. And, in case you'd forgotten, the terms of my reinstatement at the paper are not ironclad, dear. I came back because I had a killer story—no pun intended—in the Silent Death fiasco. But once I wrote that, it was back to being on thin ice. My reputation as a troublemaker didn't just disappear. And once the book money ran out—I didn't have the forethought to just save it all and get a retail job, like some people—I needed the job as much as I'd needed it the year before. So, I'm sorry if this breached our trust or whatever. Everything we did, mind you, and every conversation we conducted was under the auspices of me being a reporter. Me being an employee of the *Miami Times*. You knew I was going to make a story out of anything we found, so don't play innocent and pouty with me. I'm just not going to stand for it. Had you taken point and conducted the interviews yourself, done your due diligence—"

Pete hung up his phone. He walked through the open store door. He scrolled through his phone contacts and selected a name. He let

142

it ring. He got Emily's voice mail. It was early. She'd probably gone back to sleep.

He turned around and grabbed the one dry copy of the paper and returned to Kathy's column on the front of the local section, with a promo on the paper's front page. He read it again, sitting down at his usual spot behind the main counter. He didn't want to deal with the mess of coffee and newsprint just yet.

On second read, Pete realized the column was good—effective. She had done a fair amount of reporting Pete hadn't been privy to, including a few cops on the force speaking to her off the record. She painted a picture of an inept department that was in over its head and was now facing FBI interference on a major case. She added context. It would piss off a lot of people.

Pete still felt uncomfortable about his name appearing in print, even more uncomfortable because he had no idea it was coming. She'd been desperate and had tried to cobble something together with what little info she had. She should have called him. He heard a slight rapping on the store's glass door. He looked up and saw Aguilera on the other side, waving.

Pete got up, unlocked the door, and opened it, not stepping aside to let Aguilera in.

"We're closed," Pete said. He knew Aguilera wasn't here to buy a used copy of *Tender Is the Night*.

"Nice work in the paper this morning," Aguilera said, still with the sardonic smile. "Really appreciate you finally showing us your notes like that."

Pete backed up, letting Aguilera step into the store. The door closed behind him.

"No words, eh?" Aguilera said. "Can't say I blame you. That Bentley lady sure did a number on you. Some friend, printing all your leads on the front page of your old newspaper."

"What do you want, Aguilera?" Pete said. "Something tells me the self-righteous prick act isn't a new thing you're trying out today."

"Let me enjoy this moment," Aguilera said, raising a hand. "See, I'm not Miami-Dade PD. I could drag you in if I wanted to. I'm not scared of you. You don't have national immunity. Your little rogue mission, and Bentley's dumbass move, helps no one. Now the killer knows exactly what you know. He knows we know about the mirrors and have connected the killings. So, thanks to you, we're back to square one. In your heroic effort to top yourself, and, I guess, your weird, compulsive need to make your dad's old colleagues look stupid, you've just set us back—probably irreparably."

"I've just given you a convenient excuse," Pete snapped, "you sanctimonious asshole."

He didn't see Aguilera's swing coming, but when it connected, it knocked Pete back into the middle shelves; his body crashed against the side of the massive aisles. He slid down, more dazed than hurt.

"Fuck you, Fernandez," Aguilera said. "And fuck your friend. You stick your nose into this again—you even cough in my direction—and you'll never live a day in peace. I don't care about the FBI. Or Harras. I'll do whatever I can to make you miserable. I'm not some local punk. You may have cost some poor girl her life by traipsing around like some bodega Columbo. You make me sick, you know that? You're just another know-it-all who hasn't done shit. You're not even half the man your father was."

Aguilera turned and left, not waiting for a response from Pete.

He tried to get up, but stayed down. He'd been laid up on his back too often lately.

Pete saw Aguilera kick over the stack of newspapers still waiting outside the store, sending copies of the paper fluttering in the Miami wind again.

Pete dialed the number as he walked to his car. He had to talk to someone, and the people he would have called first were either dead, not responding, or had just been hung up on. Pete waited as the ringer went off twice. A gruff voice picked up the line.

"Hello?"

"Jack? Hey, it's Pete."

"Pete? Oh, hey," Jack said, sounding surprised. "How's it going, son? Everything all right?"

Pete balanced the phone on his shoulder as he backed his car out of the parking lot in front of the Book Bin. He pulled the car onto Bird Road, heading east. Home.

"I'm . . . I'm not doing so hot," Pete said. "I fucked up. I fucked up and I'd really just like to go to a bar, order a shot, and just destroy this day, man. It sounds so stupid and cliché."

"Where are you now?"

"In my car," Pete said.

"You heading home?"

"Yeah."

"Good," Jack said, his voice calm. "Listen to me: What you're experiencing is normal. Your body's getting used to dealing with life sober. Problems, conflict, change—the usual. The kind of stuff that'd make you recoil and head to a bar before can't have the same effect on you now. You have to fight that feeling off. Otherwise, you're back to where you started. You don't get a free pass if you go back. You return as bad a drunk as you left."

"Yeah," Pete said, trying to weave through traffic and focus on the phone at the same time. "I just feel like stuff is unraveling and I should have better control, or a better idea of what to do."

"You're just feeling life," Jack said. "Life isn't about closure or calm. You don't reach a point where everything's OK. It's peaks and valleys, and eventually you learn to manage the lows the same way you manage the highs, so you're not knocked out by either. That's the tricky part. Riding the waves."

"You're right," Pete said. He was almost there. "I'm just going to go home and get some sleep and see what I can do about this when I wake up. It'll be fine."

He turned his car onto his street. He could see his house.

"You bet it will," Jack said. "Call me if you need anything else. And Pete?"

He pulled into the carport.

"Yeah?"

"Don't talk to newspaper reporters if you can help it," Jack said. "They'll only hassle you. I heard the FBI is involved now, too? Yeesh."

"Yeah, they brought in two agents, Harras and Aguilera," Pete said, rubbing his chin. "Harras seems like a smart guy. So does Aguilera, if a bit of a hothead. He's got a temper."

"Aguilera's dad was a cop, too," Jack said. "Good man. Died too young. He worked around the same time as your father, Broche, and me."

"He died? When?"

"Not sure," Jack said. "He was Miami PD, too. Doubt his son was more than a few years old. Shame. Lots of stories from those days. Probably too many. When you're free, we can sit down over a few cups of coffee and you can humor a retired cop."

"Yeah?" Pete said, his brain wired, too agitated to really listen to Jack's rambling beyond registering that he was talking. "Anyway, thanks for picking up the phone. Sorry to bother you. I just needed to talk to someone, I guess."

"Stop apologizing," Jack said. "Just keep doing what you're doing. Answer me one question before you go."

"Shoot."

"Have you got a sponsor yet?"

"No," Pete said. A sponsor was someone who helped you work the twelve steps of the program. Pete had avoided anything that would require regular contact or anything resembling homework. He hoped that by just going to these meetings from time to time, he'd be able to keep his life in some kind of order. He wasn't sure it was working.

"I just haven't found the right person," Pete said.

"That's a weak excuse," Jack said. "But we all work this program at our own speed. Look, if you need to talk, I'm here. If you want someone to help you with this in a more formal way, I'm here too. Helping you helps me, OK?"

"Yeah, OK. Sounds good. Take care," Pete said. He hung up and turned off the engine. He sat in the driver's seat for a few seconds. He needed to take a day or two to figure out what to do next. But first, he needed some rest. Pete got out of the car.

He walked to the front of the house. He pulled out his keys and unlocked the door. The house was dark. Was Emily still asleep? He looked around. Everything seemed to be fine. He made an immediate left and headed to his—their—room. He pushed the door open slowly, trying not to wake Emily. Except she wasn't there.

He turned around and walked back down the hall to the guest room, where Emily had been storing her things and where she slept for the first few days of her stay, before they'd decided to give it another try. He opened the door.

The room was tidy—the bed was made, the dresser was cleaned off, and the two nightstands on opposite sides of the bed had been wiped clean. Costello lay in the middle of the bed, curled up and sleeping, purring to himself. Something was off, Pete thought. Why had she tidied up this room, which had been no more than a storage space for her? He walked to the closet and opened the sliding doors. That's when he knew. The closet, which had once been packed with Emily's overgrown wardrobe, was empty. He looked up at the shelf above the hangers and saw only space. Her luggage, which consisted of four or five large suitcases, was gone, presumably with her clothes in it.

He took a step backwards and then tumbled onto the bed, scaring Costello away. He felt something under him, a piece of paper. His heart beat faster. He knew what it was. Had he missed it, or just tried to deny it was there somehow?

Emily's handwriting had always been good, but this was extra legible. She didn't want to leave anything up for debate. That's just what would motivate her, legibility. He stood up, the single sheet in his hand, and walked to the living room. The page was still in his hand, unread, the sweat from his palm seeping onto it.

He sat down at the head of the small dining room table.

Pete,

I don't know what else to say besides 'I'm sorry.' You don't deserve this. You've been wonderful to me. I'm just not in the right place for this. I have a husband.

I'm so hard on you, Pete. I keep telling myself I'm trying to be strong and supportive, but most of the time I just feel mean and cutting with you, and that's a problem I can't x living in your house and sleeping in your bed. I also can't make myself accept that you will continue to put your life on the line like this, especially with what happened before. But I can also see it's not going away.

You've made so much progress in the last year. Since Mike died, since you stopped drinking.

But we don't have a future. What would we do? Get married? Have a kid? What we had together once is gone, and what we tried to have together now, while exciting and warm, was stillborn.

I do love you, in a way I probably won't ever love anyone else. And I know you care about me. But this is for the best. Please don't try to contact me.

Be strong,
Emily

He grabbed the piece of paper and crumpled it up, feeling the edges of the sheet slide against his skin. He didn't cry. That would come later, he thought. He felt cold, a strange numbness—that he'd often sought to obliterate.

He tossed the paper onto the floor. He walked down the main hall and into his room. He closed the door behind him and slid into bed. The bright morning sun crept into the room through the blinds. Pete buried his face in his pillow and closed his eyes, letting the darkness he created take him away.

PART III:
RED TIDE

CHAPTER TWENTY

He saw the light flicker on. He saw Fernandez walk across the living room and head toward the back of the house, to his bedroom. His lady friend wasn't around.. She'd been almost frantic in her packing.

Julian had chosen to pay attention to the fly swirling around his head. Fernandez was not stupid. He knew Julian had him in his sights. Luckily, Fernandez had other distractions. He still checked the liquor cabinet from time to time.

He saw Fernandez step out of the house. He waited for Fernandez to get in his car and back out of the driveway. The sputtering Toyota turned onto the street and sped off. He slipped on a pair of leather gloves. He whistled softly as he stepped out of the car and walked toward the front door.

Even under the shade of a giant umbrella, the Miami heat and humidity were still wearing on Pete. He shook his glass to make the ice move around and took a few small cubes in his mouth, crunching on them to pass the time. He hadn't ordered any food yet, despite being starved and despite being at Versailles, a restaurant with some of the tastiest and best-known Cuban food in Miami. He looked out onto the street. It was the middle of the week in the middle of the day. Not a lot of activity, aside from a cluster of Cuban *viejos* sipping coffee under an awning at the restaurant's pickup window. The fast, pitter-patter beat of the Spanish exclamations and stories being shared a few feet away comforted Pete.

"Are you waiting for a date?"

Pete turned around and saw Kathy's lanky figure standing between him and the boiling sun. She cast a long shadow.

"Kind of feels like it, no?" he said.

"I guess," she said as she dropped her purse down on the large table and sat to Pete's right. "I'm assuming this means you're not mad at me anymore?"

"I'm still annoyed at you," he said. "But I need your help."

"Well, that's encouraging, I guess," she said. "Why are we here? I mean, I'm excited to hork down some *carne asada* and all, but a fancy lunch isn't your usual way of expressing annoyance. Also, are we waiting for people to join us?"

"You'll see."

"Wonderful. It's going to be like that," she said, looking around the outside seating area, hoping for a waiter. Her eyes found two other people, though. "Who are those two dudes heading over here? They appear to know you."

"I know them," Pete said, putting his glass down and waving at Harras and Aguilera.

"I don't like this," she said. "You didn't tell me I'd have to interact with strangers."

"Just let me take the lead," he said, his voice lower as the FBI agents approached the table.

"That's fucking reassuring," she whispered back.

Harras reached the table first and nodded, sitting down across from Pete, Aguilera taking the seat to his left as he scanned Kathy and shot daggers at Pete.

"Glad you could make it, gentlemen," Pete said. "You guys know Kathy Bentley. Kathy, this is Harras and Aguilera. Two of the FBI's finest."

Kathy nodded. She looked confused. Her eyes widened at the mention of FBI.

"Get to the point," Aguilera said. "This better not be a waste of time."

Harras shot Aguilera a dirty look.

Pete laid his hands palms-down on the table and looked at the agents sitting across from him. "I want us involved."

"Involved in what?" Harras said, his tone sharp.

"In the case," Pete said, his voice clear, his eyes locked on Harras. "We knew more than you did. We know more now. Nina Henriquez is still missing—she might be alive. If you don't let me help, I'll go back to the press and we'll blow the lid off this entire thing, and show how incompetent you guys are."

"Are you fucking crazy, man?" This time Aguilera responded, half rising from his seat. "We'll throw you in jail in a second for interfering with a police investigation. Do you think we won't do that?"

"Shut the fuck up, Aguilera," Harras said, his voice low but forceful. Aguilera twitched in protest but stayed quiet.

Harras looked at Pete and Kathy, like an annoyed parent forced to discipline an unruly child.

"Forgive my partner," Harras said. "His tone is off. But he's in the right ballpark. You mess with this investigation, and it's going to be easy to lock you away."

"I'm sure," Pete said. "But by then the damage is done. The guy who brought down the Silent Death is calling the Miami PD and the FBI incompetent? People will buy it. Whether it's true or not, or whatever the details are. That can be resolved later."

Harras looked at his hands and took a deep breath.

"What's your angle?"

"You can't be seriously engaging this asshole," Aguilera said, turning to Harras, a look of shock in his face.

Harras shot Aguilera another glance before turning back to Pete and Kathy. "Fernandez—answer the question. What's your angle with this?"

"I want to help," Pete said. "I can help you. You must see that by now. I've been dancing along the fringe of this thing—these kinds of things—for a while now. I want to be an active part. I think I can help nail this guy before any other girls go missing. Or die."

Harras glanced at Kathy.

"What about her?"

"She can help, too," Pete said.

"Hold on a second," Kathy said. "You forget I work for a major newspaper. I can't just quit my day job and become an honorary deputy."

"Don't you need to write a new book?" Pete asked. "This kind of access would make for a great one."

"Assuming we give you any access," Aguilera snapped. "This is bullshit. You shot your load already with that stupid column. You don't have any information that isn't in print."

"You're wrong," Pete said.

"What do you have that we don't?" Aguilera asked.

"Enough," Pete said. "I guess now the question you have to ask yourself is, do you want to risk leaving this meeting having pissed me off? All I'm asking is to be allowed to help you. If you let me in, we can pool our information and bring this asshole down."

Harras stood up. Aguilera followed. Pete could feel Kathy's eyes on him. Harras spoke first.

"You can help by talking to some of the victims' families," Harras said. Pete took slight pleasure in watching Aguilera squirm in surprise. "But Henriquez is off limits. We're not confirming she's a victim yet. Swing by the main office tomorrow morning at nine and we'll see about getting your credentials in order." He looked at Kathy. "Any word of this in the press and we'll deny this meeting even happened. If you want this to become anything close to a book a year or two from now, those are the rules. Understood?"

Pete nodded. He stood up and extended his hand. Harras looked at it.

"You're kidding me, right?" He wiped his hands on his dress shirt, sweat rings under his arms.

The two agents turned and left. Aguilera glanced back at Pete one more time. He looked confused, Pete thought. Good.

"Well, that's not what I was expecting," Kathy said as Pete returned to his seat. "Did you take your vitamins this morning?"

"I had to take control of the situation," Pete said as he waved down a waiter. "You hungry?"

"Always."

The waiter arrived. Pete ordered a *medianoche* sandwich, which consisted of pork, Swiss cheese, pickles, and ham. It was one of his favorite Cuban dishes, and he felt like celebrating. Kathy ordered a plate of *carne asada*—roasted meat—with a side of rice and beans. Versailles was a city landmark—a nexus point for the Cuban exile community. Where revolutions were planned, careers built and destroyed, and political deals hatched. It felt oddly fitting to Pete that they'd had their showdown with Harras and Aguilera here. They ate, comforted by the sing-song voices of the waitresses and the old Cuban men arguing and joking nearby.

"So, Emily's gone?" Kathy asked.

Pete took a long sip from his tiny cup of Cuban coffee before answering.

"She left, yeah."

"Are you OK?"

"Why do you ask?"

Kathy sighed.

"Do I have to spell everything out?" she said. "It's clear something was going on. Whether it was a full-blown Relationship Renaissance or just friends with benefits, I don't know. But you two were back together in some fashion. And knowing how much real estate Emily occupies in that overthinking brain of yours, well, I just wanted to make sure you were fine."

"Not drinking, you mean?"

"Not drinking would fall under fine, yes."

"I'm fine," Pete said. "She left a note, and I haven't heard from her since. She said she felt 'overwhelmed.'"

"I see," Kathy said, fiddling with her napkin. "You don't seem totally on board with that."

"No," he said. "Not really. But I'm not surprised. I probably shouldn't have let it happen."

"That's sometimes . . . difficult," Kathy said. "Not that I know from any kind of personal experience or anything."

"I think it's good to take some time," Pete said. "I have a lot of my own issues to work out."

The waiter walked by their table and left the check. Pete took it and slid two twenties into the thin folder.

"I've got this," he said.

"I would hope so," she said, checking her phone display. "What now?"

"We start to look for Nina Henriquez," Pete said, standing up, putting the lunch receipt in his back pocket.

Kathy followed him toward the car.

"You do remember the part where the FBI told us to do exactly the opposite of that, right?"

Pete got to his car and opened the door. He looked at Kathy. "Exactly."

CHAPTER TWENTY-ONE

"I can't believe I've been reduced to drinking cheap beer," Kathy said, slurping down another gulp of Coors. She was sitting at Pete's dining room table, across from him. Stacks of papers and boxes surrounded the small area. They'd decided to go to Pete's house to combine their notes and put together a game plan, one that would hopefully save Nina Henriquez's life. Kathy's main source in the Miami PD had managed to get them copies of the Morales and Cline case files. The photos and police reports were spread over the table.

"I don't have alcohol in the house," Pete said, not looking up from his laptop. "You know that."

"Yes, yes," Kathy said. "Which is why you've forced me to shell out for this gas station piss-in-a-can beer. Oh well." She took another long swig. "I'll have to make do."

Pete ignored her and dove in, sliding some of the photos away from him. He could only stand to look at them for so long.

"OK, so what do we know? Our killer's been stalking his victims over the Internet. Victims range in age from mid-teens to mid-twenties. He uses different e-mail addresses and finds women who are looking to either move away from home or need a roommate. How do we think he does that?"

"Beyond trolling Craigslist?" Kathy said.

"You think that might be enough?"

"Well, it could be," Kathy said, opening her own laptop and typing. "The victims don't seem to be particularly special. They're all relatively pretty girls, no major problems, aside from the usual drama with parents or roommates. Nina Henriquez was on the honor roll at her school. Erica Morales had a beef with her mom—but what high school girl doesn't? It's also hard to tell when this guy started. I'm not surprised this story is only picking up traction now."

"What do you mean?"

"They're Hispanic girls, not rich, from broken homes who don't look like your generic, network television 'Latinas,'" Kathy said, her voice rising. "Even a town as diverse as Miami still has biases. People only care when the white kid is missing. People get up in arms when the white guy is shot in the black neighborhood. It's rarely the other way around. Those are the stories no one wants to hear about."

Kathy paused to scan one of the police reports.

"Also, I hate to tell you, but this guy strikes me as extremely smart and precise. He's not a rage-driven killer."

"So?"

"So, the guy that beat the shit out of you—you do remember that, right?" Kathy said. "He seems to me—based on your description—like a regular thug. It doesn't sync."

"You're right," Pete said, closing his eyes and rubbing the bridge of his nose. "But that opens up a bunch of even more terrible possibilities."

"Yes, unfortunately, investigating a serial murderer does not usually involve rainbows and butterflies," Kathy said.

"Then there's the Rex Whitehurst angle," Pete said. "Whoever this person is, he's killing girls in the same way Whitehurst did."

"Do you think the mirrors are there to imply judgment of some kind?"

"Not sure," Pete said. "It's almost like he wants to show the victim more than once."

"Like multiplying their pain?"

"That feels right, but we've got nothing to go on," Pete said, sounding exasperated. "This guy and Whitehurst, there's something between them, linking them together. What's that connection? Why?"

"Homage?" Kathy said. "Like a cover band? Sounds terrible, but these freaks are crazy, right?"

"It's definitely some kind of nod," Pete said, shuffling through a stack of printouts. "But our killer jumps around in age."

"Well, it could just mean our killer is still in control," Kathy said. "Whitehurst went off the rails by the time he arrived in Florida. Most of his focused hunting happened down the eastern seaboard, over time."

Kathy pulled out another stack of photos and spread them around a free area on the table.

"On the bright side, relatively, your friend Rick has been

exonerated," Kathy said. "Though I doubt being hounded by the police for a while has helped his standing in the community."

"You spoke to him?" Pete said.

"No, nothing like that," Kathy said. "I hear things. I'm a reporter. I sometimes make calls and people pick up. He basically went underground when all this hit, which was smart. Doubly so for someone who would do something as cliché as having an affair with his secretary."

Pete ignored her last comment. He typed a few words and scanned the laptop's screen.

"Do you think our killer started here in Miami, though?"

"No idea," Kathy said.

"Can you do a search on your *Times* Lexis account to see if you can find any similar unsolved cases on the East Coast, or nearby?" Pete asked. "If we could figure out where else this guy has killed, we might be able to track him."

"You say it like it's easy," Kathy said. "It's not. Girls go missing all the time. And remember, the only reason we know we have a killer is because the bodies have been found. Who knows how many are in a hole somewhere? I wouldn't know where to start."

"Right," Pete said, scrunching his nose as he looked at his own screen. "It's too wide a net to cast. But let's speculate for a bit. Say he has killed before. A few times. Now he's here and he's paying homage to Whitehurst. What's next?"

"Well, serial killers tend to go two ways," Kathy said. "They either go dormant for years between kills, or they increase their frequency until they start to get sloppy. Like Rory Conde—the Tamiami Trail Strangler. If these girls died by the hand of the same dude, it looks to me like he's settled into a pattern, with the exception of the floater. But who knows how long that'll last."

Pete stretched and let out a long yawn.

"I'm going to make some coffee," Pete said, standing up and walking toward the kitchen. "Need anything?"

"Another can of piss, if you don't mind," Kathy said, shaking her empty beer can.

Pete opened the fridge door and grabbed a can of Coors. The cold on his hands sent him back. He placed it on the counter and walked toward the coffeemaker near the sink. He busied himself with the preparation of the pot, trying to ignore the silver can. The coffee machine began to percolate, dripping coffee into the pot. He looked out the small window above the microwave. The dusk gave Pete's view an eerie, misted quality. The skies were getting darker. Soon, he wouldn't be able to see anything outside the tiny window. Pete didn't like it. Too much darkness. This time of year reminded him of things he'd rather forget. Mike. Emily. His father. Then he saw it. A movement—near the westernmost corner of the backyard. Pete moved closer to the window. He couldn't see anything now. Was it a dog? A possum? Probably.

He poured a cup of coffee into his old *Miami Times* mug and splashed in a bit of milk and some sweetener before stirring. He kept his eyes on the window and took a tentative sip. Nothing else. He carried his cup and grabbed the now not-as-cold can of beer. He tossed it to Kathy as he walked in. She caught it, more gracefully than Pete had expected. As he walked toward the dining room table, he noticed that the door to the utility room—where the washer and dryer were, and which led to the backyard and carport exit—was ajar. He put the mug of coffee on the table.

"Did you go outside for a smoke?"

"No, not for a bit," Kathy said. "Why?"

"This door," Pete said, motioning toward the utility room. "I haven't used it since last week, when I did some laundry."

"You do laundry? Could've fooled me."

"This isn't a joke," Pete said, turning to face Kathy. "Someone's been in the house."

Then the lights went out.

Kathy let out a frightened yelp. Pete backed away from the utility room door. The only light in the living room was emanating from the two laptops resting on the dining room table.

"This is not funny," Kathy said, standing up and walking over to Pete. "Please tell me you just forgot to pay your electric bill. I don't mind us going to my place to continue our very special episode of *Cagney and Lacey*."

They heard the sound of breaking glass coming from the guest room.

"Someone's in the house," Pete said. He darted into the utility room and came back with his gun. He flicked the safety off. He held the gun at his side and walked toward the main hall, which led to the guest room and, further down, to his own bedroom. "Stay here."

"Fine by me," Kathy said. Pete looked back at her. The laptops provided enough light for Pete to have a sense of what was around them. Kathy was leaning against the far wall, next to the utility room entrance, peering out the back window onto the backyard.

Another crash. Pete couldn't make out where it was coming from this time. Outside? His room? He crouched and began to walk down the hall, his body low to the ground. Once he got past the living room and the two laptops, the house became almost pitch black. He got closer to the guest room door. It was closed. Pete wasn't sure if he'd left it open. The last time he remembered being in the room was when he found Emily's note. Since then, he'd avoided even looking at it. His right hand tightened around his gun as he reached for the doorknob with his left. As his fingers touched the handle, the door creaked open. He couldn't see inside the room. But as the door opened, he realized that he wasn't alone. The figure—average build, hunched over, panting—stood in the middle of the guest room, in front of the bed. Pete couldn't tell if he was armed. But he knew the man had heard the noise from the door. Pete rolled away from the doorway and pressed his back against the adjacent wall. His breathing was heavy. He felt his palms sweating on the gun.

Then he heard the laughter.

It started softly at first, a low rumble, almost a growl. It came from inside the guest room—from the shape Pete had seen. Then it grew louder. More menacing. As if the man had heard the best, saddest, and most off-color joke ever. The kind of laugh that kept going well past the expiration date of any bit of humor, inching further and further away from sanity. The laughter almost masked the fact that the figure in the guest room was now trashing the room, tossing furniture around and shattering the windows. Pete inched closer to the guest room door.

He wheeled his body around, facing the entrance in a crouch, his gun pointed into the room in his best imitation of a three-point police stance. He opened his mouth and felt nothing come out. The figure wasn't moving anymore, but Pete knew he was there, in the corner of the wrecked room, poised to lunge.

"I have a gun and I know where you are," Pete said, his voice low but clear. "Come out with your hands up in the next three seconds or I start shooting. I am not fucking kidding."

Pete waited. Nothing. He tried to focus, to tune into the figure's breathing, but found nothing. His hands, holding up the gun as he stayed in the uncomfortable crouch, started to shake. He felt the sweat forming on his brow.

"You're foolish." The voice came from the room, but Pete couldn't pinpoint where exactly. It was a growl—like someone had swallowed crushed glass and was still trying to speak. "You think it's that simple? That I'd just come in here, with no plan, no goal, no concept of how to scare you and your stupid girlfriend? Did you think you'd just find Nina and that'd be that?"

Pete looked into the darkness; his eyes narrowed. He lifted the gun for a split second, unsure of where the man had gone, his voice coming in at weird levels and from different directions. He felt disoriented. The mention of Nina threw him off. *She's alive?*

Kathy's scream cut through the silence. Pete pulled back and stood up. He turned toward the scream—toward the living room—before he remembered he was leaving one problem behind. He felt the man slam into him, pushing his body into the wall across from the guest room entrance. His gun fell out of his hand and slid out of his reach. He heard the man kick his gun down the hall, away from the rooms. He felt the man's knee rise and make contact with his face. He felt his face roll off the knee as his body fell. His jaw hit the carpeted floor. The man's boot made contact with the back of his head. He rolled to the left, dodging another kick, and grabbed the man's foot, trying to pull him down. But a quick punch to the face disoriented him. Pete's vision blurred. The man darted down the hall, away from the living room—toward the guest room and Pete's bedroom on the other side of the house. The room's door slammed shut. He tried to pull himself up, but slipped and fell again instead. His head was pounding. He didn't hear Kathy anymore. He could, however, hear his room being trashed—books, shoes, and drawers being strewn about and slamming into his door. Pete strained to get to his feet.

He had to help Kathy. Whatever was going on at the other side of the house would have to wait. He started to turn toward the living room—to Kathy—when he smelled it.

Smoke.

He looked up: nothing. It was too dark. But he felt it. His lungs took in another dose of smoke and he responded with a coughing fit. He started to walk toward the living room and could see the smoke now, obscuring his vision further. He squinted his eyes. He reached the large living room and crouched on the floor, feeling around for his gun. Nothing. He was lost in his own house.

"Kathy?" Pete said, his voice low but loud enough for someone in the room to hear. "Kathy, where are you?"

The muffled whimper came from the far end of the living room, near the main window that faced the backyard. Then he did something he wished he'd thought of before: he pulled out his cell phone and let the small display light shine on the area in front of him. Within a few seconds he found her, bruised and beaten, her face red and bloodied. She was tied to the couch with what appeared to be one of Pete's own white undershirts. The same kind of shirt had been stuffed into her mouth. He pulled it out and began to work on untying her hands. The smoke was getting thicker, and he could feel the warmth of fire behind him. His father's house, the home he grew up in, was on fire. After a few more seconds, Kathy was free.

"We . . . we have to go," Kathy said.

"Stay calm," Pete said. "He's in my room, on the other side of the house. He's nuts. He's ripping the place apart. He can't hear us."

"What are you talking about?" she said, her voice shaking. "He was just here. He just tied me up."

Kathy's second scream of the night came too late to warn Pete. He felt the thud of something metallic and hard slam into the back of his head. He felt his body get heavy and his eyelids close. The last thing he saw before blacking out was Kathy's outline, moving toward him through the smoke. It felt warm all around him. His head felt light.

And then everything shut off.

"Come on, come on, come on . . . " It was Kathy's voice, slow and quiet at first, then louder. Pete heard it as his eyes opened, then closed, smoke sneaking in and stinging them. His head hurt. A lot. It was throbbing—and he felt his body moving—no, sliding. He tilted his head up and got a shot of pain at the base of his skull.

"Fuck," he said, finally remembering what had happened earlier. An hour ago? A minute ago? How long had he been out?

She hadn't heard him. Her hands were still at his ankles, dragging him across his living room floor, smoke surrounding them, flashes of fire flickering into the living room from down the hall. Pete was hot. He felt dizzy and fevered. He hadn't thought to move yet. She noticed he was awake.

"Can you walk?" Kathy said. "We need to get the fuck out of here and I don't think I can carry you."

"I . . . I think so," Pete said, pushing himself up onto his elbows, each movement causing a chorus of pains and aches. "Is he gone?"

"I don't know," Kathy said. Normally, this would be her time to quip or make a remark, but they were past that. Pete could see the bruises and dirt caking her face, even through the haze of dark smoke. His house was on fire, and he could barely move. "We don't have much time."

Pete nodded, his teeth gritting at the motion of his head. He felt her move around and get behind him, looping her arms under his and lifting him up. The rush of motion sent his head spinning, but after a few seconds he felt almost normal. He took a tentative step and stumbled, falling back into Kathy. She held him up.

"Just lean on me, but not too much," she said, a dry laugh escaping her mouth. "I'm not as strong as I look."

They took a few steps when he felt something with his foot. His gun. He knelt down, holding onto Kathy in case he fell. His hands rummaged around the floor, which was already dark with smoke, a bad sign, he thought. He felt the gun's handle and picked it up. He'd have something to remember his father by. He thought of their laptops and the piles of research they'd be leaving behind. Their entire case was lost. Nothing he could do about that now. He stood back up and gripped Kathy's hand with his free one.

"Let's go."

The first explosion seemed to come from the backyard. The house shook in response. The crashing plates and toppling furniture could barely be heard over the roar of the growing fire tearing through the house. They looked at each other.

"The fuck was that?" she said.

"We have to go," Pete said. They were about ten feet from the door, but even that seemed like three football fields of distance. Pete couldn't go a step without pain scorching his skull and neck, and Kathy looked like she'd just been run over by a few joyriding cars. He thought he heard her sigh in resignation.

The second explosion was less subtle and closer: the carport. Pete's car. Pieces of his Toyota Celica crashed through the main bay windows on both sides of the living room, sending glass, car parts, tree branches, and gravel hurtling into the remains of the house. Kathy and Pete were knocked off their feet by the force of the explosion and fell back farther into the living room, Pete's head slamming against his father's favorite chair.

The combination of smoke, debris, and utter defeat threatened to overcome what little resolve Pete had left. He let his eyes close for a second, his back on the floor. The heat of the fire and the explosion coated him. He could just let it go now. Go to sleep. He'd done his good deed for the world already; this was just another mess he'd made. Someone would find him. They'd write an obituary, probably critical and not fully accurate, but he'd make the papers, at least.

He let out a long groan and opened his eyes. He looked to his right and saw Kathy crumpled behind him, her body in a weird shape, her breathing shallow. Pete looked himself over, moving into a sitting position. He wasn't sure how long it'd been since the last explosion, but his house wasn't an armory. It couldn't take much more. He felt the adrenaline pumping inside him as he stood up, ignoring the throbbing drumbeat slamming into the back of his head. He shook Kathy. No response. He scooped her up, letting out a scream of pain as he straightened his legs. He took a step toward the door. Then another. He felt blood trickling down the side of his face. After a few steps, he tried to hold his breath; the smoke was thicker than before. He heard sirens.

A few more feet until he reached the door. He fell to one knee. He heard Kathy let out a slight cry as he toppled forward. He looked right, down the hallway, toward his old room—his father's bedroom—and only saw flames engulfing the carpet, the cheap wallpaper, the pictures on the wall of his parents, his high school graduation, his prom, Disney World vacations, and his engagement party. Pictures he'd probably never see again.

Pete was having trouble breathing. He tightened his grip on Kathy and pushed forward off his leg, slamming their bodies against the front door, his free hand jostling around and looking for the handle. The simple task of opening the door seemed impossible. The idea of giving up seemed almost appealing. Just for a second. Pete felt his hand surround the door handle and pull.

Then they tumbled outside, the fresh air whooshing into the house like a tidal wave of breathable space. When thinking back on that night, he could never remember how they got down the front steps before the third, final, and largest explosion went off. It had been as if the bomb—a poor, makeshift plastic thing that would have made a suicide bomber proud, which forensics would later reveal had been planted under the porch—had been waiting for them. The explosion sent a fireball of shrapnel up from the depths below the house. They were launched forward, their bodies thrust into midair by the power of the blast.

They landed a few feet away, close to the street and to a car that was once parked near the sidewalk but was now flipped over. They hit the grass with a thud in front of what used to be Pete's house. He looked up toward the night sky. The smoke from the fire clouded over the full moon. Had it been any other night, under different circumstances, Pete would have said it was a beautiful moon. He would have turned to Emily, or Kathy, or anyone, and noted it.

He coughed, a quick, empty cough. He saw blood on his hands as he covered his mouth. The sirens grew louder. He let his eyes close again.

CHAPTER
TWENTY-TWO

Julian stepped out of the tub and dried himself with a towel, examining his body for bruises and cuts. He was hurt. But he would be fine.

He walked into his living room/bedroom. Under his loft bed was a small office area. He dressed and slid behind his desk, booting up his computer.

A window appeared on the screen. The video feed was grainy and inconsistent, but he could see a figure at the center of the camera's view. It was a young girl, tied up, her eyes covered by a dark cloth. Her wrists and ankles were bound together. He noticed scrapes around her wrists and ankles and he smiled. She'd been trying to get out. She must have noticed the light flickering on, or heard the camera moving, because she began to move her head around, trying to look past the blindfold.

"Hello?" she said, her voice dry and low. "Who's there?"

Julian slid his chair closer to the screen and rubbed a finger over his chapped lips. How long could he let this go on? Not much longer. But he wasn't sure Fernandez had gotten the message. The bugs the Messenger provided and planted in the house had worked well. He knew where Fernandez and his friend stood. The explosion had to happen now—to destroy their evidence. He had hoped they'd be destroyed too.

The phone rang, vibrating on his tiny coffee table. He got up and opened it, waiting for the Messenger to respond.

"You're causing too much trouble," the Messenger said, sounding agitated. Nervous. "Things aren't supposed to pick up like this yet."

"This is my game," he said, his voice clear. "You gave me notes to work from. I don't need them anymore."

"Oh, really?" the Messenger said. "That's an interesting way to look at things. Seems as though you needed a little help tonight."

"You pushed for this," Julian said. "You're the one who thought Fernandez was a threat. Now he isn't. We can continue with our work."

"It's not that easy," the Messenger said. "They still know too much. We have to—"

"I'm in control now," he said, keeping his volume low and his tone measured. "I've always been in control. Understand that."

He closed the phone before the Messenger could respond. The sound of Nina's crying drew him back to his computer screen, his face bathed in the bright blue light of his monitor.

CHAPTER TWENTY-THREE

Pete let his body collapse onto the small cot in the Book Bin's cramped back office. It was close to three in the afternoon and he already felt spent. He looked over his arms and hands, still bruised and cut from the explosion. He'd walked away from it all with only a minor concussion, a few broken ribs, and a black eye that looked much worse than the last one. He was lucky. Dave had been kind enough to offer up the Book Bin as a temporary base of operations, but Pete wasn't sure how long he could take him up on that. The dank smell of the bookstore was the least of his concerns. His cat, Costello, hadn't made it out of the house. Pete only hoped he hadn't suffered much. Kathy survived, but was as much of a wreck as he was. She had an apartment, at least. He still needed to meet with his insurance company to properly assess the damage. One thing at a time. His meeting that morning had helped.

There was also the matter of Nina Henriquez. From what little Pete remembered from his encounter with the killer—or was it *killers?*—it seemed like he was referring to her in the present tense. As time passed, her chances of survival faded. Pete had avoided the press following the explosion. They were naturally curious, but he'd made himself hard to find. His job at the store wasn't on the books, per se, so without a residence it was like he'd fallen off the map.

It was harder to shake the cops and FBI. Harras had hovered over his hospital bed, waiting for the right time to begin questioning him. When that time arrived, Pete was as honest as he could be—even with the details blurry. The killer had been there. The killer had blown up his house and almost killed him. Pete hadn't mentioned Nina Henriquez. He wasn't sure why he held it back—and he knew he was putting her life at risk. But something in his head told him to hold onto that bit of info a bit longer.

He'd heard very little from Kathy since the explosion. "Shaken up" could only begin to describe her state of mind when she was discharged from the hospital—her face bruised and cut, her arm in a sling. Pete felt bad for her, which was the last thing Kathy wanted anyone to feel.

He heard the door chime and walked to the front door.

The two men—dressed in nicely pressed black suits, blue ties, and matching sunglasses—could have been twins. Both were white, tall, and clean-shaven with matching buzz cuts. One had an earpiece. The one on Pete's left nodded as Pete came into the store's front display area.

"Pete Fernandez?" Lefty said.

"Who's asking?"

"FBI—your presence is requested," said the one on the right.

"Show me some ID," Pete said.

Lefty walked up to Pete and showed him his badge. Seemed legit. But Pete wasn't exactly an expert on proper FBI agent identification. His name was Gran. Pete preferred thinking of him as "Lefty."

"My partner is Agent Davidson," Gran said. "Now, I'll ask again: will you come down to our offices?"

"That's very polite," Pete said. "What if I decline?"

"If you don't come willingly, sir," Gran said, "we'll have to bring you in anyway."

"Let me guess," Pete said, trying to stall and think over what few options he had left. "Harras sent you?"

"We're not here to elaborate, sir," Davidson said. "Please follow us."

Davidson turned and exited the store. Gran walked out and held the door open for Pete. Pete felt a tingling feeling all over his body—a mix of fear and stress. He didn't like it.

He flipped the store sign to "CLOSED" and locked the door behind him.

The Miami branch of the FBI was housed in a light gray, unspectacular office building nestled off the Golden Glades Interchange—a beautiful name for a five-highway pileup that was the nexus of nightmares for most Miami drivers. I-95, the Florida Turnpike, and the Don Shula Expressway—to name a few—all met in the same place in North Miami, and it made sense for the FBI to set up nearby. This was all built on the presumption that traffic wasn't a complete disaster and one could easily hop on any given highway to get where they needed to go. Unfortunately, traffic was always a shitshow and despite its logic-based layout, Miami was anything but an easy place to navigate. Pete would have dreaded the trip to North Miami for any reason. He was especially anxious today.

The interior of the building—from the drab lobby to the stale-smelling elevator, to the string of cubicles and utility closet–sized offices—was as dull as the soulless exterior. But Pete hadn't gotten the grand tour. Upon arrival, he was immediately ushered into a small interview room on the building's third floor. He sat at a long table, a cup of lukewarm coffee in front of him, almost daring him to drink. The air felt recycled and artificial. Pete fought the urge to close his eyes to shut out the bright lights coming from above.

Harras stepped in with little ceremony, closing the door behind him. Pete heard a lock click on the other side. He would only be leaving when they wanted him out.

This was bound to happen, he thought. He'd pushed it as far as he could and now the FBI was waking from its slumber and taking a closer look at him. Not out of any kind of admiration, but probably something closer to resentment. Who was this little shitbird mucking with their investigation? The thought of things getting any worse hadn't crossed Pete's mind until now, but the reality that, yes, things could continue to slide south seemed more possible the longer he spent in this cell-like room.

Harras sat across from Pete and folded his hands. He looked Pete over, concern in his eyes.

"How're you holding up?"

"Oh, just dandy," Pete said. "I really like roughing it. Sleeping on a cot that's about as comfortable as a stack of planks, showering at the YMCA, eating fast food, and only a gun and a bus pass to my name. Kind of romantic, don't you think?"

Harras winced.

"Cut the attitude," he said. "And I bet you've heard this a number of times, but I'll say it again: you're lucky to be alive."

"Yes, so very, very lucky," Pete said, looking down at the table for a second. "Where's your partner? He's not part of the welcoming committee?"

Harras avoided Pete's eyes.

"Aguilera is taking some time off," he said.

"For punching me at my job for no real reason," Pete said, a statement not a question. "Glad I took a minute to let his bosses know. Is that why I'm here? To file a formal complaint?"

"For a change, you're partially right," Harras said. "He shouldn't have done that, no matter how much we both wanted to."

"Well, I don't know if I'd call that good news," Pete said. "But I'll take it. I could do without that volatile twerp for—well, forever."

"Don't start planning a parade just yet," Harras said. "He'll still be shadowing me on this. So, as far as you're concerned, nothing's changed."

"A slight slap on the wrist," Pete said.

Harras ignored him.

"Well, let me clear up the whole 'why am I here?' bit for you," Harras said. "This isn't just a warning. This is a reminder. This is a gigantic Post-it note on your thick forehead: we can make your life extremely miserable. More miserable than even you're used to, which is saying a lot. We're not some banana republic local police force—we're national. We don't take kindly to amateurs bumping and crashing into things we're investigating. We tried to do it your way. We tried to loop you in. I felt like I'd made myself clear, but it doesn't seem to be working with you. I'm hoping your entire house exploding might be enough, but my guess is no."

"I feel really special," Pete said. "You invited me to your big, boring office to yell at me? I must be really getting on your nerves."

Harras sighed. "You're an idiot."

Pete's shoulders sagged and he leaned back in the tiny, uncomfortable wooden chair. He laid his hands on the table in front of him, palms up—as if to say "can we get on with this?"

"All right, now that we've confirmed you won't listen to reason, we can discuss what happened to your house. I know we've been over the particulars of the evening," he said. "And your information's been somewhat helpful. But I also wanted to bring you in here and see if anything else had come up; usually in cases like these, the victims get bits and pieces appearing in their minds days after the actual event. And call me crazy, but I get the sense that you're not always sharing information live, as it happens, as they say in TV news."

"You're right," Pete said. He suddenly felt tired. "I get little updates in my brain every so often; it's weird. But more than that, I'm baffled by how he found me."

"What do you mean?"

"Like, why me? Why didn't he torment you, or Aguilera, or anyone else working on this?"

Harras shrugged. "Wish I knew. It'd give us more insight into who this person is."

"Who knew I was working with you directly?"

"Why do you ask?"

Pete's eyes met Harras's, his stare locked into his. "Someone must have told him."

"You have got to be kidding me," Harras said, a dry laugh escaping his mouth. "I mean, I know you're a little deluded by your skills, kid, but to think someone on our end would just rat you out for jollies— that's a bit much. And insulting, I might add."

"You have an alternative?"

"Sure," Harras said. "And I'm glad you brought this up, because it's been sticking in my craw since we had our little lunchtime meet-and-greet."

"Why am I here?"

Harras slammed a palm on the table. The sound echoed around the room.

"Shut the fuck up," he said. "You're in my house now. I ask the questions and you answer them as fully and truthfully as you can, OK? We're not playing games anymore."

Pete started to respond.

Before he could get a word out, Harras stood up. He put both hands on the table and leaned in toward Pete, his voice low.

"If you think you were fooling anyone with your little mugging story, you're not so clear on how smart you are," he said. "We think the guy that attacked you may be the same guy that made your house go Nagasaki. So maybe you ought to consider that this guy had been trailing you long before you decided to put a volunteer badge on your wrinkled shirt. Hell, he probably told you the first time to stop sniffing around, and you didn't fucking listen."

Pete didn't respond.

"Am I getting warmer?" Harras said, backing off, his hands turned up, as if waiting for Pete to answer. "Good. Think about that before you decide to start accusing my people of throwing you under the bus. We have bigger shit to worry about than some two-bit wannabes. Get over yourself, asshole."

Harras turned around and walked out, slamming the door behind him. Pete heard the door click into the locked position.

Pete rubbed his hands over his face. He'd been sitting in his rental car for close to five minutes, trying to get his breathing to settle and to get a handle on what had just happened. At least they'd let him drive here. He doubted anyone would want to give him a ride after his exchange with Harras.

His exit from the FBI building had been unpleasant. After sitting in the locked room for another hour, Pete had the pleasure of being escorted out by Gran and Davidson, who seemed to enjoy dragging Pete along to the elevator. Just enough to make it uncomfortable. Just another witness in for questioning. He was embarrassed and angry, which was exactly how Harras wanted him to feel. This was a poke, and the message was clear: stop fucking with our case.

Pete was reaching for his car keys when he felt his cell phone vibrating in his jeans. The number calling was unknown. Pete picked it up anyway.

"Pete here."

"Hello, Pete? It's Melinda Farkas."

It took Pete a few seconds to remember the attractive high school guidance counselor. She noticed the delay.

"We talked a few weeks ago about Erica Morales? Remember?"

"Yes, yes," Pete said. "I do. Sorry, it's been an eventful few days."

"That's an understatement," she said. "Sorry about your house."

"Guess you saw it on the news?" Pete said.

"Well, yeah," Melinda said. "It was hard to avoid. I can't imagine how you're dealing with it."

Pete closed his eyes. He felt a migraine forming. They came a few times a day. Residual aftereffects from the concussion, the doctors said.

"So, I thought you'd want to know I spoke to Silvia," Melinda said.

Pete's interest was piqued. "Oh?"

"Yes," she said. "But remember, like I said in my office, I will deny us ever having this conversation. I'm even calling you from a pay phone. I could be fired for this. But you seem to be the only person who cares about what happened to Erica, for better or worse."

"Thanks for the vote of confidence."

"You're welcome," she said. "I'm dead serious."

"What did Silvia say?" Pete said.

"She had a lot to say, actually," she said. "She hung out with Erica that day. She was there to meet someone—a boy, Silvia thought. But Erica was being cagey, which put Silvia on alert. Erica wasn't prone to hiding things from Silvia."

"Did she see where Erica went?"

"That's the thing," she said. "They parted at Dadeland Mall, but Silvia followed Erica—she was too curious about what was going on. She said Erica went to the south parking lot and was standing around, checking her phone and texting. After a while, she was approached by an older man, who Silvia said Erica didn't seem to know. They talked, and after that, she got into a white van with him and they drove off."

A white van. Pete was distracted, still thinking about being questioned by the FBI. But the phrase played over in his head.

"But here's the weird part," she continued. "Silvia started to run toward the van, which was heading onto Kendall Drive. This kid somehow managed to catch up with the van, which she said was a Ford, whatever that's worth, and even reached the passenger-side window. But Erica was out."

"Out?"

"Yes, knocked out," Farkas said. "In the time leading up to her getting in the car or right after, this guy knocked her unconscious."

"Could she have been sleeping?" Pete said, realizing the question was silly a second after asking it.

"Do you ever fall asleep seconds after entering a stranger's car?"

"Good point," Pete said. He felt a shot of pain in his head and winced. *White van.* Why was this sticking in his mind? He turned toward the backseat of the car and grabbed a JanSport backpack from behind the passenger's side seat.

"Hold on," Pete said, putting his phone down on the dashboard. He rummaged through the backpack, which was mostly full of news clippings he'd gathered together from old newspapers Dave still had lying around the store, and pulled out a recent edition of the *Miami Times.* The more Pete thought back to the explosions that capped off the destruction of his house, the more he thought the bombs were there to get rid of whatever info he and Kathy had gathered. They had to start over completely.

The newspaper featured the first story on Erica, days after her disappearance. The photograph that ran with the story was the same one he'd seen while sitting in The Bar, when her remains were found. The picture he'd found familiar.

It all clicked into place.

Her picture.

The white van.

Where he'd seen it.

Where he'd seen her.

The dates lined up. Erica Morales had gone missing that night, and a few hours later, Pete had seen a nondescript white van drive by, a youngish girl asleep in the passenger seat. He'd crossed paths with the killer without even realizing it. He heard Farkas's questioning voice blaring out of the phone, but ignored her. He flung the backpack against the passenger-side door and screamed. His vocal chords burned. He slammed his fists into the steering wheel, and was glad when pain shot through his fingers, reminding him he was alive.

CHAPTER TWENTY-FOUR

She was alive.

Nina had to remind herself of this every so often. Despite the pain. Despite the fact that she'd lost track of time. Despite the dank smell and her restraints. She knew she was alive, at least for a bit longer.

She wasn't sure how long her eyes had been closed—or if she'd been sleeping. It all blurred together now. Her thoughts weren't in her head anymore. She felt outside of herself. There were no days or mornings or routines—it was just this dirty, wet darkness and a kind of anxiety and dread Nina had never dreamed possible.

She thought she'd imagined the clicking sound—a key entering a lock. But that disappeared when she heard the steps coming down the stairs. Calm, casual, and relaxed—frightening. She opened her eyes. The slight increase of light made her squint. She'd managed to get the blindfold off, but it made little difference in the pitch black prison she was in. She was numb. She couldn't fully register that this moment might be it. He might have gotten bored of watching her through that camera, or he might have figured out just how he wanted to kill her. She wasn't naïve. People don't normally find a way out of this kind of prison.

He was coming for her.

He was whistling—a simple, jolly tune. He was taking his time. She opened her mouth to scream but no noise escaped. Her throat was dry.

She tried again—a raspy, pained yelp escaped her lips. Then she saw his figure, backlit by the light coming from the stairwell. "Steve."

He crouched right in front of her. She could feel his breathing on her face. He smelled of mint gum and fancy aftershave. He looked like he'd just gotten off work—or, depending on what time it was, on his way to work. Clean cut. Almost handsome. He was smiling.

"Nina, Nina, Nina," he said. He didn't reach out to touch her. Instead, he slid a plastic bag toward the empty boxes of cereal that had collected over time. A refill. She felt a slight pinch of hope. Maybe he would change his mind?

He stood up. She met his gaze.

"Let me go," Nina said. Her voice cracking. "Please."

"Oh, that wouldn't do at all," he said.

"Steve" the Realtor continued: "I've been busy, which is why I've been remiss in taking care of us. But I've fixed up one last, little problem. This is going to be special. Now I'm all yours."

Then the scream came—long, pained, and from the bottom of her being. Nina screamed for what felt like a year—hurtling her body forward, pulling against her restraints, trying to reach this man who'd decided to keep her here, like some kind of misbehaving circus animal. This monster who felt like he had the right to decide if she should live or die.

"Fuck you," she said, spittle flying out of her mouth. She was scared, sure. But she was also angry. She let the anger fuel her.

He didn't even step back. She wasn't sure but she thought she heard a chuckle.

He walked over to the cereal boxes and kicked them toward her, the contents spilling around her body, joining the dirt and grime that had already collected in the small space. Her last meals were now caked with the detritus of her cell.

Her coffin.

"Actually," he said, turning around and beginning to walk up the stairs, "now you're all mine."

CHAPTER TWENTY-FIVE

Nina Henriquez's mom, Arlene, worked at a laundromat in West Kendall, off 137th Avenue, near Miller Drive. The area was pure suburbia with some Cuban seasoning—strip malls, chain restaurants, Catholic churches, and movie theaters crowded on the major streets. The further west you went, the more rural things got: horse farms, fruit stands, and lawn ornaments peppered the view. The intersection of 137th and Miller seemed almost outpost-like: a meeting point for corporate branding and cookie-cutter condominiums—all colored tan and brown.

A quick online background check—only forty-five dollars from his dwindling bank account—got Pete Arlene's current residence, marital status, and credit history. She had no job listed, which meant she was working off the books. He'd knocked on a few doors in Arlene's neighborhood and flashed some bills. Within the hour, after a few greased handshakes, he knew where she worked. He was now about a hundred bucks poorer but it seemed worth it.

The drive was tedious and fitful for Pete, thanks mostly to his timing. He'd left the Book Bin a little before five, ensuring a wave of rush-hour traffic and a migraine headache by the end of the drive. He'd spent the time in the car alternating between berating himself for being drunk the night he thought he'd seen Erica Morales in the white van and wondering what he could do with such general—and generic—info, considering every handyman and business owner in the greater Miami-Dade area owned one. He pulled his rented Hyundai Sonata into a parking space near a dingy supermarket. The laundromat was at the other end of the tiny shopping center, but Pete still wanted a few moments to think about how he was going to approach Arlene Henriquez.

The news would almost certainly filter back to the FBI that someone was asking questions. He hadn't even bothered to call Kathy. He was running on instinct. He knew he had to talk to Arlene.

The strip mall was long and narrow—anchored by a main thruway with satellite stores spreading out toward the east and west. For every active storefront, there was an empty, abandoned one. These kinds of buildings—hodgepodge collections of small businesses set up on the cheap—were commonplace in the suburban outskirts of Miami; even the layout seemed like it was pulled from a template some architect had saved. You could find them off every major intersection for miles.

The smell of fresh Cuban coffee and pastries distracted Pete as he walked past the Futuro Supermarket. He turned a corner and almost missed her.

Emily was walking away from her car, her purse slung over her shoulder and a concerned, pensive look on her face. She hadn't seen Pete yet, but he had nowhere else to go. A moment later she noticed him. She hesitated for a second before starting to walk over. Pete stayed where he was.

"Hey," she said.

"Hello."

"Did you just get out of your car?"

"Yeah," Pete said, confused by the question. "I'm heading to the laundromat."

Emily didn't answer. She was looking at Pete with a distant, glazed stare. She seemed nervous, almost scared, Pete thought. He waited a beat before talking again.

"How are you?"

"I'm, well, I'm fine," she said. "I heard about the house . . . I'm not sure what to say. Are you OK? What happened?"

"I'm OK," Pete said. He'd rehearsed this moment in his mind dozens of times, and each time he had at least one, maybe two, catchy retorts he could sling back at her. He was coming up blank now.

A few seconds passed. Emily looked toward her car, then back at Pete. She couldn't look him in the eyes.

"I'm sorry," Emily said. "About all this. I was confused. I needed some space."

"You didn't seem confused," Pete said, his tone flat.

"I guess I deserve that," she said.

"Where are you staying?"

"I'm home," she said, not elaborating. But Pete knew what it meant. "I'm going to work on my marriage. I need you to accept that. There's another person involved in this, and I can't . . . complicate anything anymore."

"Huh, all right," he said. He looked away from her and coughed into his hand. "Look, I have to go. I guess I'll talk to you later."

Pete watched Emily head down the strip mall's main walkway. She seemed upset. Pete felt bad for taking some pleasure in that. He didn't realize he was following her until his feet started moving.

Pete tried to keep his distance. The mall was mostly empty, which made it hard to go unnoticed. He felt angry. Angry at himself for not laying into her enough, and angry at her for letting their exchange end when it did.

She was close to the back of the mall. As Pete started to wonder if she was leaving the mall entirely, she cut into a small shop. He picked up the pace and darted by the storefront. A Realtor's office. *So much for wanting to fix her marriage,* Pete thought. Or were they looking for a new place together? The office wasn't in their neighborhood. It was at least forty minutes north, and it didn't strike Pete as the kind of place that merited the detour. Had she made a point to go outside her neighborhood because she didn't want people—or Rick—to know she was looking? He kept walking. The Realtor's office had a giant glass window in the waiting area, making it easy for those sitting around to people-watch. He wasn't sure if Emily had seen him, so he had little time to stare. She was chatting with a man around their age—nondescript and boring.

He turned around, intent on going back to his initial plan: visiting Arlene Henriquez's workplace.

"Are you following me?"

Her voice didn't surprise him. It was almost as if he'd wanted to get caught.

"I was, but then I decided I had nothing else to say," Pete said, turning around to face Emily. She'd come outside when she saw him, he realized. The man Emily had been speaking to was now watching them through the office window, probably wondering why his pitch had been interrupted.

She hesitated, not expecting such an honest response. "Why?"

"Why what?"

"Why were you following me, Pete?" Emily said.

"Why are you even here, Emily? Visiting a Realtor?"

"Oh, Jesus," Emily said. "First of all, it's none of your business—but that's obvious. I was in the area and swung by because this Realtor's been calling nonstop about some kind of deal he wants me—us—to check out." She let out a long sigh. "Look, I don't want to get into this here."

"Get into you and Rick looking to buy some real estate?" Pete said. "Rick, the guy who cheated on you? The guy you left?"

She shrugged. "What do you want from me, Peter?"

"I miss you," he said.

Her features softened for a second and she looked away, down the direction they'd come from, toward the parking lot.

"Don't do this to me," she said. "Please. I've made my decision."

"You've said that before," he said, and the desperation in his voice shamed him. "And you came back."

She turned to face him, her eyes red. "Did you ever consider Rick in all this?" she said. "You knew I was married. You knew I was vulnerable. Yet you let it happen. You knew I wasn't myself, yet you let things develop. You pursued me."

"That's not true."

"I know you'll rationalize this to no end when you walk off,"

Emily said, her voice rising. "Because that's how you can live with yourself, and all the stupid shit you do. We're not friends. We stopped being friends when we started having sex. You let me move in. You wanted this to happen. And when it finally did you started to act like you were having reservations. You're not an adult. You're not a good person. Fuck you, Pete. Fuck you for messing with my emotions and acting like I'm some kind of monster. You're the monster."

She didn't wait for a response as she turned and walked to her car, giving up on the real estate visit. The sound of her flats hitting the dirty concrete matched the painful pounding in Pete's head.

CHAPTER TWENTY-SIX

Miami Purity was a tiny, nondescript, and unremarkable laundromat tucked away on the north end of the small strip mall. Pete pushed open the door and walked into the empty shop, his senses overloaded by the flowery scent of cheap detergent, the whirring sounds of the washers and dryers, and the television perched above the washing machines playing a *Diff'rent Strokes* rerun. There was no one behind the counter. Pete walked up and looked toward the back of the space, seeing and hearing nothing back there. The door chime cut through the other noise. Pete turned around.

"I'm just going to pretend you're picking up your dry cleaning for work tomorrow," Harras said. His eyes had a "gotcha" look—like a cat realizing it'd just cornered an injured mouse.

"That works," Pete said, trying to remain calm. "Except the dress code at the Book Bin is pretty lax."

Harras walked up to Pete and looked around the laundromat.

"What the hell are you doing here, Fernandez?"

"I'm trying to help you."

"Help me?" Harras said. "You have a weird way of helping. Do you usually do exactly the opposite of what people ask you to do?"

"Nina Henriquez is alive," Pete said.

"How the fuck would you know that?"

"The killer made that pretty clear," Pete said, his mind flashing back to that night, surrounded by fire and smoke.

"You are a real trip, you know that?" Harras said. "How many times did I or someone on my team ask you about what happened that night? Never once did you share that little nugget. Now you're cornered and you suddenly have a lead?"

Before Pete could respond, a low, confused voice cut through their conversation. "Can I help you?"

Pete and Harras both turned to find an older woman standing behind the counter, her eyebrows raised, waiting for a response.

Before Harras could speak, Pete interjected, "Arlene Henriquez?"

She nodded, her eyes on Pete.

"We're with the FBI, ma'am." Pete felt Harras's stare burning into the back of his head. "We want to talk to you about Nina."

Her expression changed from detached confusion to sad relief. She placed her palms on the counter, as if to balance herself. "Oh, OK," she said. "Yes, yes. How can I help you?"

Harras stepped forward, shooting daggers at Pete before clearing his throat. "I'm Agent Harras, Mrs. Henriquez," he said. "This is Pete

Fernandez. He's an associate of mine. We're sorry to interrupt your day, but we wanted to ask you a few more questions about Nina's disappearance. Can we sit somewhere and talk?"

"Yes, of course," she said and motioned for them to come around the counter and toward an office in the back. Harras shot Pete a look that promised intense physical harm to him in the not-so-distant future. Pete shrugged in response. He'd deal with Harras when the time came. For now, they were talking to Arlene Henriquez.

The back office was tiny and offered little wiggle room. Arlene went in first and left the door open. Light from a medium-sized window lit the room. She sat behind a tiny desk with no computer and let Pete and Harras fight over the remaining chair. Pete motioned for Harras to take it.

"Now, Mrs. Henriquez," Harras began.

"Please, call me Arlene," she said.

"All right, Arlene," Harras continued. "I want to talk to you about your daughter. You reported her missing a few days ago. I know someone from Miami PD came by and got a report, but I wanted to make sure there wasn't anything you may have forgotten that could be of use to us."

Mrs. Henriquez nodded. Pete could tell English wasn't her first language. She was trying to keep up with Harras without letting on how difficult it was.

"*Hablas español?*" Pete asked.

Her eyes lit up. She nodded at Pete. Harras frowned.

"I don't *habla español*, Pete," Harras said, mis-conjugating the verb for emphasis. "So let me handle this, OK?"

Pete looked at Henriquez.

"*Quiere hablarte en inglés,*" Pete said. She responded with a gracious smile, thanking Pete for trying.

Harras cleared his throat and continued. He'd pulled out a tiny notepad and began taking notes.

"Mrs. Henriquez, when was the last time you saw your daughter?"

"Not for a long time," Mrs. Henriquez said, her voice low, almost ashamed.

Pete fought the urge to blurt out a question. Harras responded quickly and with more precision. "Your daughter," he said. "Nina. She's missing. When was the last time you saw her?"

"Saw her?" Henriquez said. She paused and looked toward the ceiling, as if to focus her thoughts. "I no see her for a long time. Six month. Year."

Harras let out a deep breath and rubbed his temples. "Mrs. Henriquez, did Nina live with you?"

"No, Nina live with her father and brother," Mrs. Henriquez said.

"But you reported her missing, didn't you?"

"Yes, yes," she said. "Her father tell me she was missing, so I call the police."

"Have the police talked to her father?" Pete asked her, ignoring Harras's glare.

Mrs. Henriquez looked at Pete, then back at Harras, smiling, her nerves showing through. Her body was saying what she couldn't: *How would I know?*

Harras stood up and walked out of the office. Pete was left alone with Henriquez, who looked more confused than when they started. Pete nodded politely and followed Harras, catching up with him outside the laundromat. Harras turned around, his face red from anger. He took a step closer to Pete.

"Why are you wasting my time?" Harras said, his teeth gritted.

Pete took a step back. "How would I know she didn't live with her mother?"

"You're not supposed to 'know' anything," Harras said, using air quotes in a way Pete would have found obnoxious under normal circumstances. "This is not your case. This is not your job. This is not your life. I followed you because I knew you were going to do something stupid, I didn't expect you'd go into this with no idea."

Pete didn't respond.

"You're the worst kind of know-it-all, you know that?" Harras said. "You think this lady wants to relive the fact that her daughter is missing and we have zero leads? You probably didn't even think about that. You self-involved prick."

Henriquez's scream cut through the empty strip mall before Pete could respond.

Harras stepped into the laundromat first, gun drawn. He didn't protest when Pete followed, his own weapon out, holding it awkwardly in comparison with the more polished Harras. The place seemed quiet, especially compared to a few moments ago, when all Pete could hear was Harras berating him. As they tiptoed toward the tiny room in the back of the Miami Purity Laundromat, he prayed it would be that simple.

They reached the office and each took a stance on one side of the door, which was now closed. No sound was coming from inside and nothing had been heard since the scream a few moments earlier. Harras reached for the handle and gave it a quick turn. It was unlocked. The door swung in with a slight, whining creak. Pete swallowed and closed his eyes for a second.

By the time Pete turned around to enter the office, Harras had let out a long sigh of relief. She was alive, Pete thought.

He peered over Harras's shoulder and saw Henriquez, crouched on the floor, sobbing. The cries were low but wracked her tiny body. She hadn't turned around to face them. The window above the small desk had been opened—by force. Shattered glass covered Henriquez and the floor under her.

It took another second for Pete to notice the piece of paper a few feet away from Henriquez's hand. It was crumpled. Harras gave Pete a freezing stare that said, *Look at what you did*. The FBI agent backed out of the office and walked into the tiny laundromat's main area. Pete could hear him shouting orders over his phone, probably calling the main office. Pete kept his feet in place, his eyes frozen on the still sobbing middle-aged woman, her body shaking. He took a small, tentative step forward. Still not in the office, but closer. Close enough to read the hastily written letters on the piece of paper: **NINA'S DEAD. EMILY'S NEXT.**

The words sent a cold snap through Pete's system, blocking out Harras, blocking out everything as he ran back to where he'd last seen Emily.

CHAPTER TWENTY-SEVEN

"**A**re you fucking crazy?"

The Messenger was agitated. Julian had stepped out of the Realtor's office to take the call. He'd been expecting it.

"I can't talk—I'm at work," Julian said. He had ducked away near a garbage area, surrounded by massive metal bins full of trash, keeping his voice quiet and his movements casual. He'd let his ego interfere. There'd been no upside to leaving the note. It had been tricky, too. He enjoyed that. Hearing the woman scream. He'd left work without a word, which raised some eyebrows. The edges were beginning to fray.

"People are figuring it out. I can't believe you dealt with her without letting me know. You've ruined the moment," the Messenger said. "That note was stupid. There were prints! I'll take care of that. But Fernandez is heading over. I'm ahead of him, thankfully. I'm going to resolve my end of the bargain, because we have no choice."

"I kill on my schedule," Julian said. "Do your part. Fix my Fernandez problem. Execute the task I've written for you. Don't let this fall apart."

Julian slammed the phone against the garbage dump. He turned to go back to work when he saw her. She looked up from the compact she'd been using to check her makeup. The girl couldn't have been over twenty, and stood just outside the garbage area. She looked scared, her big brown eyes open wide in fear. Her hair was cut short, almost like a boy's. A cigarette was at her feet. She'd come out for a smoke to find this.

He took a step toward the girl. "Sorry you had to hear that," he said, his voice sweet and welcoming, a warm smile on his face. "Give me a second to explain."

CHAPTER TWENTY-EIGHT

"**M**eet me at Emily's house," Pete said, his breath short. He hadn't even waited to hear Kathy say hello.

"What? In Homestead?" Kathy said. She sounded annoyed. They hadn't talked in a few days.

"Hurry," Pete said and hung up, tossing his phone on the passenger seat. He'd been trying Emily's number nonstop but it was going straight to voice mail. Harras had assured him a cruiser was on its way to Homestead—but Pete hadn't heard from him since then. A cruiser with sirens blaring had a distinct advantage over most people, but this guy wasn't "most people."

Pete felt his foot press on his rental car's accelerator, its engine groaning with the strain. The radio was off. The windows were down. The drive to Homestead was not a quick one—the suburb was the last vestige of civilization south of the city of Miami before you hit the swamplands of the Everglades and the first hint of the Florida Keys. It was mostly agrarian, large farms and miles of unblemished land that were slowly getting populated by people looking for more space and cheaper housing. Pete hated it there.

His mind veered back to the exchange with Emily. Pete cursed himself under his breath. The sociopath who'd been stabbing teen girls to death to get his rocks off was on his way to do the same with Emily. The car was stopped at an intersection, the light red. Homestead was at least forty-five minutes away, even at top speed. The intersection was a busy one: Sunset and 137th Avenue. Cars were whizzing across. Pete felt a chill cover him. He imagined Emily working on her garden. He pressed the horn and let it ring out, a long, droning squawk. Then he pushed down on the accelerator.

He'd looked both ways enough to discern a lull in the oncoming traffic, but not much of one. He ignored the horns from behind and both sides and pushed the car forward. He made it across the intersection and let out a quick sigh of relief. He was pushing seventy in a fifty-five mph zone. He kept his eye on the road, checking the rearview mirrors for cops.

There were two police cars in the driveway at Emily and Rick's house when Pete pulled up and parked in front, leaving the driver's side door open as he ran to the front door. He was met by a uniformed police officer.

"Hold it, bud," the cop said. "Can I help you?"

"Is she here? Is she OK?" Pete said, out of breath. "I want to make sure she's inside."

The officer walked toward Pete and motioned for him to move to the side of the walkway, concern in his eyes.

"Say that again?"

"I think my friend is in trouble," Pete said, starting to get frustrated. He tried to look over the cop's shoulder to see what was happening in the house, but could only see a few other uniforms. "I need to find her."

He started to move past the cop when he felt the man's firm hand grab his left arm.

"You're not going anywhere just yet," the cop said. "I need to have one of our detectives talk to you. You don't just waltz in here and—"

Pete pulled his arm away and sidestepped the officer. The cop was only doing his job, Pete realized, but that wasn't Pete's problem. He ran for the front door and made it inside the house before he felt his body slam into the hallway entrance. He hadn't seen the man coming, but his voice was familiar. He felt the knuckles of a fist as they made contact with his chin.

"Where is she? Where is she, you motherfucker?" Rick screamed. It was pure luck that Pete turned his head to the left and noticed Rick's arm careening toward him. Rick's face was red and his eyes wet. He looked wobbly and rough.

Pete shoved Rick back and raised his hands up. He wasn't here to fight.

"Where is she?" he asked.

"She's gone," Rick said, his voice a charred whisper. "She never came home. Her phone's off. The cops found her car on the side of the road, blood on the front seat."

Before he could say anything else, Aguilera appeared. He got between Pete and Rick, his hand pushing Rick away from Pete.

"Gentlemen, take a deep breath and try to relax for a second," Aguilera said, his tone calm if a bit condescending. Pete looked around at the house. It seemed very little was out of place. Pete tried to weave farther into the home, but was met by Aguilera's other hand. Pete fought the urge to twist Aguilera's arm back and move ahead anyway.

Aguilera seemed to notice the flicker of violence in Pete's eyes and turned his gaze on him. He seemed calm, Pete thought. He didn't care about what was happening. This was his job. Just another day for him. Pete tried to push the resentment out of his head.

"We need to stay calm," Aguilera continued. "Pete, why are you here? What's going on?"

"Did you talk to Harras?" Pete said. "I thought you were off the case."

"Don't worry if I'm on or off the case. Yes, he called me; then we got the call from Rick," Aguilera said, looking to Rick briefly, as if to confirm he was still there. "Emily's gone. We have no idea what state she's in or where she may be going. Someone pulled her off the road and kidnapped her. Do you have any idea who that might have been?"

Pete took a half step back. Aguilera's tone bothered him. It was a positioning question; he was asking as if he knew the answer already, which was not what Pete wanted to hear.

"I have no fucking idea, man," Pete said, shrugging Aguilera's hand away. "Harras saw the same thing I did. Someone left a note on the floor saying 'Nina's dead. Emily's next.'"

"We're still checking that note for prints," Aguilera said. "But Harras says they've got nothing so far."

"Well, I'm not a big pro like you are," Pete said. "But considering I had just finished talking to Emily before meeting with Harras, I put two and two together and figured he was going after her."

"Who's he?" Aguilera continued, his tone still calm and probing. He ignored Pete's annoyed look.

"I don't know," Pete said. "But he might be the same guy who beat the shit out of me, blew up my house and car, and killed all these girls."

"This is your fucking fault," Rick said, his voice a low, menacing growl. "You got her into this mess. You got her involved. It was bad enough when he took Alice, but now this . . ."

Pete could already see Rick shoving Aguilera aside and charging for him, but before that scene could roll, another uniformed officer approached, the same one who'd stopped Pete out front. His appearance slowed Rick's momentum.

"There's a reporter from the *Times* outside, sir," he was talking to Aguilera, ignoring Rick and Pete. "Says she knew the victim. Wants to talk to this guy." He motioned his head to signal Pete, and not in a positive way.

Aguilera nodded and turned to Pete. "Come with me," he said. "Let's talk to your partner and see what we can figure out."

They both walked past Rick and toward the front yard. Pete looked past Aguilera and could see Kathy standing alone in the fading light of dusk. She was wearing a black T-shirt and slim jeans, her face scrubbed and eyes curious. She'd made it. Pete felt a great warmth toward her.

She reached for him and grabbed his arm. She looked Pete over, as if checking him for any bruises or wounds.

"Hey."

"Hey," Pete said. "Emily's gone."

"I figured as much," she said, looking at Aguilera for a second. "What happened?"

"Harras and I were talking to Nina Henriquez's mom," Pete began.

"No, you were talking to her," Aguilera said. "If Harras hadn't been following you, you would have talked to her alone."

Pete cleared his throat and kept going. "We talked to her, but got nothing—she hasn't had a relationship with her daughter in at least a year," Pete said. "Harras and I went outside to regroup. That's when we heard her scream."

"Oh God," Kathy said.

"When we came back, she was on the floor wailing, crying," Pete said, not enjoying having to repeat the story. "She had a note in her hand. It said 'Nina's dead. Emily's next.' I'd just seen Emily—by chance—minutes before, in the same mall."

"This is your fault." Aguilera's words cut through the night and left Kathy and Pete frozen for a few seconds.

"What?"

"You heard me," Aguilera said. His look and demeanor hadn't fluctuated beyond the calm, collected, and sharp vibe he'd given off when Pete arrived. "You shouldn't have been at the laundromat. You know this. Your pretty friend might have made it home to tend to her garden, or to a nice dinner with her husband if you hadn't decided to play cowboy."

"Since when are you so serene and matter-of-fact?" Pete said.

"Do you have any leads?" Kathy said, cutting him off.

"A few," Aguilera said. "But none I'm going to share with a delusional wannabe and a newspaper columnist."

Aguilera seemed to relish the opportunity to put them down. He pulled out a cigarette and lit it. He slid the lighter into his coat pocket and let a puff of smoke leave his mouth.

"I suggest you both go home, or wherever you live," Aguilera said, looking at Pete as he said the last part. "And wait. She may reach out to you if she can. Or we may have some more questions. But we don't need you here. Frankly, we don't want you here. This is the last time we let you interfere with our investigation."

"Fuck you." The words left Kathy's mouth seconds after Aguilera finished. By the time Pete had registered them, she was halfway to her car. He took a slight bit of pleasure in seeing Aguilera's feathers ruffled again. The agent looked at Pete before turning back and heading to the house without another word.

Pete saw Rick coming toward him. He turned to face him, his hands balled nervously into fists. Rick's approach was not menacing, though. If anything, he seemed defeated and tired. He stopped a safe distance from Pete.

"I'm sorry about how I got in there," he said.

"It's fine," Pete said.

"I need you to find her, Pete," Rick said. "Find her for me. We were finally getting back to—back to where we were. To being together. I can't lose her now."

Pete swallowed. His throat was dry. *He has no idea what went down with me and Emily.*

"I don't think these guys want my help," Pete said, motioning to the police still looking around the house. "But I want to find her. We have to find her."

Rick looked around before talking again. "They left another note," he said. "And I think it was meant for you. It was in Emily's car."

Pete felt himself begin to shake. The dusk had turned to darkness, leaving only the dim porch light to illuminate the front yard. Rick's eyes wide and searching, desperate for anything that could help him. Pete didn't want to hear anything else from him. He didn't want this to be real. He rubbed his sweaty palms on his jeans.

"It was written on one of her business cards," Rick said, his voice cracking. "I told the cops but I don't know what they're going to do. I don't know what's going to happen. I—"

"What did it say?" Pete asked, his curiosity trumping his fear.

"'You lose.'"

CHAPTER
TWENTY-NINE

Pete held the silver can of beer up to the kitchen light and turned it in his hand.

He leaned back against the counter in Kathy's kitchen and placed the can on it, still within reach. It was late. Close to three in the morning. Kathy had offered up her couch, a marked improvement over the small cot in the back of the Book Bin.

He'd been in the apartment before. It was a cozy two-bedroom on the fringes of Coral Gables—"Little Gables" as the Realtors called it, hoping to lure unsuspecting tenants into paying Coral Gables prices—that had seen better days. The paint was peeling and it looked like a hurricane "after" photo—file folders, printouts, Blu-rays, a few empty wine bottles, and notepads scattered around the living room in various piles. It was very much Kathy's place.

Pete could see Nigel, Kathy's tiny cat, jump from the couch in the living room to a nearby table. He'd rescued the small gray feline when he first set out to find Kathy. It felt like ages ago. It sent him thinking back to his own cat, Costello—now just ashes mixed with the rest of his life.

He sat down on the couch, next to the sheets and pillows Kathy had hastily set out for him. His father would have known what to do. He'd been a cop's cop—a stellar homicide detective who was also a stellar person, good father, and loyal friend.

Pete grabbed a small notepad from the coffee table next to the couch and pulled out a pen from his pocket. He began to jot down names. *Alice Cline. Erica Morales. Nina Henriquez. Emily Sprague-Blanco.*

Then the list began to evolve and include clues that were relevant, or should be, in Pete's mind. White van. Internet. Mirrors. Knives. Sex. Apartment. E-mail.

He underlined Cline, Morales, and Henriquez. Those were the stable victims, the ones the killer had wanted, Pete reasoned. Emily was an offshoot—a byproduct of his annoyance with Pete. She didn't fit the mold of the killer's victim profile. Yet he'd gone after her anyway. Why?

Both Cline and Morales had been e-mailing with someone purporting to be a Realtor, promising a good deal and the chance to move quickly. From what little he'd learned about Nina Henriquez, he could at least assume she came from an unhappy home. Mothers leaving children was not a recipe for success.

He started another column on the same page. Memorial. House. Laundromat. Assault. Fire. Note. The methods of attack didn't add up, Pete thought. They didn't seem right. A killer kills, sure, but does he use so many different means? So many weapons? He wasn't sure. And if there were two men, one was an expert at bomb-making, hand-to-hand fighting, and knife-play.

Pete's hand guided the pen over an open part of the page. He was drawing. The outline seemed random at first, but as he let his mind wander, he realized he was drawing his own house. Just the basics. Pete wasn't an artist. The living room. The guest room. Pete's bedroom. The utility room. *Where he got in.*

Pete thought back to that night. The confrontation in Emily's room, the guest room. Kathy tied up in the living room. No one was that fast. He saw Kathy's face. The look of fear she had when Pete told her not to worry. Not to worry because he'd left the killer behind, on the other side of the house. One of the killers, at least.

He stood up, letting the pen and pad drop to the floor.

"I was definitely two people—but where does that leave us? This serial killer has a sidekick? We don't even know who he is. Now we have to figure out who he rolls with?"

Kathy's question hung in the air. It was close to six in the morning. Pete hadn't slept. Kathy had slept little.

Pete frowned. "It's right and it's not right," he said. "The attack on the house. The differing methods. One killer took the first few; then it seems like another person left the note for Nina Henriquez's mom. That was a message. To stay away. Then that person took Emily. It's almost like the 'B' killer is protecting the main one."

"What do you mean?"

"He wants..." Pete paused. "He wants the main killer to continue.

He's defending him. We're an obstacle. Emily might be alive."

Kathy waved her hands as if to get Pete's attention. "Hold up," she said. "We don't know any fucking thing about this killer. Now we're speculating that he has a guardian angel who may not be a killer, or as much of a killer?"

Pete let himself lean back into the couch. He was exhausted. He ran his hand through his hair. He needed sleep. But he needed to find Emily—and he had nothing but a theory.

"I don't know," he said, his voice quiet.

"Look, sometimes killers change the type of victim—slightly, but they do," Kathy said. "Ages go up or down, usually because they have to hunt elsewhere. It comes down to availability."

"Go on," Pete said.

"So, maybe this guy just ran out of high schools to troll," Kathy said. "Or Craigslist postings to scour. I mean, there can only be so many teenage girls looking for an apartment."

Pete felt a sharp pain through his body. He closed his eyes and his mind drifted back—back to his walk through the strip mall. Catching sight of Emily. The initial confrontation. His following her.

"Pete?" Kathy said. "Are you OK? What is it?"

Pete stood up and checked his pockets for his keys and phone. "We have to go," he said. "Now."

"What?"

"Emily," he said. His words were coming out slow, dragging. "She was at a Realtor's. She was looking for an apartment. Like the other girls."

CHAPTER THIRTY

This was becoming an unpleasant habit, Pete thought, as he pressed the gas and pushed his wheezing rental car down Bird Road. He glanced at the passenger side and saw Kathy wrap her hand around the armrest. She was anxious. So was he. They could be heading straight into the belly of the beast with no idea what to expect.

"Check the glove compartment," Pete said, not taking his eyes off the road.

"What?"

"Open the glove compartment and make sure my gun is there," he said.

She did as she was told. The gun was there, where Pete remembered leaving it. They might be going into this blind, Pete thought, but they wouldn't be defenseless.

The early morning drive would have been pleasant under any other circumstances. The sun had not yet fully peeked out, and the usually packed thruway was littered with only a few cars.

He pushed the car a bit faster. He looked at Kathy for a second. She was leaning on the passenger-side window, looking at the stores and houses speed by, still holding on to the door—probably a combination of tension and fear. She looked worn down. He wondered if this was what she'd envisioned for herself as a kid. Probably not. She was talented but perpetually unhappy, living in a cloud of chaos that she seemed to thrive on. How long could you sustain that, though? There has to be something else, he thought, as the car skidded to a stop at a red light. 107th Avenue. They were almost there.

"What are we going to do when we get there?" Kathy said, breaking the silence, which Pete realized had taken up most of the drive.

"I'm not sure."

"Excellent," she said, more tired than sarcastic.

The light changed before Pete could respond. The morning haze had morphed into bright, seething sunlight. Pete turned onto 137th Avenue and felt the weight in his chest get heavier.

Pete slid his gun behind his back and hooked it through his waistband as he got out of the car. He scanned the empty parking lot and saw nothing out of the ordinary. They walked toward the Futuro Supermarket at the front of the tiny strip mall.

This place is usually empty, Pete thought, trying to reassure himself as they headed down the smaller walkway that would lead them to the tiny Realtor's office. He reached out and grabbed Kathy's hand, giving it a strong squeeze and letting it drop. They exchanged a knowing glance and continued.

Pete could see where the walkway split; shoppers were given the option of continuing down the abandoned strip mall or turning into it, to discover more empty spaces or barely-open hair salons and discount clothing stores.

"Are you fucking serious?"

Pete turned around, fighting the urge to go for his gun immediately. He heard Kathy let out a frustrated groan.

Aguilera was a few paces behind them, holding a paper cup of steaming coffee and looking haggard. It had not been a relaxing night for the FBI agent. He also looked pretty pissed, Pete thought.

"Where's Harras?" Kathy said.

"What are you two idiots doing here?" Aguilera asked, ignoring Kathy.

"We need to talk to Harras," Pete said, "We have a lead on who this guy is."

For a moment, Aguilera's expression changed, from complete annoyance to concern. Pete would have missed it had he not been looking straight at him.

"Come with me," Aguilera said, turning around and motioning for them to follow.

They walked down the main stretch of the strip mall until they reached a turning point, the same place where Pete had run into Emily, within sight of the Realtor's office. Aguilera moved past it, to a smaller parking lot at the far end of the stretch of tiny stores. Pete fought the urge to correct the FBI agent; he didn't know what Pete suspected. Pete wasn't sure if that was a good thing.

Aguilera walked into the parking area. As Pete reached the end of the mall, he saw why Aguilera was leading them there. At the far end of the lot was a medium-sized garbage bin. It was surrounded by crime scene tape and police. Pete could see Harras standing the closest to the metal container, a worried frown on his face. Pete could make out a human hand, stained with blood, hanging out of the metal garbage bin.

"This what you guys were here for?" he said. "Another peek at the action? Well, you got it."

"What are you talking about?" Kathy said.

"Whoever this guy is, he's lost it," Aguilera said. "He isn't putting in his usual thought into his victims. This girl—who worked in this mall, at the market near where you guys parked—was killed less than a day after Nina Henriquez's mom got the note about Emily. We're thinking it's less than that—maybe a few hours. In this same mall."

"Something's not right," Pete said. His mind was whirring. Why would the killer come back to the same place? Why would he kill so close to the laundromat, where he'd just poked the FBI? It was foolish, and this guy was anything but dumb.

"What's not right?" Aguilera said. "The guy's lost it. He's no longer cherry-picking victims. He barely had time to set up a few mirrors. That's the only reason we know it's him. He couldn't help himself."

"No," Pete said. "That's only part of it. Don't you get it? He didn't plan on this girl. She took him by surprise. Why else wait so long between kills if he was actually on a spree?"

Aguilera's nose scrunched up in judgment. He didn't appreciate Pete's dose of advice. Pete began to open his mouth to continue when he saw Harras approach.

"This is becoming a habit, Fernandez," Harras said, not a sign of humor in his voice. He turned to Aguilera. "Where'd you find them?"

"Right around the corner," he said.

"Care to explain?" Harras asked.

Pete and Kathy exchanged a look, her eyes shoving Pete forward into the spotlight.

"Well, we didn't expect to find another dead body," Pete said. "But we were up talking last night and comparing notes—"

"Notes?" Aguilera said.

"Yeah, notes," Pete said. "You know, those little things you write down to help you remember? Or make you think? Those?"

Aguilera stepped forward. Harras put his open palm on the other agent's chest to hold him back.

"Go on," Harras said.

"Did you notice that office we walked by?" Pete said.

"Which one?" Harras said.

"'The Realtor.'"

"What of it?" Aguilera said.

"That's where I saw Emily go," Pete said, his voice cracking as he finished the sentence. "We argued. She'd told me she was back with her husband, but then I find her here of all places. Later that day, she's kidnapped."

Harras rubbed his chin and looked at Pete. "So you're telling me this psycho's been running an ad hoc realty operation from his job, and cherry-picking his victims that way?"

"Well, he could do the online trolling at home," Kathy said. "And most of the legwork. But if he was looking to expand his base, why not pick some apples from another tree?"

"Let's not forget he knows you're on his ass," Harras said. "If it's all the same guy, he already tried to beat you away. Failing that, he blew up your house and car."

"What are you saying?" Pete asked.

"That Emily was an opportunity," Kathy said.

"An opportunity for what?"

"To teach you a lesson," Harras said, his voice low and vacant.

A few calls later and Harras had a search warrant for the Realtor's office. Pete was surprised at the speed with which Harras and Aguilera worked their respective phones, calling in favors and making sure the news didn't leak. Less surprising was the FBI agents' exclusion of Pete and Kathy in the search. The majority of officers tasked to the murder scene remained there, inspecting around the body and surrounding area as Aguilera and Harras entered the vacant Realtor's office, which was a fairly generic-looking storefront, from what Pete could tell. The sign hanging by the window, Penagos Realtors, was blocky and unremarkable, giving Pete little insight into the people that might work there.

"Think they'll find anything?" Kathy said, between long drags of her cigarette. She'd been smoking since the body had been found, taking a few puffs and then tossing the butt away. She'd probably gone through a pack, he guessed.

"Not sure," Pete said. "I mean, it's not like this guy was just working out of his office. He must have gone home to plan his kills."

"If this is our guy."

"What's that mean?"

"I just . . . " She hesitated. "It seems too easy, is all. On paper, it's perfect—I mean, location-wise, too. Some of the victims lived around here. But still. Easy."

"Easy how?" Pete said, his tone sharp. "We haven't found him. We haven't found Emily. We're just standing outside."

"Don't get snippy with me," she said. "I'm just saying it'd be too easy if they walked in there, found a bunch of bloody rags pointing to some guy who worked there, and then the case was closed. Serial killers are smart. They kill people over decades. And this guy is no fool; he's studied killers that have prowled this very area."

"So what do you suggest we do? Give up?"

Kathy sighed and met Pete's eyes for the first time in what seemed like hours to Pete.

"Yes, let's give up," she said. "Of course not. Jesus. I'm just saying there's got to be more to it. He could be playing us. Maybe this is a distraction ploy of some kind."

As Kathy finished her sentence, Pete caught Harras and Aguilera walking out of the Realtor's office, yanking their plastic gloves off with disgust. Nothing.

The officers working the area had opened umbrellas and tried their best to secure the crime scene from the surprise Miami rain shower, but it was messy business. Pete stood off to the side, Harras on his left, as Aguilera and the other investigators scanned the area surrounding the girl's body. Melissa Saiz had worked in the strip mall at the Futuro Supermarket. She was barely thirty. Pretty, going to Miami Dade to finish her degree. She'd probably come outside for a bit of fresh air or to make a phone call to her boyfriend or mother.

"How bad was it?" Pete asked, more to avoid the thoughts careening through his head than to talk to Harras.

"What do you think?" Harras said, before taking a sip of coffee.

Pete watched as Kathy, across the small lot, wandered away from the crime scene, pulling out her cell phone. Calling the paper? He hoped not. Their standing with the FBI and police was tenuous enough as it was. Having her report what was going on would destroy any chance they had of helping find this guy. He felt his hair begin to mat against his scalp as the rain got stronger, becoming less of a shower and more of a storm.

"It's not one guy," Pete said.

"What?" Harras responded, his eyes still on the officers working the crime scene.

"I've crossed paths with him a few times," Pete said, his eyes squinting from the droplets of rain hitting his face. "And he hasn't come at me the same way twice. First, he beats me up in a parking lot like some kind of thug. Next, he destroys my house with bombs."

"A guy can't kick your ass two ways?" Harras said, a laugh buried under the growl of his voice. "You need a serious reality check."

"No, it's not that," Pete said, his voice trailing off. "But when I was in the house, it felt—I dunno . . . it seemed like he was moving so fast. First he was in one room, then he'd tied Kathy up in another. Then he surprised me from behind. It was almost like some kind of supernatural creature."

Pete thought he heard Harras fight back a scoff.

"We can't discount it," Harras said. "But think about your perspective: You've been beaten to hell, your house is on fire, you're inhaling who knows how much smoke, and you can't see for shit. Not the most ideal way to gauge how many people are in your house, right?"

"I guess you have a point," Pete said.

"Plus, these guys," Harras said, his chin motioning toward Saiz's body. "They don't run in packs. Not usually."

Pete saw Kathy walking back toward them. She looked tired, Pete thought. Her shoulders sank and her expression was unreadable.

"I'm leaving," she said.

"What do you mean?" Pete said. "I drove here." The words spilling out of his mouth before he realized how silly they sounded.

"I'm taking a cab," she said. What she meant by "leaving" was becoming clearer the more she spoke. Pete's eyes squinted as he forced his mind to comprehend what was happening.

"Where are you going?"

"Home."

Harras raised his hands slightly as he walked off. "You guys do whatever you need to do," he said. "Fernandez, we need to talk. If you've got some theories bouncing around in your brain, I want to hear them. But for now, I have to finish up here."

He flicked his card in Pete's direction, as if Pete wouldn't be able to contact him otherwise. Pete grabbed at the card and missed, watching the tiny light blue piece of matte paper fall on the wet gravel. He bent down to pick it up, looking at Kathy as he stood.

"What's going on?"

"Nothing," she said.

"It doesn't seem like nothing," Pete said. "You were fine two minutes ago; then you go and talk on the phone and suddenly you're in a hurry to go home."

"I'm just—I'm done with this," Kathy said, her voice cracking as she motioned her chin toward the Dumpster and the body being slowly pulled out from it. "Death. Murder. Girls in Dumpsters. Friends missing. It's been two straight years of it and I don't have the stomach for it."

"Who was on the phone?"

"It doesn't matter."

"Then tell me."

"Work," she said. "It was work. Steve Vance called me. He said they got a call about me. They wouldn't say from whom, but I can guess. Whoever it was let them know about the deal we struck with Harras and Aguilera. The one where I wouldn't report any of the information I learned right away, but save it for a book that would have nothing to do with the *Miami Times*. Believe it or not, the newspaper I work for was not too keen on that. It also didn't help that they had no idea I was here."

Steve Vance was Pete's old boss at the *Miami Times*, and far from his favorite person. The word "tool" came to mind. Vance was the type who knew how to climb the corporate ladder, but little else. He'd had a role in getting Pete fired the previous year. Pete's own distracted and half-baked work hadn't helped matters.

"Fuck Vance," Pete said. "We're on the verge of something here."

"Listen to yourself," Kathy said, her eyes watering. "We're on the verge of nothing. Deep down, you know that. This isn't some minor league weirdo you're chasing. This is a mass murderer who tried to have us both killed. Tried to have you killed a handful of times already. Someone who has your ex-girlfriend tied up somewhere, if she's even alive. And all you can think about is unlocking the Rubik's

Cube? Then what? What happens if you find Emily and we catch this guy? You're still doing nothing."

Pete took a half step back. "What? Where is this coming from?"

"I got fired," she said. "I just got fired. The deal with the FBI was unacceptable to them. I'm not surprised, but I didn't think they'd figure it out so fast. Lying to my employer and withholding information that would probably help my job as a local columnist, coupled with the fact that I'm just hanging out at a crime scene with no clear press role, plus a million other tiny little things, was the end of the line. I have a month's severance and I get to say I resigned. But I just got fired."

"Look, I'm sorry," Pete said. "That's terrible. But Vance is a prick and an idiot. I mean, he fired me, and look, it all turned out fine. I—"

"It didn't turn out fine," Kathy said, her voice loud. Pete noticed a few of the surrounding officers' heads turning in response. "Look at you. Look at yourself. You think just because you quit drinking nothing else is wrong? That's not how it fucking works. I've spent the last few weeks traipsing around with you, trying to find this monster because it seemed like a good idea. Well, it wasn't. We're not equipped for this, Pete. We are not the police. We're not the FBI. Your ego won't let you see that. You have nothing: no home, no friends, no job, no life. Just this weird, backward delusion that you have some innate ability that no one else can tap into. Well, newsflash—you're not fucking smarter than everyone else. And this is it for me. I tried. I wanted to find this guy because, let's be real, I made my name the last time we did this sort of thing. But that's never happening again."

"You're upset," Pete said. "I can understand that . . . "

He reached out his hand. He was surprised when she swatted it away and moved backward. She was crying now, her makeup mixing with her tears.

"Don't patronize me," she yelled. "I'm done. This is over. Emily is dead. She's probably in a ditch somewhere, too, and we'll never find her. And this is all your fucking fault. If you hadn't stuck your nose in it, dragged me along, fucked around with everyone who was fine and happy and doing things apart from you, none of this would be happening to us."

She didn't wait for him to respond. She turned around and walked toward the parking lot. The rain had started again, a soft drizzle that most people would normally ignore. But as Pete watched his friend's figure grow smaller and drift farther into the tiny, decaying strip mall, he felt every drop sting and stab at his tired body.

CHAPTER THIRTY-ONE

It had stopped raining by the time Pete arrived at the Book Bin. It was nearly eight in the evening and the store was closed. He opened the front door and locked it behind him. He hadn't bothered to swing by Kathy's to try and gather what few material possessions he had left. At least there was a cot in the back office here, he thought. Somewhere warm to rest his head. Tomorrow he'd figure out what to do. Tomorrow he'd find Emily. He felt his throat clench at the thought. His mind bounced back to what Kathy had said. About Emily probably being dead. *Probably chopped up in a Dumpster somewhere.* He felt weighed down, his body suddenly heavy as he dropped onto the tiny cot in the small office. He didn't bother to turn the light on. He wasn't sure if Dave would be opening the store tomorrow, but he wasn't concerned.

He didn't give what he was doing much thought until he'd pulled the bottle of Stoli vodka from the small desk's bottom drawer. How long had he known Dave kept it there? Probably since the first night he'd slept in the back room, scrunched onto the tiny cot, his feet dangling over the edge. He set it on the desk and found some comfort in the way the mostly full bottle hit the cheap, imitation wood. The liquid inside sloshed from side to side. Pete opened another drawer and pulled out a small Dixie cup. He set it next to the bottle and paused for a second. Was this when he would feel a pang of guilt and stop himself? Run out of the shitty used bookstore that was the only roof over his head and find Emily? Negate all the damage he'd done and fix things?

Kathy was right. As he considered what was left of his life, he heard the familiar sound of liquor pouring into a glass.

He lifted the flimsy cup up to his face and stared at it, smelling the alcohol.

The first sip sent a wave of warmth and electricity pulsing through him. He was back. He was home. He felt complete. The buzzing in his brain had erased the sadness, worry, and anxiety that had set up shop. He didn't care about anything anymore, and that's what he wanted. The second and third—and fourth, fifth, and sixth—sips were more like gulps, and soon the cup was gone, his throat burning from the vodka. He stood up and refilled his cup with one sloppy flourish. He downed most of it immediately.

He fell onto the cot, the paper cup falling on him, spilling a few remaining drops of vodka onto his shirt. He didn't bother to wipe it away. His head was already hurting. He felt his mouth drying up and he didn't give a shit.

He leaned forward, stretching to reach the bottle. He grabbed it and brought it back to bed with him, no longer bothering with the pretense of a cup or pacing himself. He heard the sounds of Bird Road outside the store—the honking of horns, the blaring music blasting from expensive stereos, Spanish and English dancing together in the sweat and humidity of Miami—and he took a long, choking pull from the bottle.

Pete opened his eyes. He figured about an hour had passed. The words and pictures that had crossed his mind brought a cloud of sadness over him. He wanted to laugh at how silly that sounded—how silly his drunken logic had become. How little anything had changed. How little progress he'd made. How he'd fooled himself into thinking he'd beaten back whatever sick demons were residing inside him. But all he could find in himself was a quick, jagged sob. Sweet oblivion.

PART IV:
THE DEVIL NEVER SLEEPS

CHAPTER THIRTY-TWO

Pete looked around the empty room. The Jamaica Motel was a rundown shithole on Calle Ocho, on the westernmost fringes of Little Havana. It was one of many such places on the strip, offering free cable TV and no questions asked. You could rent rooms by the hour, day, week, or month. Pete had paid for the room in cash. The pink paint coating the motel's exterior had faded to an off-peach shade and the pool had developed a layer of green paste over the water.

The bed smelled of cigarettes and sweat. The TV was on, blaring the Channel 7 news. Pete was sitting on the floor, his body leaning on the nightstand next to the bed, his face looking toward the door, a bottle of cheap vodka in his hand. He'd rented the room that morning. Dave had asked him to leave the night before. "If you're not going to work, and you're just going to hide back here and sneak drinks, you have to go." Pete hadn't argued. This was what he wanted anyway. To be alone.

He took another long swig from the bottle of Popov vodka. It was cheap and strong. Felt like he was downing acid. The kind of vodka that would kick the hangover in earlier. He was already feeling the first effects. He didn't even bother going to a bar. Why? Why go somewhere when he could just spend a few twenties and be set for the night? The television said something about the murders and Pete felt a click in his brain, like the sound of someone flipping on a light switch a few rooms away. Something easily ignored, but still there. Better to lie here, alone, in dirty clothes, a week-old beard, and less than a hundred dollars in his pocket. This would be his last stand. This would be his epitaph. Pete Fernandez, a washed-up hack, known for being able to down over a dozen drinks and still drive home, for the innate ability to lead his friends to an early grave, and for an undeserved ego and deluded sense of self-importance. A waste of space. A monster. His memory trailed back to the year before, when he'd run into his father's old partner on the Miami-Dade police department. What was it Carlos Broche had said? "What would your father think if he saw you now?"

His dad would be glad he was dead. Happy he didn't have to see his son wash away what was left of his sad life. He let out an empty laugh. The truth hurt. His head throbbed as if in response.

He didn't even have any music. Nothing. The room was stale and empty and dirty. But what would he listen to? No sad song would make him feel better, much less feel anything. What could Morrissey or Paul Westerberg offer? What trivial advice would Lou Reed have to share? No one knew what he was feeling, and no one ever would. It was his pain. His fault. He deserved this black hole.

He took another drag from the bottle and felt his sadness wash away. Felt the lukewarm liquid invade his mouth and seep into his pores. His vision glazed over. He remembered putting the bottle down and laying his head against the bed frame. Then everything went dark.

A new day. More of the same. He tried taking a long shower in the afternoon. His head was a constant ache. His bones hurt. He'd awoken on the floor, what little had been left in the bottle spilt on the cheap carpet. Vomit on his shirt, dried drool caked on his face, and stubble. He wiped at his shirt, as if that would clean off the dirt and bile that were now coating everything around him, in reality and in his head.

He changed into his last clean shirt, from a stack of polos he'd grabbed at a discount store a few days after the explosion. He felt better from the shower, but knew it wouldn't last. He looked out the cloudy window of his room and saw that the sky stood out in stark contrast to the gray, musky room. The day was bright, orange, neon, and candy-coated. Miami. Even at its worst, it shone the brightest light on the dankest and darkest corners of any street. Pete allowed himself a wry smile as he left the room and walked out of the motel.

He had some cash left in his pocket and called a cab from the lobby. He'd been forced to return the rental, and he didn't anticipate getting a new car anytime soon. The cab came. He got in and gave the driver directions in a flat monotone. He could smell the wine on his own breath and realized he hadn't brushed his teeth, nor had he done much of a job when it came to showering. He could tell the cabbie noticed. He didn't care.

He could hear Willy Chirino coming from the cab stereo as the car wheeled onto Calle Ocho and inched east, toward the 836. Willy was singing about a mysterious woman wearing black socks. After about fifteen minutes, they were in Coral Gables, near the art galleries, glitzy shops, and five-star restaurants of Miracle Mile. He directed the cab to drop him off near Giralda and he paid the driver, leaving a decent if unspectacular tip. He counted the bills in his wallet. Sixty bucks. Enough for a good time at The Bar and possibly a bottle for the rest of the night.

It was close to four in the afternoon. On Friday? Saturday? Pete wasn't sure until he walked into the dark bar and noticed the day on the television that was showing ESPN sports highlights. Sunday. His hands gripped the bar for support. Had he really lost all sense of time? His tongue ran over the inside of his mouth, picking up the taste of wine and vomit from the night before. Had it ever been this bad before? He didn't want to answer himself.

He sat down at the bar in his usual spot and looked around for a bartender. Lisa met his eyes from the other end of the bar. She could do little to hide her reaction to Pete. Her shoulders slumped and her mouth went from a grin to a flat, resigned expression. She wiped her hands on a rag and walked over, in no hurry, as if steeling herself for something terrible.

"Hey there," she said.

"I'll have a vodka soda. A double, if you can swing it."

She looked him over in the same way Pete thought she'd scan a homeless guy trying to scam a drink.

"You sure?"

"Yeah," Pete said, trying to smile, but instead coming across with a creepy, distant expression. "Of course I am."

She shrugged and walked back to the other end of the bar. He watched her as she prepared the drink—a little light on the vodka—and dropped a few straws in it. She brought it over and plopped it down on a coaster. She lingered, watching Pete as he hungrily gulped down part of the drink, like a thirsty sailor on shore leave. He looked up at her.

"Can I keep a tab open?"

The look she gave Pete almost broke his heart. "I'd rather you pay by the drink," she said. "If that's cool with you."

"Never had to do that before."

"Pete . . . " she started, her mouth quivering a bit. He'd known Lisa for years; he'd been a regular at The Bar since before he'd moved to New Jersey with Emily. He'd talked to Lisa about going sober. She'd been supportive, even while ribbing him for his weird Mike-photo ritual. She seemed defeated. "You look like shit, man. Are you OK?"

"What do you mean? I feel fine. I'm fine. Can I open a tab?"

"Look, I'll serve you as long as you can pay and as long as you don't disrupt my place," she said, her voice wavering a bit as she reached the end of her sentence. "You're not a stranger. This isn't you anymore? Are you sure this is what you want to do?"

Pete took another long swig from his drink, leaving it about half full before responding. He let the vodka slosh around, the liquor stinging the inside of his mouth, raw from vomiting, his throat burning from the speed with which he drank it down.

"I'm fine," he lied.

The back of the woman's car smelled of cigarettes and bleach. He felt her breath on his neck as she fiddled with his belt and undid his pants. Her mouth was warm on his. She bit his lips and pushed his body down further onto the back seat of her tiny Sentra. Her name was Michelle, Pete remembered. She'd sidled up next to him around seven o'clock, which was right around drink eight. She worked next door at Randazzo's. She'd just finished her shift and was looking to relax for a few hours.

He didn't remember much about what they talked about. Pete complained about the jukebox. Lisa had since left. He remembered watching her talk to the incoming bartender—a burly dude named Carlos—and motion toward Pete. "Watch this guy," her lips had said, close to his ear. Pete scoffed. He was fine. He'd done nothing but sit at his stool and down his drinks. A few vodka sodas. A shot of Southern Comfort. Had there been a Jager in there? Yes. Some FIU grad students had been celebrating something—an exam? Who the fuck knows. They'd bought him one, yes.

He ran his hands over her body, his senses dull. He felt her warmth on top of him as they connected. Did he put on a condom? He almost laughed at the thought. Why bother?

The sex was quick, uncomfortable, sweaty. Pete felt his soaked shirt sticking to his skin and recoiled at how he smelled. He felt dirty. She continued to shove him around the tiny car's back seat, cursing under her breath, saying things Pete hoped to never remember. She'd seemed nice at the bar. Right? Or had he imagined that? He'd never see her again.

"You wanna fuck me, right?" she said, her voice low as they moved in a weird, synchronized rhythm. "Then fuck me."

Pete didn't respond.

A street lamp turned on. The light flashed into the car and illuminated them for a second before flickering out. Pete saw her, saw himself. Half-naked, sweaty, drunk—in the back of a car, fucking a girl he'd just met. Ten dollars in his pocket and nowhere to go. He'd been drinking alone in a shithole motel for a week and had probably missed Emily's funeral. The girl he thought he'd marry and be with forever was six feet under, and he was having sex with a stranger in a parking lot. He felt his eyes watering. A sob came out of his mouth. He tried to make it sound like a cough.

"Yo, are you falling asleep on me?" Michelle's words snapped Pete back to attention. He didn't think. He grabbed her and moved her off him. She protested.

"The fuck are you doing?" she said. "Did you finish? Fuck, you didn't even pull out?"

Pete didn't respond. He felt her closed fists connect to his shoulder and back as he zipped his pants and opened the car door. He walked out, ignoring the yells and curses being flung at him from the car. He stumbled as he walked toward Giralda, covered in sweat, his head pounding, an aching feeling in his hips and no idea what to do.

He felt around in his pockets. His wallet was gone. He didn't have house keys anymore. He almost missed the scrap of paper that had somehow survived in his back pocket for weeks.

He read the note. Jack's phone number.

"Do you have a sponsor yet?" Jack had asked him. It felt like they'd talked years before.

He didn't have anything, not anymore, he thought. He pulled out his phone. It'd been shut off for days. It took a few moments to power up. The display screamed at him—dozens of texts, missed calls, and voice mails. He ignored them and dialed the number. He'd never bothered to put him in his contacts.

"Hello?" It was Jack.

"Hey." Pete's voice came out like a croak.

"Pete? Is that you?"

"Yeah, it's me," Pete said. He'd managed to put a few blocks between himself and his angry new friend. He was leaning on a lamppost. It was dark. He was in a pseudo-industrial area that consisted of empty parking lots and poorly lit bodegas.

"Where are you? Shit, Pete. I've been looking all over for you," Jack said. "She's alive, Pete. Your friend—Emily—she's alive."

"Alive," Pete said. The word sounded foreign to him. Over the last few days—clouded by drink and darkness and dirt—he'd managed to create a buffer between himself and the reality: that Emily was dead. Now, finally reaching his bottom, he'd connected with someone who told him otherwise. Alive.

"She's alive," Pete said. He pushed a button on his phone, ending the call.

He stumbled over the sidewalk and onto the dark street before he started to sprint, his breathing heavy, his feet propelling him toward the lights of Miracle Mile.

CHAPTER THIRTY-THREE

It was around four in the morning when Kathy picked him up, standing outside the closed Barnes & Noble on Miracle Mile, the lights a bit dimmer than when he first made the call. The pristine sidewalks and high-end outlets made Pete feel even grimier. It was a five-minute drive for Kathy from her apartment, but the wait felt like hours.

Kathy had just found out about Emily, too. They agreed it didn't make sense for Pete to show up at the hospital smelling like a gin mill and looking half-dead. He showered at her place and changed into some spare clothes she had. He didn't ask who they belonged to. He tried calling Rick but got his voice mail. He thought to leave a message but wasn't sure what he'd say.

Kathy didn't ask him where he'd been. She didn't seem to care. Her kindness was there, but distant and mechanical, as if she'd had too many experiences like this—where someone she cared for made a terrible mistake and spiraled back into bad, old, and dangerous habits. The silence was fine by Pete. He was still processing the shame and embarrassment that coated him in the absence of a buzz or hangover.

According to Kathy, Emily was at Baptist Hospital, about twenty-five minutes from Kathy's apartment and further west on Kendall Drive. Emily had been brought in late the night before and was in intensive care, albeit in some kind of stable condition. She'd been found beaten and left for dead on the side of Coral Way, near the on-ramp from Le Jeune Road. They were going to the hospital. They'd just show up and see what happened. It was all they could do.

After a few detours and some unhelpful front-desk employees, Pete found her room. Kathy followed him onto the elevator.

"Thanks for your help," Pete said. His eyes focused on the elevator doors.

"I'm just glad you're alive," Kathy said. She wasn't looking at him. "I thought you'd gone and done something stupid."

"I did," Pete said. "A lot of stupid things. Too many."

"We have bigger things to think about," she said, pushing the fifth floor button again, willing the elevator to go faster. "But at least you're alive. Emily's alive. Those are good things."

Pete started to respond, but the doors opened up, interrupting him.

There were a few seats set up outside of Emily's room, 521. Pete recognized Rick; then as they got closer, he noticed Aguilera and Harras were there as well. They hadn't seen him yet. He wiped his hands on his black, borrowed T-shirt and looked himself over: clean, but rough. That was how he felt, too. A new start, but not without the baggage of what came before. Maybe they'd put that on his tombstone. Kathy looked at him and moved her chin in the direction of Emily's room. *Go.*

Pete took a few steps and saw that Rick had noticed him, as had the two FBI agents. Pete recognized Emily's mother walking out of her room, looking ashen and despondent. Rick got up with a start and made a beeline to intercept Pete. In a few moments, they were face to face.

"What are you doing here?"

"We came to see Emily," Pete said, his tone flat.

"Why? Where've you been all this time? She doesn't want to see you."

"I think I'll let her determine that," Pete said, trying to look past Rick, who stepped to his left to block Pete's view.

"We don't want you here."

"Oh, for fuck's sake," Kathy said, stepping between Rick and Pete. "Now's not the time for a dick-measuring contest, OK? Let us through. We want to see your wife. Is that so wrong?"

"I want you both gone," Rick said.

Pete looked up and met Rick's gaze for the first time.

"I don't give a shit about what you want," Pete said, surprised by how controlled his anger was. "Now, either let us pass and see Emily, or do something."

Rick waited a few seconds before responding. He sized Pete up. Pete could feel the tension rising. Was he going to hit him? Would he end up having to fight Emily's husband in the middle of a hospital? He hoped not.

Rick stepped back and made room for Pete and Kathy to walk down the hallway. Pete nodded and continued toward Emily's room. Kathy motioned for him to go in first. He could feel Harras's and Aguilera's eyes on him as his hand turned the door handle.

He hadn't given himself a second to prepare for what he saw. The room was dark, the lights dim. The only sound Pete could recognize was the beeping coming from the machines hooked up to Emily—or what he thought was Emily. He stepped closer. There she was. Lying on the bed, her face bruised and puffed up, scratches and cuts littering her cheeks and forehead. Her left arm in a cast, and her visible skin mottled with blue, black, and yellow bruises. For a moment he wasn't sure if she was breathing, but then her chest moved—a tiny, half-breath that did not inspire any confidence that she would make it. He felt a tear stream down his face.

Pete pulled up a chair next to her bed and slid his hand into hers, which was hanging over the bed. She didn't grasp his hand back, but her hand felt warm. He felt a wave of relief each time he saw her breathe. He could stay here forever, he thought. Until she was OK again.

"Jesus," Kathy said, behind him.

"Em," Pete said, his voice a whisper. "I'm sorry. I'm so sorry."

He let his mind wander. The killer had been on one path—tricking teen and college-age girls into renting apartments, and then murdering them—before Pete became involved. Once Pete and Kathy started sniffing around the case, it was as if the killer felt threatened. Could that be possible? Then the killer had reacted: threatening Pete at Mike's memorial, destroying Pete's house, taking Emily. But now, with Pete out of the picture, things had calmed down, at least according to Kathy. There'd been no new murders and Emily had been spared. Nothing else since Pete and Kathy stepped away. The killer considered him a threat, Pete thought. Or was that his ego? Pete put that aside for a second. If Jack and Kathy were right, the killer's actions had been echoes of another killer, from another time. Rex Whitehurst had tormented South Florida and the surrounding areas for years before being caught and put to death. Was this killer paying homage? Trying to connect or commune with an idol? There was a factor Pete didn't know enough about to formulate a conclusion. He had been too quick to act, hadn't spent enough time trying to learn about his foe and his methods. His impetuousness had cost lives and almost ended up with Emily dead. Something outside was affecting the killer. But Pete was in no shape to figure it out. Yet he still managed to stumble further and further into this mess.

Pete was certain there'd been two men in his house on the night it was destroyed. Despite Harras's doubts, it just didn't make sense. Someone was helping the killer.

He glanced up at Emily for a second. She looked terrible. He had no idea what was going on inside her body. He looked at his hands, clutching her limp one. How had she survived, though? The killer had murdered each of his victims viciously, yet he had left Emily on the side of the road, as if the job were done. She was beaten, but not stabbed—like the others. It didn't add up. Serial killers don't suddenly develop qualms about murder.

Had Emily been taken by the killer, or by someone helping the killer push Pete aside? It seems their plan to scare them off—blowing up Pete's house—had backfired, as it made Pete work harder on the case. Even Kathy pressed on. But someone let her bosses know that her investigation—which the *Times* was aware of, to some degree—wasn't on the up-and-up. Allegations were made and it became the last straw. The fact that Kathy had struck a side deal with the FBI to feed her information for a book to be written later did not sit well with her bosses, so she got fired and, in effect, lost any credentials when it came to helping Pete. But who tipped off the paper?

Pete didn't have any answers, but he had a lot more questions, and that was a start. His father used to say something along those lines when Pete was a boy. After a grueling night of work—often arriving home in the morning, exhausted, just as Pete was getting up—he would sit in the living room, with Pete sitting by him, listening.

"Sometimes the best break is just the right question," Pedro had said, sipping a cup of coffee, even though he should have probably been trying to get a few hours of sleep before he was due back at work. "If you find the right question, it's like hitting a good note—it'll take you to the next one. And then you're moving along."

Who wanted us out of the way? That was the question. He needed to find the answer.

He was startled by the sound of the door opening. He and Kathy turned to see Aguilera stepping into the room, trying to be quiet. He nodded at them and walked toward Pete, stood next to his chair, and looked Emily over.

"Where've you been?"

"I had some problems," Pete said, unable to meet Aguilera's eyes. "But I'm better now."

"Your friend is lucky to be alive," Aguilera said. "Had that couple not found her and called us when they did, she'd be dead."

"Is this the part where we all hug and thank you? Or realize we're all on the same team?" Kathy said, standing up. "If so, I may have to politely decline."

She wove around Aguilera and walked out of the room.

"Can't win 'em all, I guess," Aguilera said.

Pete didn't respond.

"We've hit a wall with this," Aguilera said, waving his hand toward Emily. "We've got zero leads and we just got word on another body."

Pete looked up, surprised.

"Yeah," Aguilera said, reacting to Pete's expression. "We think it's the Henriquez girl—but we haven't gotten a proper ID yet. We have to go with dental records. That's not official. We haven't alerted the press yet."

Pete didn't have to ask any more. Resorting to dental records for a murder victim meant that the body was so severely burned or destroyed there was very little that the naked eye could see in regard to identification. The little bit of hope he'd held out for Nina was gone. She was dead.

"It's gotta be her," Pete said.

"Yeah," Aguilera said. "What are you going to do with yourself now?"

Pete was surprised by Aguilera's sudden concern over his well-being. "I'm going to keep tabs on Emily and try to get on with my life," Pete said. "What's left of it, I guess."

"That sounds like a good idea."

"What do you mean?"

"I just mean it's good to work on yourself," Aguilera said, looking at Emily's body on the bed. "To become what you were supposed to, in a way. Leave the crazy shit to the crazy cops and agents like us."

Before Pete could respond, he heard a strange noise from Emily—a tiny, almost childlike whine, like a toddler fighting off a nightmare. She turned on her bed, moving away from Pete and Aguilera. She seemed frightened.

"What's wrong with her?" Aguilera said. The whining got louder, forming a frightened howl. She began to thrash her arms, lifting them to protect herself.

Pete stood up. "Go get a nurse," he said, his hand holding onto Emily so she wouldn't hurt herself. "She's having some kind of bad reaction."

Aguilera nodded and walked out of the room. Almost instantly, Emily calmed down, the whimpering slowly dropping in volume. *What the hell had set her off?* Pete ran a hand over her head and hair. She was warm—sweating. He hadn't noticed that before.

A few moments later, a nurse came in. She stepped in front of Pete and began to check Emily over.

"What's wrong with her?"

The nurse gave Pete a look which seemed to say, "What's not wrong with her?" before continuing her work. Finally, she stepped back and put her hands on her hips.

"She had some kind of episode," the nurse said. Pete could see her name tag, ELISA AYALA. "Something made her anxious. She's been floating in and out of consciousness for most of the night. The doctors are hoping she comes out of it soon, but the most we've seen from her is that: frightened noises and sudden movements."

"How lucky was she?"

"Lucky?"

"I mean, to have been found when they found her," Pete said, trying to clarify. "Do you think she was left for dead?"

"What kind of question is that?"

"I'm trying to figure out why she was spared at all," Pete said. He could see the confused look on nurse's face. She thought he was some kind of freak. He was, he guessed. But a freak who had an idea.

"Whoever left her like this didn't think she had much time to live," Elisa said.

"So, they either think she's dead or want her to be dead," Pete said.

"I'm not sure what you're asking me," she said, heading toward the door. "And I don't like it."

She stepped out of the room. The door closed with a firm click. Pete turned around to face Emily, who seemed to be sleeping. This wasn't over. Despite what he'd told Aguilera, he had no intention of leaving things be. It was too late for that. He closed his eyes and tried to ignore the feeling that things were about to get much worse.

CHAPTER
THIRTY-FOUR

The West-Dade Regional Library was a bit of a dump, Pete thought, as he took off his sunglasses and entered the large building off Coral Way, less than a ten-minute drive from where Pete's house used to be. It was close to noon. He'd allowed himself to sleep in, for whatever that was worth, considering that he'd spent the evening curled up once again on the flimsy cot in Dave's office. He felt rested but not completely back to normal. Maybe there was no such thing.

He walked up to the reference desk and was greeted by a tidy-looking librarian. He wondered what she made of him: unshaven, in a gray Rush T-shirt Dave had lent him and faded blue jeans, his eyes probably bloodshot; at the very least he looked worn-out and beaten.

"I need to do some research," Pete said.

"Well, you came to the right place," she responded, her voice cheery and almost melodic. Pete cringed inside. *People actually talk like this?*

She took Pete's silence as a cue to continue. "What can I help you with on this lovely afternoon?"

"I'm trying to find all news articles pertaining to Rex Whitehurst," Pete said. Her expression changed from perky to perturbed in a second. "I've done some basic research, but I need to go farther back into the archives to learn more about him."

"Well, sure," the librarian said. "I can set you up on one of those terminals which are connected to our microfiche databases. You can search via keyword. Not everything is digital, though, so I have to apologize. It will let you know where to go to pull the hard copies, though."

She seemed to be in a hurry to leave the conversation. Funny how mentioning one of the state's deadliest serial killers could sour an otherwise chirpy Tuesday afternoon exchange. "Not light reading, I know," Pete said.

She nodded and led him to a computer terminal toward the back of the reference area of the library. As a kid, instead of making friends or playing sports, he'd spent most of his time at the other side of the building, devouring bad sci-fi and horror novels after school.

She showed him how to log into the library system and moved away.

"If you need anything, I'll be over there," she said, motioning to her desk, which was visible from Pete's terminal.

Pete got to work. He pulled a tiny reporter's notebook from his pocket and set it next to the keyboard. He wasn't sure what he was looking for yet, but he knew where he wanted to start. After this, he'd swing by the hospital and see Emily again. He prayed she was doing better. After the visit, he'd only spoken to Kathy very generally. He could tell she was hesitant about continuing to work on the case. He didn't blame her. He could use her help now, though, especially with research. He'd always been a decent reporter, but he'd never enjoyed being a library jockey.

He began with a basic search for Rex Whitehurst. He got hundreds of articles. Although much had been written about Whitehurst's murders, Pete knew very little about his life before he'd been caught.

According to stories written soon after Whitehurst had been captured for what would be the final time, he had been working as a carpenter in South Miami, doing odd jobs on the side and splitting his time between his rented house and an unnamed girlfriend's residence. The rental house had provided the most damning evidence that Whitehurst was a serial killer. Pete focused on the sentence. He'd never read or heard anything about Whitehurst having a girlfriend. Who was this woman? Could she still be alive? Probably, Pete thought.

He refined his search to "Rex Whitehurst, girlfriend" and saw the number of articles that matched his query was minor in comparison to the hundreds that appeared initially. There were only three. One was the original story Pete had seen, the first mention of this woman. Another was a quick recap story following Whitehurst's execution a few years later, which noted that his now ex-girlfriend had not been in attendance. The last piece was more recent.

It was a local column by Alexandra Trelles. It had been written before the recent spate of murders, but after Pete and Kathy's run-in with the Silent Death the year previous. Trelles was filling in before the paper would decide to hire Kathy to fill her father's old job as the

Miami Times local columnist. The piece was good—very emotional and colorful—and touched on the lives of the many people who had "survived" Rex Whitehurst's murderous rampage, who Trelles had interviewed on the anniversary of Whitehurst's execution. One of them, Ana Gallegos, was revealed to have been Whitehurst's girlfriend of many years. Trelles didn't quote Gallegos directly— but to Pete's journalistic eye, it was clear they'd at least spoken on background. For whatever reason, the story revealed her identity and even that she was now living in a Brickell high-rise, in a ritzy area near downtown Miami.

That didn't sound right, Pete thought. Why would the reporter screw over a source like that? It reeked of bad editing. The editor had probably requested Trelles's notes and inserted facts that were not meant to go beyond her conversation with Gallegos. He allowed himself a judgmental moment at his former workplace's expense. The once-proud newspaper of record had become a cheap, slapped-together rag with little regard for posterity or ethics. Pete also realized that the story hadn't come up when Kathy searched the *Miami Times* archive. He could see it now because the microfiche terminals dealt with actual, hard copies. But someone had apparently tried their best to remove the story from the paper's electronic files. Had Gallegos sued? Had someone at the *Times* gone back and erased the column?

Pete did another search, this time for Ana Gallegos specifically. Who was this woman? Why hadn't anyone else researched her life? It was almost as if she had been purposely tucked away. Was someone trying to hide her? Or protect her? Too early to tell.

He didn't realize what he was doing until he'd finished dialing Kathy's number. Under normal circumstances, Pete would text—but this felt more urgent. The phone rang a few times before going to voice mail.

"Does the name Ana Gallegos mean anything to you? I think it's important. Call me back. I'm on my own on this and I could use your help. Thanks."

Pete hung up and slid the phone into his pocket. What now? He longed for the access that being a newspaper employee provided. If he were still at the *Times*, he could have accessed their database and figured out where Ana lived, and if she had any kind of record.

Why had the columnist mentioned Gallegos's name in the story? Why hadn't anyone else followed up on this person, especially when a string of mirror murders were happening? It was gnawing at Pete.

He almost didn't feel his phone vibrating in his pocket. Kathy spoke before he could say anything.

"You rang?"

"Did you get my voice mail?"

"No, you know I hate voice mail," Kathy said. "What are you up to?"

"I need to see you," Pete said. The librarian was giving him disapproving looks. He had to get off the phone. He stood up, waved at the librarian and walked toward the library exit. He made it to a few steps outside the library before Kathy responded.

"Oh boy," Kathy said. "What now?"

"Ana Gallegos."

"Who?"

"What do you know about her?"

"Nothing," Kathy said. "Should I know her? Is this some kind of trivia game?"

"You didn't think it was worth mentioning that Rex Whitehurst had a girlfriend?" Pete said as he walked toward Dave's car, which he'd let Pete borrow for the day.

There was a pause before she responded.

"I had no idea," Kathy said. Pete believed her. "I know the paper had a column about Whitehurst a while back and the idiot editor let slip something that was supposed to be off the record, and that led to Alexandra Trelles—my predecessor—leaving, but I didn't know what it was. This must have happened when I was off working on the Silent Death book, or during one of my many 'probationary periods.' When I pulled pretty much everything we ever printed on Whitehurst for our research slumber party a while back that column didn't come up."

"Where does Gallegos live?"

"How would I know? I'm in the same spot as you—a *former* staffer at the *Miami Times*."

"Can you call Trelles? Do some research. Whatever you can," Pete said, sliding into the car. "Whoever is behind these murders wanted Emily dead. They left her for dead. So, either they think she's already dead or they're going to try and finish the job. I have to stop it before it gets to that point."

"Pete, you need to go to the police," Kathy said. "This isn't your job."

"Tell me where she lives and meet me there in an hour," Pete said. He wasn't budging.

Kathy sighed. "Fine, let me call you back," she said. Pete could hear her typing something on a computer before she hung up.

A few minutes passed. Pete watched the digital clock change numbers. He hadn't started the engine. He waited. Kathy called back.

"Alex Trelles is a professional friend—I don't want to screw her on this, OK? She got burned by this whole affair. Needless to say, she was extremely curious as to why I was calling her out of the blue," she said.

"Did you get the address?"

"Patience is not your strong suit, I take it," Kathy said. "Ana Gallegos lives on Brickell and Seventeenth. In a fancy complex, Brickell Bay. We'll be lucky if she even lets us in. There's a reason people live behind those kind of fences, you know. I'll meet you across the street from the complex in half an hour."

Pete hung up without responding and pulled the car out of the library parking lot.

If you lived in Brickell, you had money and weren't afraid to flaunt your bank balance—whether it was in a one-bedroom apartment or a suite atop a luxury high-rise, nothing in the neighborhood was cheap. South of Miami's downtown, Brickell had it all—close to the beach, great restaurants, and enough distance from the riffraff to make it appealing to the deep-pocketed.

Getting past the Brickell Bay security had been easy. It helped that Kathy had come along. Pete doubted he would have been able to smile his way past them alone. Her story—that she was invited to a surprise party but had forgotten her guest pass—seemed flimsy to Pete, but held enough water for the chubby security guard to smile and push a button allowing them both into the complex, which seemed more like a big, luxury hotel than an apartment building.

"Now we just need to figure out her apartment," Pete said.

"One-one-six-seven, Tower D," Kathy said, without looking at Pete. She was walking toward what Pete assumed was the elevator bay at an accelerated pace.

She punched in the floor button as they entered the elevator and leaned against the wall. She had barely spoken to Pete since they'd met outside the complex.

"Why are you here?"

She met his eyes with a "Did you really just ask me that?" look.

"I'm here because you, for once, made a logical argument," she said. "Whoever did this to Emily is still out there. I'm also feeling a little protective of you. Don't let it go to your head."

The elevator doors opened and Pete let the conversation dangle as he followed Kathy down the hall. When they reached Ana Gallegos's apartment, Kathy knocked. They heard someone shuffling around inside the luxury condo.

The door opened a few inches and Pete could see an older woman, probably in her sixties, peeking through the barely open door.

"Yes?"

"Hi, Ana Gallegos?" Kathy stepped in front of Pete and took charge.

"Who are you?"

"I'm Kathy Bentley," she said. "I'm a reporter for the *Miami Times*."

The door closed with a slam, forcing Pete and Kathy to hop back.

"You have a lot of nerve coming here," Gallegos said through the closed door. "I'm calling security."

Kathy stepped closer to the door.

"Ms. Gallegos, before you do that, I wanted a few minutes of your time," she said, her voice loud so she could be heard through the door. "We're working on an apology in the paper and a retraction to make up for the mistake we made."

Pete nodded his approval at the lie. Kathy scowled at him.

"The damage has already been done," Gallegos said. "Your organization took what I said and violated it. I don't want to speak to you."

"Part of the apology, Ms. Gallegos, involves a monetary reward," Kathy said. She was freestyling now, hoping that the growing lie would become more believable. Pete wasn't sure, but he had little choice. "We'd like to make you an offer as a show of good faith."

Pete rolled his eyes, but caught himself as the door opened again, this time without the latch holding it back. Behind the door stood Ana Gallegos, a small, waifish woman. She was wearing black slacks and a dark blue blouse, her hair made up as if she'd just stepped out of the beauty salon. She nodded and motioned for them to follow her into the apartment.

"Who's your friend?" she asked, not bothering to turn around and look at Pete.

"He's an editor at the *Miami Times*," Kathy said, enjoying her fictional reality more than she probably should, Pete thought. "He's representing the editorial board and our decision."

Ana sat down on a dark brown recliner and pointed to a small gray couch across from her.

"Well, it's about time," Ana said. "What your paper did to me was terrible. I had to quit my job and I lost so many friends. All because I dated a man who I thought was a gentleman. How was I to know he was a murderer?"

Pete bit his tongue and let Kathy continue to take point.

"Yes, we're very sorry about that," Kathy said. "We'll discuss the specifics of the monetary settlement shortly, but I'd like to ask a few background questions about your relationship with Rex, along with my colleague, for clarity's sake."

"Why is that necessary?" Ana asked, sensing the first chink in their story's armor.

"It's not for publication, ma'am," Pete said. "We just need to make sure we covered the story with you and have all the information to relay it to the board."

Ana nodded. She still seemed confused but had apparently learned enough to continue.

"First off, Ms. Gallegos, how long were you with Rex Whitehurst?" Pete asked. Kathy had pulled out a notebook and pen.

"Well, Rex and I got together a few years after my first husband died," Ana said, a hint of sadness in her voice. "I'd met him at the Publix near my house. I lived in South Miami at the time. I was shopping and so was he. We chatted about silly things. I kept running into him around the neighborhood—at the store, church, restaurants—and we just kind of hit it off. After a while, he asked me out to dinner."

"How long were you together?" Kathy asked.

"It was a slow relationship," Ana said, her voice thoughtful and methodical. "I had just lost my husband. I wasn't in a hurry to meet anyone. But he wore me down. You know how men can be. After a year or so, he moved into my house, but kept his apartment. So, overall, we were together for over ten years, until he was . . . well, captured. Until the police found him."

"Did you ever have any inkling about what he was doing?"

Pete asked, trying to dance around the macabre reality of who Rex Whitehurst was. "Did you ever think he was acting strangely?"

"No, not really," Ana said, a dry smile on her face, as if she realized how silly she sounded. "I mean, he was always distant and aloof, but I just thought that's how men were. He spent a few days a week at his old place and he traveled a lot for work, but I didn't leap from that to think he was killing children."

"So, you were surprised when the cops arrested him?" Pete asked.

"I was," Ana said. She didn't sound convincing, Pete thought.

"Did you ever talk to him after he was arrested?" Pete continued.

"No, no, not at all," Ana said. "He wasn't the man I thought he was. He was a monster."

"Did you write?" Kathy asked.

"Write? Letters? Oh, no," Ana said, letting her voice trail off.

"Now, Ms. Gallegos, we need you to be fully honest with us," Pete said. "Are you sure you had no contact with Rex Whitehurst after his arrest?"

"No, I never spoke to Rex again," she said, uttering the killer's name slowly, as if savoring a word she hadn't used in a long time. Her eyes scanned the floor. She began to rub her hands together. "But I knew how he was doing."

"How?" Pete asked.

He felt Kathy's fingers jabbing at his side. She wanted him to cut it out. Pete couldn't. He knew this was going somewhere.

"Rex—and this sounds terrible—had a way with children," Ana said, her voice hesitant. "And the more I think about this, the more insane it sounds, but I never thought he would hurt him, even after all those terrible things about Rex came up."

Pieces started to click together in Pete's head. Just enough to put him on alert.

"Hurt who, Ana? Who wouldn't Rex hurt?" Pete said.

Kathy had stopped distracting Pete. Her hand was now on his arm as they watched the older woman wipe tears from her eyes. She was still looking at the floor.

"My son, my little boy," Ana said, her voice low and hollow. "He loved my little boy, from my first marriage. I let him keep in touch with Rex. I explained everything to him. He was happy to have a father figure of any kind. He's very smart. He knew Rex had done bad things, but he still cared for him."

"Your son?" Kathy said.

"How long did your son keep in touch with Rex?" Pete said, his voice clear and forceful.

"Until they killed him," Ana said. "They wrote letters back and forth for almost a decade."

"Where's your son now?" Pete asked. He could feel Kathy inching closer to him. She was scared.

"My son is a good boy," Ana said. Her eyes were glazed over. She realized this had been a sham, but she couldn't stop talking anymore. "He just loved Rex."

"Where is he?" Pete asked again.

She didn't answer. Her head was in her hands. She was sobbing now. Kathy gave Pete a confused look.

Pete's mind was buzzing. They were close to something. He ran over Ana's words. What was he missing?

"Is Gallegos your maiden name?" Pete asked. It was a gut reaction question. She brought her head up. Her eyes were suddenly clear. Her mouth slightly agape.

"What?"

"Gallegos. Is that your maiden name?"

"Yes."

Pete felt Kathy's nails digging into his arm.

"What's your son's name, Ms. Gallegos?" Pete asked. He felt his stomach turn. He hoped the answer would be something other than the name he already knew was coming.

"Raul . . . Raul Aguilera," she said. "My little boy. Raulito."

Pete could barely hear Kathy's sharp intake of breath over the ringing in his ears.

CHAPTER THIRTY-FIVE

"**W**e need to meet," Pete said to Harras over the phone, his voice more of a hiss than anything else. They were speeding down 836, heading west. Pete watched as Kathy navigated the crowded expressway. They'd left Dave's car parked on the street near Ana's condo, thinking it'd be better to ride together. Soon the traffic would become unbearable; they couldn't risk being stuck or separated. Pete tried to concentrate on the road and on Harras, ignoring the phone's vibrations—signaling another obscenity-laden text from Dave complaining about the status of his vehicle.

"Where? What's going on?"

"We know the killer," Pete said. "That's all I can say on the phone. Where are you? Can you meet us somewhere? Where's your partner?"

"I'm at home," Harras said, sounding annoyed. "Not sure where Aguilera is. Probably on break, too. They've got some uniforms stationed at the hospital. Look, this better not be bullshit, Fernandez. I don't have time for it. Not now. Meet me at La Carretta on Eighth Street, off Le Jeune. I'll be there in twenty minutes."

"See you there," Pete said, then hung up. Kathy looked at him.

"He's game to meet," he said. "La Carretta."

"Why do we always meet cops at Cuban places?"

"You're complaining?"

"Well," Kathy said. "I guess not. But still."

Pete allowed a smile to crack. They'd done it. They had figured it out. The killer had been under their noses all this time, and now they had the ammo to take him down.

"Wow," Kathy said. "Aguilera's the last person I would have thought of for the killer, you know?"

"Well, you wouldn't usually suspect the person investigating the crime," Pete said, looking out the passenger side window as Kathy took the Le Jeune exit. "But it fits. He was close to Rex, probably admired him, and now has some weird fixation on paying homage to him. Emily also had a meltdown when he went into her room—once she heard his voice, she went nuts."

"Is it that easy, though?"

"What do you mean?"

"I mean . . . " Kathy said. "Well, I don't know. Let's hope it's him. It just seems very neat. Although it would explain Emily flipping out when Aguilera came into her room."

"Exactly. More evidence. Some things have to work out for us, don't they?"

"When do they ever work out like this?" Kathy said.

263

Pete knew something was wrong the moment they turned left on Calle Ocho. The parking lot to La Carretta, which was usually bustling at this hour of the day, was strangely quiet. He couldn't spot Harras's car, a late model Mazda Miata, anywhere in the lot, and the usual crowd of aging Cuban *viejitos* was nowhere to be found. He put his hand on Kathy's arm.

"Turn around," he said.

"What? Why?"

"Something's weird," he said. "It doesn't feel right."

"Well, you haven't even eaten yet," she tried to joke.

"Think about it," he said. "Who's Aguilera's mom going to call the second we leave? And what power does he still have?"

"You think she called him?"

"We're walking into a trap."

She slammed on the brakes and made a U-turn in a few quick, smooth motions. Pete gripped his door handle to keep from slamming into the dashboard. He felt the car accelerate in the opposite direction of the restaurant. He didn't realize he was holding his breath until the car turned back toward the expressway. Kathy's eyes were focused on the road. Pete looked back and didn't notice anyone following them—so far.

"Where to now?" she asked, her eyes still on the road.

"I don't know," Pete said. As he finished the sentence, he felt his phone vibrating in his pocket. He looked at the display. Kathy turned to him for a second.

"Who is it?"

"Harras," Pete said.

"Pick up."

"This is Pete," he said, his voice straining to sound casual.

"Where are you guys? You call me in a panic and now you're dragging ass?"

"We should be there soon," Pete lied. "We got caught in some traffic."

There was a pause before Harras answered. "Lay low," Harras said, his voice a quick whisper. "I'm not sure what's going on, but they're after you."

"What?"

"There's an APB on you and your girlfriend," Harras said. Pete could tell he was conflicted. Betraying the confidence of his fellow officers went against his very nature. "Something's not right about this. I can feel it. Lay low and let me figure it out. But they're on your trail."

Pete hung up the phone without responding. He lowered his window and tossed the cellular out.

"What happened?" Kathy said, confused. "Why the hell did you just do that? You could have just tossed the SIM card, you psycho."

"They're looking for us," Pete said. "The police think we're involved somehow."

"How do you figure that? Another premonition?"

"Harras just told me," Pete said, trying to think. "We need to go somewhere they won't find us."

"Call Dave," Kathy said, handing Pete her phone.

Dusk had settled into night as Kathy pulled into the grassy parking lot across from Churchill's Hideaway in Little Haiti, a formerly poor part of town that was known more for its crime rate than anything else. But Little Haiti was now squarely in the sights of investors looking to gobble up land as close to the trendy parts of town as possible. While still far from flush and home to a large part of Miami's Haitian community, the area was gentrifying at an alarming rate—with bodegas and creole restaurants replaced by pop-up stores and nightclubs. The streets were going from dark and seedy to bright and artsy—with Churchill's as a fossil of an edgier, more dangerous era.

Inside, the bar was a dive's dive: loud music, grizzled drunks, and grimy glasses. Outside, torn flyers, stickers, and graffiti covered every bit of wall space, and Pete's mind instantly went back to his younger days, when a night wasn't complete without hitting Churchill's for a show or a nightcap pint of Boddingtons. They got out of the car and Pete paused for a second to take in the landmark of his youth.

"Leave your keys in the car," Pete said.

"What? Are you high?"

"Just do it," Pete said. "One of Dave's friends is going to drive it somewhere and leave it. We have to throw them off our trail. If they find your car here, we're caught."

"If they're here, we're caught," Kathy said. Still, she did as Pete requested. "What sort of master plan does your trust fund–thug friend have, anyway?"

"We'll see," Pete said as he held the door open for her.

They were greeted by the loud, jagged chords of a local power punk band, Corky. They'd been playing around the bars and clubs of Miami since Pete was in college. He had seen them play more than a few times—blurred memories that were now almost gone with time.

The crowd was sparse, but the music reverberated around the two-room bar. The main area, with two pool tables and soccer on the big-screen TVs, was empty. The showroom, with the band playing, a busy bar, and a few tables, was more crowded. Pete nodded at the bartender—a big, burly Dominican named Escala, his arms decorated with what looked like prison tattoos—who pointed toward the back with his chin. Pete and Kathy headed past the stage and through a narrow hallway that would have probably dissuaded anyone who wasn't familiar with the venue.

"The fuck was that?" Kathy whispered.

"Dave's here," Pete said.

"Well, I would hope so," Kathy said. "I mean, what was that little knowing look you got from Tony Montana over there? This is a whole different side to you. You hang out with these guys?"

Pete turned around, his hand on the door to the outside patio.

"I used to," he said, his expression flat. "Dave still does."

Pete opened the door and they found themselves in a dark, dank garden area. The music from inside the bar could still be heard through the thin walls, but it did little to mask the humid, uneasy feeling that hovered over the empty garden. A few pieces of dirty lawn furniture were all the decoration Pete could see. Dave appeared suddenly, as if cutting through the darkness itself. He seemed totally at ease, his belly visible under his too-tight Def Leppard shirt. He had some kind of crumbs in his beard. He was also wearing large sunglasses.

"You guys are in some deep shit," he said, skipping pleasantries.

"Are we?" Pete asked.

"Yeah, dude. You're all over the news," Dave said. "They're saying you're 'persons of interest' in this serial killer shit."

Pete and Kathy exchanged glances.

"I need your help," Pete said.

"You don't even have to ask," Dave said, almost offended. "What's the deal?"

"We think Aguilera is the killer," Pete said, looking around to make sure there was no one else around.

"The FBI agent? Holy fuck," Dave said.

"Yeah," Kathy interjected. "Crazy, right?"

"Why him?"

"His mom dated Rex Whitehurst," Pete began. "The killer from way back. Turns out her son and Rex were tight. When I was visiting Emily, she freaked out when Aguilera showed up and started talking, as if she recognized his voice."

"So what do we do?" Dave said as he scratched his chin absentmindedly. "Go to the cops and explain everything? I mean, they're on your ass."

"First, we need to get rid of Kathy's car," Pete said.

"Gomez is already driving it to Coral Gables," Dave said. "It'll be outside her apartment in no time."

"Can you get someone to keep an eye on Emily's room in Baptist?" Pete said.

Dave nodded.

"I'll call some people, see what we can do," Dave said. "It's going to be tough, especially if there are cops around her all day. But we'll try."

"If it is Aguilera, then he thought Emily was dead when he dumped her on the side of the road," Pete said. "Now he knows she's alive—and he knows she'll pin this on him. He'll try to kill her first chance he gets."

Dave pulled out his cell and walked away from Kathy and Pete. He could only make out a few words of what Dave was saying in Spanish.

"What's going on?" Kathy asked. She was nervous.

"If we don't hear what he's asking them to do, we can't be implicated," Pete said.

"That is some loose-ass logic there, Petey," Kathy said.

Dave flipped his phone shut and walked back to them.

"What else?"

"I dunno," Pete said. "That's all I worked out on the way here. We need to think. I need to figure out how we can put the spotlight on Aguilera before we get arrested, because if we're locked up, that gives him time to bail."

"Follow me," Dave said, motioning them toward a gravel walkway near the back of the patio.

They walked along the narrow path for a few feet until they arrived at a shack about the size of a college dorm room.

"The fuck is this?" Kathy said.

Dave opened the door. Inside was a small, well-lit room, with a few chairs and a table that served as a dining area. There were no windows. On the table was a Mac laptop. It was cold in the tiny space.

"I come here when I need a break," Dave said. "Computer's all yours, just don't judge me if you stumble across anything dicey in my Internet history. I got my car back, by the way. No thanks to you."

"How long do you think we have before they find us?" Pete asked, ignoring the jab.

"Couple hours at least," Dave said. "Probably a few days if you stick it out here. But knowing you, that's probably not going to happen."

"No," Pete said. "But this'll do for now. Thanks, man."

"What do we know?"

Pete's words echoed around the tiny room. It was close to three in the morning. He and Kathy had spent the last few hours doing as much research on Raul Aguilera as one could with just a laptop and an Internet connection. Luckily, the usually slothlike *Miami Times* had yet to revoke Kathy's database access, giving them a bit more maneuverability than they'd expected. It probably had to do with the please-don't-sue-us "exit package" they'd given her, which meant she got part of her salary for a few weeks but didn't have to report to work—something to tide her over until she found a new gig. Still, the search results were nil.

"We know that Raul Aguilera was a model student," Kathy said. "And he went on to be a well-regarded and respected FBI agent. No criminal record, no professional missteps and, aside from what we learned today, no links to Rex Whitehurst or any other serial murderers, aside from the ones he tried to put away. We have a lot of ground to cover, so let's focus. We don't exactly have the option of going home and sleeping on this."

"No, we don't," Pete said. In the last few hours, they'd seen numerous news reports—on the Internet and television—with their photos featured. The cops were doing a full-court press to find them, and if they were caught with nothing to back up their claims, whatever hopes they had of stopping Aguilera would be under the bus with them.

"Any chance we could find some of those ads?" Pete said.

"The ones the killer posted?"

"Yeah," Pete said.

Kathy didn't respond right away, but began typing.

"Let's see how far back we can go," she said. Pete leaned over her, his eyes scanning the screen as she flipped through pages and pages of the Craigslist's site history.

"I wish we had the stuff we got from visiting Alice's roommate," Pete said. "It's going to be impossible to figure out which ad one of these girls responded to."

"Wait," Kathy said. She lifted her hands from the keyboard for a second. "Didn't one of the posts come from a weird e-mail address?"

"Yeah, you're right," Pete said. "A Hotmail account. Alice's roommate got defensive when you made fun of the poster for using one."

"It was something cheesy but sort of official-sounding," Kathy said. "Like, MiamiApartments@hotmail or something?"

"MIAapartments4rentSOON@hotmail. Try that," Pete said.

She typed in the address and waited for the slowish Internet connection to kick in. After a few seconds, a single listing appeared—from a few months before.

"Bingo," Kathy said.

She clicked on the listing. They both scanned the text quickly.

"This is it," Pete said.

"Are you sure?"

"Yup. This is the ad Alice Cline read and responded to," Pete said. "This is the ad that killed her."

$800 / 1br—430ft²—APARTMENT IN KENDALL
(7320 SW 80TH ST APT J402)
Nice clean apartment, for rent starting June 1st.
By appointment only. Ideal for first-time tenant
or college student. Located near restaurants
and laundry. No broker fee, great deal. Contact
Steve via email.

"OK, but there's no number with it," Kathy said. "We know it's him, but that doesn't help. We're grasping at straws here."

Pete motioned for Kathy to step away from the laptop. They were both tired and cranky, but he had an idea.

"Let me get in there for a second," he said.

He went back to the main search option and typed "miaapartments4rentSOON"—minus the Hotmail domain. He got a handful of search results.

"They're all from the same time period," Pete said.

"So?"

"So, our guy was creating e-mail addresses with different service providers," Pete said. "But he couldn't be bothered to change up the login names."

"Again, so what? How does that get us any closer to anything?"

"Not sure yet," he said. He cursed under his breath. Why hadn't he thought of this sooner?

Pete clicked on each ad from the list, opening each one in its own browser tab. He scanned them, one by one. They were identical, except for the second-to-last one.

"We've got a number," Pete said.

"What?"

"There's a phone number with this ad," Pete said. "None of the others have one, but the text is identical otherwise."

"Why have a number on this one?"

"Not sure," Pete said. "This is one of the later ones. Maybe he was hoping to expand his client base?"

"Victim base, you mean," Kathy said. He could see the weariness in her eyes. She wanted no part of this anymore. Pete couldn't blame her.

Pete grabbed Kathy's phone from the table and began dialing. She didn't protest. After a quick exchange with someone on the other end, Pete hung up with a long, frustrated sigh.

"What happened?"

"False alarm," Pete said.

"How so?"

"The number's for a disposable phone," Pete said. "Whoever had it before knew that. The number itself is worthless."

"True, but the clue is valuable," Kathy said. "It means he didn't want to be traced, which implies he was doing something wrong. Not a smoking gun, by any means, but still. Something."

Pete pushed himself away from the table in frustration and stood up. He was tired. His head hurt. They'd been holed up in this tiny, sketchy room for hours and all they had was a temporary cell phone number and a few Internet postings. He felt helpless.

"Something isn't going to help us here," Pete said. "We need more. This guy was going after girls. He had a fixation with his mentor, Rex Whitehurst. What else? What else can we pin on him?"

"How do killers pay homage to other killers?" Kathy said. "What methods did Rex Whitehurst have that Raul Aguilera could mimic?"

Pete nodded, starting to pace again.

"What did this killer do?" Pete said. "What did Rex do differently?"

"Rex's kills were similar, but not the same," she said. "He didn't use ads, he'd troll neighborhoods and entice kids to come into his car . . ."

"Wait," Pete said. "That's it."

"What is?"

"His car," Pete said. "Rex drove a white van. That was his signature move. Erica Morales's friend Silvia said she saw Erica get into a white van. But saying someone owns a white van in Miami is like saying you have sunglasses in LA. Still, what if Aguilera adopted that part of his stepdad's MO?"

"That would make sense," Kathy said.

"Can you find out what kind of van Rex Whitehurst used for his crimes?" Pete asked.

"Sure," Kathy responded, already back at the laptop and typing. "Shouldn't be too hard. Let's see. Okay, here we go. A Ford Aerostar, 1983, white."

"Ford stopped making the Aerostar a few years back, no?"

"How should I know?" Kathy said.

"It's true," Pete said. "They changed the name—to the Windstar. So someone still driving a Ford Aerostar, especially one from 1983 that's white, has got to be rare."

"Thank you so fucking much for being incompetent, *Miami Times*," Kathy muttered as she continued to type. "Let's see how far into the DMV records the *Times* system will take me before it raises a red flag and they realize I'm not exactly an employee anymore."

Pete nodded. He'd done something similar the year previous during the Silent Death case, also with Kathy's account, no less. The *Miami Times*, as the city's paper of record, had unprecedented access to public networks, databases, and information, the Department of Motor Vehicles being one of them. But even that had its limits. If a user account was flagged for browsing sensitive sections of personal records, it could be shut down.

"Bingo," Kathy said. Pete felt his stomach tie into a knot. "There's a handful of 1983 white Ford Aerostars still registered and active in Miami. Most seem to be in the hands of older folk, or in junkyards—which means they won't get their registration renewed or they've been on the garbage pile for years."

"Anyone actively using one, though? Any person seem out of the ordinary?" Pete asked.

Kathy took a sharp breath.

"What is it?"

"Fuck," Kathy said.

Pete moved in closer to the laptop and looked over her shoulder.

There was one person who owned a white Ford Aerostar from 1983 that wasn't pushing it in age. His name was Julian Finch. He was thirty-five, white, male, and worked as a Realtor for Penagos Realtors in West Kendall.

Penagos Realtors.

Pete could see the shop's neon sign as if he were standing in front of it. His mind jumped back to seeing Emily waiting inside. It jumped ahead a few days—to the body of Melissa Saiz being pulled out of a garbage dump behind the building. The fruitless search. They had been so close.

"Who the fuck is Julian Finch?" Kathy said.

But Pete wasn't around to answer.

CHAPTER THIRTY-SIX

S he wanted to die.

Nina Henriquez could hear her heart beating. Slower now, it seemed. She'd lost track of time. All she knew was that she was running out of water and had finished the last few crumbs of cereal yesterday.

The whirring sound—the camera, she figured—hadn't come to life in a while. She wasn't sure if that was a good thing. The man that brought her here—Steve, the real estate guy—was gone. Was he real? Her head was still foggy. But she had pieced together enough.

How could she have been so stupid? The thought crossed her mind throughout the days—weeks—she'd been here, in the small, musty-smelling room.

He'd planned her capture well, Nina mused. Tying her hands just so. She was able to stretch her fingers and reach the food—sometimes even the water—but it was almost impossible to yank the cloth wrapped around her face. Almost.

Her legs felt dead under her. She rocked back and forth, trying to get the blood circulating again. She knew it was only a brief respite. Her wrists—tied to her ankles—were rubbed raw. Her fingers massaged her toes.

She'd stopped crying a while ago. Not because she didn't think anyone could hear her. She'd figured that out soon enough. She didn't want to give him the pleasure. This asshole had manipulated her. Taken advantage of her. For what? She wasn't sure. She might never know. But she wasn't going to feed his sick fantasy. She wasn't going to just be a notch on his wall.

Every day, she'd allow herself to think about her brother for a second. A minute, if she needed to. She wondered where he was. What he was doing. If he was mad at her. He probably thought she'd up and left like her mom, found a better life. She hoped he didn't think that. She would never leave him. Even if she didn't survive this.

She gritted her teeth and held her breath. This was the worst part. The painful part of her daily ritual.

The cords wrapped around her wrists were not smooth. They felt like rope, but weren't. Maybe Velcro, she thought. She rubbed her wrists together, fast at first, but slower as the pain kicked in. The scabs—from the previous days' work—were gone now.

She felt the blood dripping around her wrists. It was warm. A trickle at first, but more than last time. The scrapes and scabs and cuts she'd collected under the cords were something now. For the first time since she'd been taken into this dark pit, she felt motion. She allowed herself a tiny sob. She felt the tears running down her face but refused to acknowledge them. She was crying, but she wasn't going to *cry*. Not for help. Not for anyone.

It happened faster than she thought. The blood soaked the cord wrapped around her wrists and ankles. She felt light-headed. She scrunched her hands into tiny, lean shapes—like two long triangles—and pulled. The first tug hurt like hell. The scrapes being dragged toward her palm and creating new abrasions. The second gave her hope. By the time she'd managed to put her toes between the cord and her hands, she wasn't sure she'd have hands for much longer.

Her right hand popped out first and she let out a yelp of surprise. It was throbbing, but she ignored it. The room was dark, but even the minimal light emanating from the small bulb above her was enough to cause her to squint. She took a few deep breaths and let her eyes adjust.

She looked at her free hand. It looked like a wild animal had taken a nibble and passed because it was too light on flavor. She would have laughed under better circumstances.

She looked at the tiny room and felt a wave of disgust. The smell and temperature she'd become accustomed to hit her as if for the first time.

She noticed the camera. It wasn't on—or the lights weren't flashing.

She was able to free her other hand soon after. It was then just a matter of figuring out her captor's knot style. This guy was good, but Nina had basically been a Boy Scout, or so she liked to think. Hell, she'd helped her brother with his scout work and gone on enough camping trips to know a square knot from a bowline.

She managed to free her legs after a bit. She made the mistake of standing up in one motion. The shock to her system—which had spent who-knows-how-long sitting basically cross-legged—was painful and jarring. The blood rushed through her body and sent her back down, screaming.

"Fuck," she said. Her voice was dry and it felt strange to hear herself.

She got to her feet. It still hurt, but less so as long as she took it slow.

That's when she heard the knock.

The knocking turned into banging. Someone was trying really hard to get in. Just outside the tiny closet-sized room she found a small set of stairs that led up to a door—the noises were coming from there. She walked up and put an ear to the door. She could hear panting on the other side. Cursing.

Nina struggled to find something—anything—she could use to defend herself. She held the ropelike cords that bound her.

Her breathing quickened. It wasn't meant to be like this. She'd almost made it out of an unthinkable prison. She was about to escape. But who was on the other side? It wasn't "Steve"—he'd just waltz in, and that would mean the end of Nina.

She didn't have more time to think about it. She tried to position herself somewhere that would give her an element of surprise, but there was nowhere to hide that wasn't in plain view of anyone coming down the stairs. She settled for flattening herself against the wall, hoping that the door opened inward and she'd have a few seconds of a head start.

The words she did manage to hear from the other side made her rethink the plan—and jump down the stairs three at a time.

"Coming in . . . shoot . . . door . . . back," the person said. It was definitely male. She waited at the bottom of the stairs. This is it, she thought. She wasn't going to just roll over and die. She'd come too far for that.

The gunshot echoed around the small room and Nina covered her ears and closed her eyes for a second. The door opened and she heard footsteps speeding down the stairs. Nina bolted toward the stairwell—arms flailing.

She felt her fist connect with a face and heard a groan of pain, then the weight of someone falling onto her, pushing her back. She clawed, felt a face, and took some pleasure in the man's scream. More footsteps. Another person?

"Holy shit." The other voice, female. "Holy fucking shit."

Nina's head was spinning and her hands were pinned down at her sides. She felt the man keeping her on the ground, his heavy breathing hot on her face. She couldn't open her eyes. No. She couldn't deal with this. To taste freedom for a second and then have it stolen. It was over. She'd been so close.

She heard the woman approach and kneel down beside her head. "Nina? Nina Henriquez?"

Nina opened her eyes. The man holding her down rolled off her and was panting, out of breath. He was fat and had a scraggly beard. Nina slid backwards, toward the wall, facing them.

"Who the hell are you?" Nina croaked.

"My name is Kathy," the woman said. She was older. Thirties, probably. She seemed worn out, like she hadn't slept in a few days.

Nina froze. She felt her mouth moving but the sounds—mutterings—coming out of her mouth weren't words. Somehow, her brain and body realized that these people—these strangers—weren't there to kill her and began an immediate shutdown of defenses, leaving Nina shaking and on the verge of tears.

"It's going to be fine," the man said. He didn't try to get closer to her. His hands were up, trying to calm her. "We're not going to hurt you."

"You're safe now," the woman said. "It's all over."

CHAPTER THIRTY-SEVEN

Pete pulled into the strip mall parking lot and parked near the little bodega he'd walked by so many times in the last week. The sun was out, and Pete realized it was close to eight in the morning—still too early for anyone to be getting to work. Or was it? He felt something vibrate in his pocket. He pulled out Kathy's cell phone and answered.

"Hello?"

"Not only do you dart off without saying anything, but you steal my phone?" Kathy said. "And Dave's car? What do you do to people you don't like?"

"I wasn't going to drag you along any further," Pete said, his eyes on the front door of the real estate office, which was still dark. No one home.

"How very kind of you," Kathy said. "While you ran off to play hero, Dave and I found Nina."

"What?"

"She's alive, Pete," Kathy said, all humor gone. "We cross-referenced properties owned by either Aguilera or Finch and came up blank, but dug a bit deeper and found out that Aguilera was renting a storage space in Homestead under his mother's name. That's where Nina was. She's tough—she'd already gotten out of her restraints."

Pete took in a sharp, surprised breath. He wasn't sure what to say.

"That's . . . holy shit—that's a miracle," Pete said. "Kathy, I . . . can't believe . . . where is she?"

"Well, I'm technically still wanted by the police, so I felt it wasn't in my best interest to walk into headquarters with a girl that's believed dead," Kathy said. "So one of Dave's goons dropped her off at Homestead Hospital."

"She's alive." Pete felt his eyes welling up. Not everything was lost.

"Where the hell are you? Or do I know the answer?"

"I'm in the car, waiting outside," Pete said.

"I'm going to assume you have not notified our colleagues in law enforcement about this," Kathy said.

"That's a safe assumption."

"So, what are your plans if and when you run into this Julian Finch? Did you ever stop to consider that he might just be Joe Regular, who happens to drive a white Aerostar? What then? Citizen's arrest?"

"Hadn't thought past coming here," Pete said. Then he hung up.

Pete checked the time on the dashboard. 7:45. He hadn't slept in almost two days. The energy that had propelled him from Dave's hideout to West Kendall would fade soon, and he'd be left exhausted and with no plan. He leaned his head back and stared at the car's ceiling. It didn't help that he hated and was terrible at stakeouts. He let his eyes close. Just for a second.

Pete woke up with a start. It took him a second to remember where he was. He rubbed his eyes. He had a vague, fading memory of a dream. He checked the time on Kathy's phone. It was almost 9:30. The iPhone's battery was dying. He'd slept for almost two hours. Pete cursed under his breath. So much for staking out the scene. He looked over at the real estate office and noticed the lights were now on. Someone had opened the door. Someone was inside. Pete exited the car. He looked around the small parking lot. No one else was around this early. He felt for the gun resting behind his back, supported by his jeans waistband. He walked toward the small real estate office.

The door chime went off and startled Pete as he opened the door. The office, though small, was divided in two. Pete was in the main lobby area, which was cordoned off by a reception desk. Pete assumed the Realtor offices were past the reception area. There was no one around. The lights were on.

He walked up to the desk and pushed the button that would alert the receptionist. He heard some rustling in the back room. Voices? He wasn't sure. After a few minutes, a short, stout woman of about fifty made her way to the front desk and took a seat. She eyed Pete. He could tell she was having a hard time smiling.

"May I help you?" she said. The nameplate on her desk said MYRNA.

"Hi, I'm looking for Julian Finch," Pete said, trying his best to sound casual, probably failing.

He noticed something in her eyes. Pete wondered if it was normal, or if he'd tripped some kind of alarm in her head.

She cleared her throat. "Julian isn't in yet," she said. "Most of the agents are either out in the field or not here until later."

Pete put on his best neighborly smile. "Ah, gotcha," he said. "Any idea when he'll be in?"

"Probably later this afternoon," she said. "Can I take a message?"

Pete noticed her hands were shaking as she rummaged through her desk for a pen.

"Sure, but I can wait," Pete said.

"He won't be here for some time," she said, her voice firm. "I wouldn't want you to be stuck here for hours."

"Can you call him?"

"What is this concerning, Mr.—?"

"Fernandez," Pete said. "A friend of mine was here recently and I wanted to follow up for her about an apartment she was looking at."

She jotted down his name and a few other words Pete couldn't make out.

"I'll be sure he gets this message," she said. "Does he have your phone number?"

"No need to give that," Pete said, backing away from the reception. "I'll swing back later in the afternoon."

He heard a palpable sigh of relief as he turned around to head for the front entrance. He wasn't sure if Myrna was just the world's most jittery secretary or if he'd missed something. If the office hadn't been totally silent, he wouldn't have noticed the low, wheezing sound. Pete slowed his progress to listen, but the noise was gone. It could have been anything.

He left the office and walked toward the car. He had to remind himself there was an entire police force looking for him and Kathy. He felt stupid. While the Julian Finch lead was something, there was very little Pete could do on his own.

He glanced back at the office. The lights were off. Strange. Why would Myrna come in, open the office, and take his message, just to shut things down? Pete stopped. The strip mall was still relatively empty. He turned around and headed back toward the office. Locked. He cupped his hands around his eyes and tried to peer inside, but couldn't penetrate the darkness. He thought he saw a figure moving in the background. He tried the door on the right, and was surprised when it responded. It made a squeaking sound as Pete slid inside. He winced as the door chime went off. It wasn't very loud—but enough of a signal to frighten someone away. Myrna hadn't locked both doors. Why? Was she hoping he'd come back? Pete crept into the office and stayed close to the far wall, his eyes focused on where the reception desk was. He couldn't see or hear anything beyond the sliver of light coming in through the blinds behind him. He pulled his gun out as he walked toward the reception desk.

Pete recognized the sound of a silenced gunshot. He couldn't pinpoint where the sound was coming from. He gripped the handle of his own gun as he felt his way toward the reception desk with his free hand.

He walked past the reception desk and found the door that led to the main part of the office after a few minutes of fumbling. He was relieved to find that someone had left at least a light or two on down the short hallway, which, Pete presumed, led to a larger office area. He almost tripped a few steps past the door, steadying himself on the wall. He looked down and saw what had caused him to slip. An arm. Myrna's eyes were still open—her face turned up in a weird expression, blood seeping out from the precise bullet wound in the middle of her forehead. Her body lay on the floor at an odd angle. Pete recoiled in surprise and tried to keep from yelling. He felt for a pulse. Her body was still warm, but she was dead. He had just seen her. Had just spoken to her. Pete was thankful for the dim light in the hallway as he stepped over the secretary's body.

The hallway ended and revealed another nook with two offices on the left side, with a door at the far end marked EMERGENCY EXIT. It was open. Pete wondered why the alarm hadn't gone off. He walked past the first office—he tried the handle, but the door was locked—and picked up his pace. He reached the final door, half-open.

The office was small and sparse. Pete could tell it was a shared area. Two desks were set up facing each other at the center of the crowded room. The light from the hallway was muted in the room, and it took him a second to register that someone was sitting at the far desk. Pete couldn't make out his face from where he stood, but he knew it wasn't going to be good. He took a cautious step toward the body, walking around the two desks to approach from behind. He tapped his leg with his gun, as if to remind himself he was still armed and ready in case anything jumped out at him. But he was also certain nothing was going to move. Dead people don't move.

The man was hunched over the desk, blood splattered on the computer monitor, which had also taken part of the blast. The man's face was partially blown off, but Pete knew who it was. His eyes seemed frozen in fear, even as his face slid down from the monitor and landed on the keyboard.

Pete was close to the body now. His eyes scanned Raul Aguilera's familiar features. He'd been too late. Right, but too late. He felt his stomach turn at the sight of Aguilera's exposed brains and skull, pieces of which were stuck to the destroyed computer screen and desk. He almost failed to notice the blood-stained Post-It note that had landed near Aguilera's feet.

Pete crouched down to look at the paper. The message was scrawled in blue ink. Pete only had to read it once to understand what the killer meant, and where he was heading.

NO LOOSE ENDS.

CHAPTER THIRTY-EIGHT

The drive to Baptist Hospital was a blur. Pete couldn't be bothered with the speed limit, red lights, or any traffic laws that would slow him down. The hospital was to the southeast of the strip mall, in a more residential area—surrounded by seasonally decorated four- and five-bedroom houses, doctor's offices, and parks as opposed to condo complexes and hair salons—a long trek across major intersections and smaller neighborhoods. Though technically on the same southwest quadrant of Miami's gridlike layout, the real estate office and hospital were on opposite ends, which didn't bode well for someone in a rush, like Pete. After about twenty minutes, he found himself on Kendall Drive—the main street that would take him directly to Baptist—and said a silent prayer. He needed to make it down this last stretch of road and get to Emily before anything else could go wrong.

He dialed the number without looking and hoped someone was around.

"Hello?" Dave said. Pete sighed in relief.

"I need your help," Pete said.

"Where the hell are you, man? Your girlfriend is flipping out over here."

"The killer is on his way to get Emily," Pete said, ignoring Dave's joke.

"Who?"

"Finch," Pete said as he abruptly changed lanes and went through a red light on 107th Avenue. "Kathy knows what I'm talking about. Her phone's at, like, two percent. Tell her to get in touch with Harras—with anyone—and let them know he's heading over to the hospital. He's going to kill Emily."

"OK, OK, where are you?" Dave asked.

"Heading over there."

"You got your piece?"

"Yup," Pete said, checking his rearview. "Not sure how much good that'll do me, though."

"We'll head over there," Dave said. The thought was nice, but Pete knew they were too far—a drive from Little Haiti to Kendall was an hour affair, at best. They didn't have that kind of time.

"We need the cops there, now," Pete said. "He's at least ten minutes ahead of me, and I have no idea what he's driving. I thought you had people watching her, man?"

"Calm down," Dave said. "We did. But the cops didn't let them stick around. They kept ushering them out for some reason. It was really—"

The line cut off. Pete looked at the phone. The battery was dead.

Julian parked his car in the lot adjacent to the Baptist Hospital Intensive Care Unit.

The Voice had lied to him. The Messenger was a false prophet. Now he'd have to finish what Aguilera could not.

This was a test, Julian thought. A challenge brought upon him just as he thought the path was clear. He'd almost felt the vibrations of clarity. He'd been so close. Aguilera was an amateur, paying homage to a man he had no right to know.

Julian thought back to when he had found a worn copy of the book years ago, in a used bookstore in Nashville. The bold, red letters called out to him from a shelf on the brink of overflowing. REX WHITEHURST: THE METHODICAL MONSTER. Julian was intrigued. After a few chapters, he knew he'd found a kindred soul—a guide, even. He spent whatever time he had researching Whitehurst—his methods, his victims, his message.

In his final days, Rex spoke of a "mass action"—a series of ceremonies performed so fast, so close together, that they merged to create one vibration—a chorus of pain and fear. This unified force would then give Rex a peek into his own future, and allow him to alter it. Rex knew that there was no way to absorb them simultaneously. So the mirrors appeared. As he progressed, his chosen ones began to be discovered in intimate poses. Brutal poses. Bent over with their eyeballs in their mouths. Hands tied to their thighs, their tongues cut out and shoved somewhere unmentionable. And mirrors. Always surrounded by mirrors. The only way Rex could fight back the whispered urges driving him to the next event was by turning the volume so high, he'd be able to eliminate all evil from his mind and the world. He just needed to know how to do it. He needed to see it. Julian could feel it too. His bond with Whitehurst grew the more he read about him. He longed to reach out to him. To be near him.

But the man Julian had discovered as his own god, his Voice, had died at the hands of the Florida legal system a few years earlier. Still, something inside him urged that he push on, almost as if it knew what was next.

Then he found out about her.

Julian packed his things and used the last of his savings to buy a one-way bus ticket to the tropical wasteland of Miami. To find the person who had communed with the Voice. To create his own twisted family.

He found more than just an ex-flame. She had a son. A son that had known Whitehurst. He was close to Julian's age—a few years younger. Even the discovery that Aguilera was working toward becoming an FBI agent didn't deter him. He followed him. Watched him from afar. He could tell Aguilera was angry, emotional, and hot-headed. One night, following him out of a dive bar in Florida City, Julian witnessed Aguilera reveal himself—his true self. The future FBI agent, feeling slighted by a beggar asking for change as he walked toward his car, throttled and dragged the homeless man into a nearby alley and proceeded to beat him bloody, the man's screams muffled by the shattered teeth and bruised mouth Aguilera had demolished. He didn't kill him. He wasn't crossing that line yet. There was anger there, and Julian meant to find out how to reach it.

The first box was ignored. A brief note and a burner cell phone with instructions on how to reach Julian. He'd expected that. He tried again a few months later, having learned more about his new friend during the interim: He was a loner, not very close to his mother or his long-dead *father. Prison logs showed he had visited Whitehurst sporadically, as if he were struggling with his own desire to stay connected to the man. At the same time, he chose to honor the life of his biological father in public, becoming an FBI agent—a stern operative of the law. He went through the motions socially, dating and partaking in the company of friends and colleagues. But Julian saw more. He saw the darkness inside Aguilera and felt kinship.*

The third gift was more direct. The burner, instructions, and a simple note: **HELP ME REACH HIM.**

The call came the next evening.

They spoke a few more times. Despite never seeing each other, they had built a bond stronger than blood. Julian knew Aguilera wanted revenge on those who had hurt his true father, but he didn't have the means or skill to execute them. Julian did. Aguilera became his Messenger, his connection to their shared idol. And together, they killed in his name.

Before Julian could move on, everything had to be wiped away. He remembered sliding a finger over the back of Aguilera's head. He tasted his blood. He had had such high hopes for him.

He entered the hospital with ease. He put on a pleasant smile and looked like an everyman. He was wearing a pressed shirt, tie, and slacks. He found the reception desk. The receptionist was older, pushing fifty and overweight.

A soft smile, a pat on the hand was all it took.

He made sure to let his eyes linger over her as he walked toward the elevator, the room number written in swirly numbers on a scrap of paper.

The trip up to the fifth floor was uneventful. He scanned the hallway and saw no one in the waiting area. Where were her friends now? Her stupid husband? Harras? Julian would be happy when this was resolved and he could move on. He hadn't decided where to go yet, but it would take at least a day to get out of Florida by car. He'd decide then. After he'd created some distance between him and this sun-soaked hellmouth.

He turned and began to walk down the hall. He almost didn't hear him. He slid his hand into his left front pocket. He waited a second before he heard another footstep behind him. It was never going to be easy, he thought. He turned around, unable to hide the smile on his face. But the smile was soon replaced by a surprised snarl.

"Stop right there, you son of a bitch," Harras said, his gun aimed squarely at Julian. "Put your hands where I can see them."

By the time he reached the front desk of Baptist Hospital's Intensive Care Unit, Pete was drenched in sweat and unable to fully formulate sentences. The drive from West Kendall to the hospital had gone much faster than Pete expected, but he still felt behind— and any time lost to Julian Finch could mean lives. Emily's life. He wouldn't allow another friend to die because of him. He motioned for the stocky receptionist to get off the phone and recognize him.

"Yes?"

"I need to see Emily Sprague," Pete said between gasps. "She's on the fifth floor. I'm a friend."

"Well, she's not supposed to be seeing any visitors," the lady said. "I'm sorry, but you'll have to come back later."

Pete didn't have time for this. "It's an emergency," he said. "I need to see her. She could be in trouble."

"Well, she's in a safe place," the nurse said, her voice trailing off. "I'm sorry. I can't let you up. I've already let one friend past, and I really shouldn't have."

Pete felt his blood run cold. For a brief moment, while speeding over to the hospital, he hoped he'd misread Finch's message—that maybe, for whatever reason, he was heading somewhere else.

"Wait, you said you let someone go up to see her already?"

"Yes, a friend of hers," she said. "A very nice man. He was very polite."

Pete didn't bother to listen to the rest of her explanation. He turned and bolted toward the elevator bank, jamming his fingers at the UP button. After a few moments, one of the cars opened and he was gone.

Pete heard nothing as he stepped out of the elevator. The floor's small reception desk was empty. Odd. Pete walked toward Emily's room, picking up speed as he got closer. After a moment, he found Emily's hallway.

The red smear of blood stood out in stark contrast to the off-white tiles that covered the floor. Harras's body was splayed out in front of Emily's room at an odd angle—his legs spread in front of him as if he'd been dragged, his arms dangling awkwardly at both sides. There was blood everywhere. His eyes were closed, his face spasming in pain. He was alive, but barely.

Pete ran over to the fallen FBI agent and knelt down next to him. Harras tried to move his mouth, but he was having trouble breathing. He didn't have long, Pete thought. His eyes fluttered open and closed. He let out a pained cough.

"Here . . . " he said, his voice sounding like it'd been dragged over broken glass. The pool of blood under him was spreading.

"It's OK," Pete said. "I'll get some help. You'll be fine."

Pete didn't believe his own words. Harras closed his eyes, his mouth still open. He was still trying to talk.

"Aguilera cleared . . . the floor. That's . . . why I came. Something wasn't . . . right," Harras said. "He's . . . here."

Harras's eyes pointed Pete toward Emily's room. He gripped Harras's hand for a second before standing up. He looked away from the grisly scene. He felt his fists clench. Harras was a good man. He didn't deserve to die like this—alone, bleeding out, no one to help.

Pete took a deep breath and leaned against the wall opposite Emily's room. He could see inside. She was gone. Where, though? How far could she move? Obviously Finch was armed, probably with the same silencer he had at the realty office. Pete pulled out his own gun and walked in the opposite direction from the elevators. Emily was basically comatose; Finch would have to carry her to get her anywhere. Unless he meant to just finish her off. Pete shuddered at the thought. That was possible. Anything was possible.

Emily's scream cut through the silence that had enveloped the hallway. Pete sprinted left, toward another set of rooms and the emergency exit stairs.

He looked to his left and noticed one of the rooms was open, a pair of feet on the floor, just outside the door. There she was, he thought. He panicked until he reached her and confirmed that she was alive—in pain, but alive. She was curled up in a fetal position, her hands covering her face, her hospital gown strewn around her body and tears streaming down her cheeks. But she was alive. Pete pulled her toward him.

"Em," Pete said. "Jesus Christ, Em. How did you get away?"

She was shivering next to him. He could feel her heart racing. She was clutching him, her nails digging into his arms. She looked up at him.

"No, no," she said between muffled sobs. She buried her face in his shoulder. "Oh, Peter."

"It's OK," Pete said. "Can you stand up?"

He felt her shivering increase, as if she was trying to pull away. Not from him, but from the room. It was only then that he noticed the man standing over them. And the gun pointed at his face.

CHAPTER THIRTY-NINE

"**Y**ou misunderstood my note," Finch said. He seemed calm, Pete thought. He was dressed well, his hair combed, and even the slight stubble on his face seemed intentional in a way that Pete could never master himself. Was he really mentally complimenting a serial killer on his style before he got killed? Probably.

"Did I?" Pete said, hoping to keep him distracted long enough to formulate some kind of escape plan.

"Yes," Finch said, keeping his eyes and gun on Pete's head. "You're the loose end, Pete. Coming here, tossing your ex around like a stupid prop, was only part of it. It was all about getting you here. You're the bow that can finish wrapping this little parting gift for me."

Then he saw it all come together. The APB on him and Kathy. Harras bleeding to death. Aguilera's murder. Finch was going to set

298

him up. Pete would be the raging alcoholic ex-fiancé/serial killer who, after murdering the two agents who'd been doggedly hunting him down, killed his one true love before killing himself. It was nice, neat, and left no room for the existence of a Julian Finch. Pete shook his head in disgust. He'd walked right into it.

Finch noticed Pete's reaction and let out a chuckle—more menacing than humorous. Pete felt Emily slump in his arms. She was resigned, he thought. This was it. He could still feel her breathing.

"You don't think I'd just show up here without any backup, do you?" Pete lied.

"I don't think much of you at all," Finch said, his tone more annoyed than intimidated. "You've been a nuisance from the beginning. I'm surprised you made it this far."

"I've got files saved all over pointing to you and Aguilera," Pete said. "And Kathy Bentley's got them, too. You don't think they'll be all over the *Miami Times* tomorrow?"

Pete noticed a slight hesitation in Finch's eyes. He pressed on. "You think Harras and Aguilera were the only cops I spoke to? Or that I don't have friends with connections to other places?" Pete said. He tried to rein himself in. He couldn't lay it on too thick, for fear of blowing the top off his own tall tale. "You may be able to kill us, and you may be able to get a decent head start, but it's over. Your face will be plastered all over every news channel from here to Alaska. You'll have nowhere to run."

The kick to his face caught him by surprise and sent him reeling back into the hallway.

He felt blood trickling out of his mouth, warm and slow. Emily had rolled off to the side. She was out cold. The movement, action, and fear had shut her down. Pete needed to move this away from her. Finch took a step toward him. Pete stood up and darted right, toward the elevator bank. He made a silent prayer and realized that he could be dead on the floor at any second. His gambit was a long shot: if, in fact, Finch wanted Pete's death to look like a suicide, he couldn't just shoot him in the back. No, that would throw his entire plan in disarray. Finch had to grab him.

Pete heard Finch curse, but for a few seconds his heart hung in place. If Finch didn't come after him—if, instead, he took out his psychotic rage on Emily, everything was lost. His gamble would have been pointless. He heard Finch's feet begin to race after him. He allowed himself a quick sigh of relief and then returned his attention to getting away—at least for now. He had to figure out how to escape and still save Emily. He had no idea what to do. Not yet.

On instinct, he leapt over the empty reception desk and hunched behind it. But he soon realized that was a mistake. There was no clear exit that would give him cover, and it was an obvious detour. He'd painted himself into a corner.

"Story of my fucking life," he said.

He was tired. He was tired of running. Tired of putting his friends in danger and wondering what to do. He was tired of dealing with psychopaths who had no respect for what was around them. Most of all, he was tired of being afraid.

He leapt onto the reception desk and waited a few moments before Finch ran by, and without much hesitation, hurled himself at Finch's back, knocking them both to the ground with a loud thud.

Finch's face slammed into the tile, making a sound akin to boots on gravel. The scream came after, and it frightened Pete to the core.

A guttural, low yell that was a product of both pain and surprise. For a fleeting second, Pete saw Finch's gun skitter out of his hands and out of reach. They rolled across the hall, each man gripping the other to get the upper hand. Finch's face was covered in blood. He probably had a broken nose. Through the dirt and blood caking his once pristine face, Pete saw hatred—a seething, primal hate. Pete had gone from a pesky annoyance that Finch had to eliminate before he went on to more important things to being an actual threat. Someone that had to be crushed with relish. It was a compliment and a death sentence rolled into one.

The bite came out of nowhere. Finch's teeth clamped down on Pete's chin, and the skin tore off with surprising ease. The pain was sharp and spread quickly. Pete saw his own blood gush out of his face and mix with the killer's. His vision blurred and for a second he feared he'd black out. Then it would truly be over.

He didn't even think about his actions anymore. He felt his face move forward and slam into Finch's battered and broken nose, and felt a sick satisfaction as the murderer yelled in pain.

Finch moved back, releasing Pete and covering his face with his hands. Pete took the moment to regroup. A mistake.

Finch stood up and hovered over Pete for a moment before giving him a quick kick in the midsection. He folded into himself in response to the pain. He'd lost Finch. The pain from his face and kick in the gut had made him lose balance. When his vision cleared, he saw Finch standing. His gun in hand.

"I don't care anymore," Finch spat out. "Let them think whatever they want. I want this over and I want you to suffer."

Pete had little time to move, yet it was almost like he saw the bullet's entire trajectory before it hit him, shattering his left knee. The pain shot through his leg and up to his brain in less than a second. The scream came soon after, and it took Pete a second to realize the noise—a loud, frantic cry—was coming from him. He felt his head spin. He didn't dare look at his leg. He couldn't move. He felt behind him for his gun. It was there. It hadn't fallen out. The throbbing in his leg felt endless. At the fringe of his vision he could see a large pool of blood forming. Farther still, he saw Finch, running down the hall. Away from Pete.

Toward Emily.

He wants me to suffer, Pete thought. He was going to kill Emily and Pete had no way to go after him. He stifled a scream as he stood up, his entire weight on his good leg.

Pete didn't hesitate as he lifted the weapon—the same gun his father had carried for years as a homicide detective in Miami and the same gun Pete had used to kill someone a little over a year before— and pointed the barrel. He pulled the trigger and felt the blowback from the gunshot. The pain in his leg doubled as he moved backward, losing his balance. His head crashed into the dirty white linoleum. He turned his face and saw Finch on the ground. He wasn't moving.

The last thing Pete remembered before closing his eyes was the sound of the elevator doors opening and a woman's scream.

CHAPTER FORTY

Pete tried to reach for the pile of paperbacks. They were too far. He grabbed his crutches and sidled over to the stack, leaning against the science fiction section near the front of the Book Bin. He tried to crouch down, using one of the crutches for support, but realized he couldn't. His leg would take some time to heal, and it was far from functional—even now, four months after Julian Finch.

Finch. The name lingered in Pete's brain for a second too long. He rubbed his eyes and hoped—in vain—that Finch's face wouldn't be on his mind when his eyes opened up again. Maybe he'd never go away. Never leave Pete alone.

The death of an FBI agent—revealed as an accessory to a murdering psychopath—shook Miami for weeks. After two days in surgery and in varying states of medicated haze, Pete spent the next few days talking to myriad police officers and federal agents, each one trying to piece together what had happened, and how a low-rent, washed-up journalist could have figured it out with only the help of a laptop and a local columnist with a *Miami Times* password.

Pete had answered their questions to the best of his ability. It was then, in the early days of his recuperation, that he decided what he would do next. Or, rather, what he would do next once he was fully able. He wasn't there yet. In the meantime, he went to meetings. He talked to Jack, who was now his sponsor. He had lunch with Harras—who'd somehow survived the bullet to the stomach. He drank too much coffee. He started making plans and putting things in place—some literal, like books, others more theoretical.

Kathy was on a more definite path, working on an outline for another true-crime book. She'd already signed a book deal. This one about the legacy of Rex Whitehurst—his connection to Raul Aguilera and how Rex's vicious murders had inspired another, deadlier killer to roam the streets of Miami and prey on young women. Harras, over lunch with Pete and Kathy a few weeks after his release from the hospital, let them know as much as he was comfortable with in regard to his wayward partner. How the FBI had learned of his relationship with Whitehurst, raising a red flag that, coupled with his rage issues in regard to Pete and in other, more egregious situations, led to his watered-down "suspension." Harras expressed some regret that they hadn't dug deeper. Pete regretted it, too.

Most of Kathy's book consisted of interviews with the victims' families and extensive talks with Nina Henriquez, the only known survivor of Julian Finch's killing spree. Pete had only met the girl briefly, with Kathy, a few months before. He was amazed by her strength and bravery, but also by her ability to remain young and

ALEX SEGURA

optimistic about a world that had dealt her such a disturbing set of cards so early. Kathy now also had information on Finch's bloody swath of victims, including the body they originally thought was Nina Henriquez, and other cases that were confirmed as Finch's work in nearby states.

And then another healthy chunk of the book came from conversations with Pete, conducted in Pete's hospital room. Pete was happy for her. From time to time she'd go on about missing the *Times*—especially when she'd get the occasional offer to return—but Pete hoped this was it for her in terms of the daily newspaper grind. They had dinner once a week. She, Dave, and maybe Jack were his only friends. He wasn't sure what to make of Harras yet.

He didn't turn around when he heard the door chime. He used the wobbly shelves to leverage himself up from his partial crouch and get back onto his crutches. Only then was he able to turn around.

"We need to talk."

Emily walked into the Book Bin and headed toward the back, to Pete's makeshift office. Well, not so makeshift anymore.

Pete watched her walk away before starting to shuffle behind her. The crutches were cumbersome, embarrassing, and annoying. Even though some time had passed, he still hadn't mastered them. He winced as his bad leg touched the ground.

By the time he'd reached the office Emily was sitting across from his desk. She was wearing a business suit, dark brown, with a beige blouse. She was coming from the office or a meeting or an interview, he thought. He tried to avoid thinking about how beautiful she looked. He missed her.

"I don't have a lot of time," she said as Pete hobbled around his desk.

305

He'd cleaned the office up. It was his now. Dave still ran the store, but he let Pete have his way with the place.

"Just give me a sec," Pete said.

He moved his crutches away from him and maneuvered himself onto the rolling desk chair he'd reminded himself daily he should replace. The last thing he needed was to fall on his ass now.

He managed to land on the chair with minimum pushback. He rubbed the bandage that he still had on his chin. That bruise would take a while to heal.

He swiveled the chair to get a clear look at Emily for the first time. He could still see the faint echoes of the bruises and cuts that had almost covered her face the last time he saw her. The visual was etched in his memory.

It seemed to Pete like she'd been crying. But he wasn't sure if that was him projecting. She looked tired. Not even angry, which was what Pete would have expected if someone told him this morning that his ex, who he'd failed to save from being kidnapped and beaten by a serial killer's assistant, was going to swing by and chat.

"The office looks nice," she said, stalling. "Clean."

"Yeah," Pete said. "I've had a lot of time on my hands. I can hop around and organize with the best of them."

He thought better of even trying to laugh a bit. His body heat was higher than normal. He'd start sweating soon. He was nervous.

"I can't talk to you, Pete," Emily said. "Ever again. I just wanted to be here, in person, to tell you that. I realize that just running away and leaving you that letter—that was immature. And even with everything that's happened since . . . and even though I have more than enough of an excuse to never talk to you again . . . I, well, I felt like I needed to do this. To come close this chapter in person."

"OK."

"OK?"

"I don't blame you," Pete said. "I'm surprised you're even here. I wish I'd known. There's a lot I want to say. But yeah, I don't blame you at all, Em."

"Please don't call me that," she said.

"OK."

"I was left for dead, Pete," she said. "Left for dead by some sociopath who thankfully wasn't as good at it as he thought. He kept me in his trunk—while he was at my house pretending to be a cop. He pulled me off the road and put me in his trunk. I could hear you and Rick and I knew I was going to die. Can you imagine what that felt like? And when I came to, in a hospital room, surrounded by strangers and my fuckhead of a husband—when I asked where you were? They tell me you were out getting lit while I was who-knows-where. You'd been holed up in some shitty motel drinking yourself to death, with no idea where I was, or where this killer was. You were gone, Pete. You didn't help find me. You left. You disappeared. You showed up too late."

The tears started streaming down her face but she refused to acknowledge them. She pressed on.

"Don't ever call me. Don't ever visit me. Don't even think of me. Don't ever try to contact me through our friends," she said, her teeth gritted. Pete had never seen her like this. Sure, he'd seen her upset, but never like this. Never fueled by rage. Hate, even.

She stood up.

"We loved each other once," she said. "And I thought we could again and that was . . . that was stupid. I was being stupid. Stupid for thinking we could just be friends. I realize that now. I'm not innocent. I made mistakes, too. With you and us. And I get you have a problem. But it's not my problem anymore. You're not my problem anymore. And I hope you stay alive as you continue to do stupid things to yourself—because you think you're the smartest person in the room and—"

"You're right," Pete said. "OK? You're right. Saying I'm sorry will never be enough. You have every right to hate me."

Emily opened her mouth as if to respond, but no words materialized.

Pete fell back into the chair. He sagged. She stood over him. The anger was gone. She wiped the tears away with a quick motion, as if she were trying to do it fast enough for Pete not to notice.

She wasn't looking at him anymore, but past him. "Take care of yourself."

"Don't worry about me," Pete said. He saw her eyebrows pop up and her eyes come into focus, as if she were just now realizing he was in the room, too. "You never have. I've made mistakes, but don't use my fuck-ups to whitewash your own shitty behavior. Goodbye, Emily."

She looked stunned but then turned around and walked out of the office without another word. He didn't have the chance to see her full reaction to his parting shot. That was fine. His eyes followed her down the aisle and past the front door.

The phone rang. He picked it up.

"Fernandez Investigations," he said.

He grabbed the yellow notepad and pen that were resting on the left side of his small desk and began to jot something down.

"Slow down," Pete said. "Your husband did what?"

He wrote down a phone number. He checked his watch. There was a meeting near FIU in about an hour. He'd see if Jack was going.

"Ma'am," he said, interrupting her. "Can we touch base in a few hours? I can meet you. OK, great."

He jotted down her address and hung up the phone. He looked at it, resting on its base. The red message light was blinking. He'd missed a call. Probably another client. Another case he'd have to work on a gimpy leg. He smiled.

About the Author

Alex Segura is a novelist and comic book writer. He is the author of the Pete Fernandez novels *Silent City* and *Down the Darkest Street,* both available from Polis Books. He has also written a number of comic books, including the best-selling and critically acclaimed *Archie Meets Kiss* storyline, the "Occupy Riverdale" story, and the upcoming *Archie Meets Ramones.* He lives in New York with his wife and son. He is a Miami native. Visit him online at www.AlexSegura.com and @Alex_Segura. He is currently at work on the next Pete Fernandez novel, *Dangerous Ends.*